MW01233389

FOR THE
LOVE OF FAMILY

The second book in the For the Love series,
following *For the Love of Charlotte*

A M A N D A   J .   G O W I N

ISBN 978-1-0980-5696-4 (paperback)
ISBN 978-1-0980-5697-1 (digital)

Christian Faith Publishing, Inc.
832 Park Avenue
Meadville, PA 16335
www.christianfaithpublishing.com

Printed in the United States of America

In tragedy there is beauty and healing.
The heart of what family is all about.

PROLOGUE

Once Charlotte woke up from her medically induced coma, she was moved to a rehabilitation floor of the hospital. As the week wore on, Charlotte was gaining strength and not only was awake enough to open her eyes; she was also beginning to talk. It was a struggle, but she gained more strength and speech ability into the next week.

During this time, she was hearing all about the changes and reconciliations in the family. It was as much to take in as was the news and realization of her accident and inability to move, talk easily, and even eat and drink. She needed help to do everything. It was very frustrating, and when she wasn't struggling, the physical pain and headaches were almost too much to bear.

After two weeks on the rehab floor of the hospital, Charlotte could talk pretty well and could feed herself and hold her own cup to drink. She was sitting up but couldn't try to walk until her broken legs and broken arm healed more. At this point, they moved her to a rehabilitation center for recovery until she could go home to her family.

Elliott and Emma were wonderful at being her cheerleaders and right at her beck and call every time she needed anything. If they weren't there, it was her parents or Marissa and her new boyfriend Dan. Dan was evidently the officer who arrived at her accident first. Dan was also the son of the chaplain who had been with her family and become very good friends with Elliott while she was in her coma. She had met him briefly a few times, but he was busy helping families, and she hadn't seen much of him. Someone was always there trying to help her or asking her dozens of questions.

It was appreciated and frustrating at the same time. Charlotte knew she needed their help but resented needing it, and every time she tried to move, they were right there offering help or asking her how they could help her. It was maddening, but she tried to keep smiling and be polite. It was getting harder, and sometimes she wasn't so polite.

Charlotte realized she was not being as polite as she thought she was, once she realized how often everyone started to apologize to her. This just made her feel worse. What was wrong with her? Why was she so ungrateful and such a horrible patient? It wasn't fair to her family either. She loved them all so dearly, but for some reason, she was just so angry—angry about the accident, angry about being so helpless, angry about everyone's life going on as normal, if not better than before her accident and her life felt ruined.

All these thoughts and feelings were just swirling around inside Charlotte and she didn't know how to verbalize it or understand it. She just wanted to scream, or get away from everyone, but she couldn't. She was trapped inside her own body.

Recovering

Elliott walked into the coffee shop and looked around; he spotted Lewis over in the corner at a small table waving to him, two coffees on the table.

"Hello, Elliott, how are you?" Lewis asked, standing to shake his hand.

"I should be great, right?" Elliott asked, feeling a little defeated. Lewis smiled kindly as they sat down.

"Recovery is hard on everyone," Lewis said softly.

"You can say that again. I thought once Charlotte woke up, everything would be back to normal. Dr. Lemons warned us it wouldn't be like that, so we thought we were prepared on what to expect…"

"You weren't. No one is. How could you? None of you have ever been through anything like this. Not you or Emma or the others, and especially not Charlotte," Lewis said and let out a deep sigh.

"You are right. I just don't know how to help her. I try and that makes her angry. I try to give her some space, but she needs the help and the inability to help herself frustrates her. She snaps at everyone, the nursing staff, the family, and what is hardest is to see her hurt Emma. This isn't my wife! We all know that. I find myself apologizing to the medical staff and telling them this isn't like her. They nod and seem to understand and tell me it is okay, but I hate thinking what they must think of her. She is the sweetest soul I have ever met and this is not her. I want them to know that. I want them to love her too. I want my wife back…" Elliott began sobbing into his hands.

Lewis leaned forward and put his hand gently on Elliott's shoulder. He let him collect himself.

"They do understand. Charlotte isn't their first patient. They understand that the patient is dealing with their whole life altered and they are dealing or not dealing with it very well. It is normal. It just isn't what you know as normal. Be patient with her. She needs you all now more than ever to just love her. Don't take it personally, and keep letting Emma know you are her ally and one day her mom will be back," Lewis soothed.

Elliott nodded and wiped his tears. He hadn't planned on crying, but he just couldn't hold it in any more.

"Everyone at work and church ask how she is, and I tell them she is recovering. I try to hold it all in and be strong for Emma and apologize to Charles, Delores, and Marissa. They are very supportive. They tell me they aren't going anywhere. It is hard for all of us to see her like this, it isn't our Charlotte, but we hold on, just hoping she comes back one day," Elliott said, still shaking a little.

"It is hard. I have seen so many families go through this. I wish I had a way to make the process go faster or better, but I can listen and I am here," Lewis said honestly.

Elliott nodded and smiled at his friend and sipped his coffee.

"That is all anyone can do. Thank you," Elliott said, smiling, then sighed. "She comes home tomorrow from the rehab center. She is getting around in her wheelchair well now. She doesn't talk to anyone much, and if she does, it is short and comes out angry."

"I see," Lewis said, nodding. "How do you feel about her coming home?"

"Scared to death and elated too." Elliott laughed. "Charles and Delores will be there. Emma is back in school, so that gives her a break now. She spends a lot of time in her room alone. She is hurting that her mother is back, but not back. She feels like she is doing everything wrong because of Charlotte's reactions. It breaks my heart. I feel for both of them. I just don't know how to make it better."

"Are you praying?" Lewis asked.

"Yes, Emma and I pray together, and I pray for her a lot on my own, not only for Charlotte but to help us and give us strength and comfort too," Elliott said.

"Good. Don't try to do this alone. You can't," Lewis advised and Elliott nodded. "Just keep praying and let God touch her heart and body."

One Week Later

Delores worked away in the kitchen making dinner. Charles came through and took in a deep breath and smiled big.

"That smells delicious, Delores. You have always been the best cook I have ever known," Charles said cheerfully.

"And you have always been the best flatterer I have ever known, Charles Medlock!" Delores laughed.

"Well, thank you, ma'am," Charles said with a bow. Delores laughed harder. She smiled at him.

"Charles, why is it that you have always been the one to make me the happiest?"

"A God-given talent, my lady," Charles said, beaming, then grew serious. "May I call you 'my lady'?"

Delores was surprised by his question and began to blush. There was definitely no denying the chemistry between them was as strong as ever. She tried to ignore it and just enjoy it as they focused on Charlotte, Elliott, and Emma.

"I guess that seems appropriate." Delores blushed deeper. "I am your wife, I suppose."

"Yes, and I would like to begin dating you. I was hoping that we could see where this leads. Maybe one day I will really be your husband again," Charles said honestly.

Delores smiled and nodded. Her lips felt dry, so she licked them and her throat felt tight.

"I would like that too," Delores whispered.

Charles smiled and kissed her forehead.

"Great, now I need to go pick up our granddaughter from school. Maybe after dinner with these kids we can go grab some dessert. Just the two of us." Charles winked at her and headed out the door whistling.

Delores giggled and began whistling herself.

* * * * *

Charles pulled up to the school and saw Emma standing near the door waiting. She looked surprised to see him instead of Elliott. She smiled and jumped in his car.

"Hi, Grandpa," Emma said, shutting her car door.

"Hi, Emma, your dad called and asked if I could pick you up. He needed to work over to finish a report. Splitting time between work and home has him a little behind at work. He said he would be home in time for supper."

"Grandpa, do you think it would be okay if I ate dinner in my room tonight? I have a lot of homework and…" Emma felt guilty lying, but she just couldn't bear the thought of sitting at the table tonight listening to her mother bite everyone's head off. It wasn't who she knew as her mom, and she just didn't want to be yelled at tonight. She was sure she would do something wrong.

"Is it your homework, or is it your mom?" Charles asked softly. Emma burst into tears.

"Oh, honey, it is okay. It isn't easy for her or for us, is it?" Charles asked. Emma nodded.

"I just don't seem to do anything right for her. I try but she just gets so mad. Why is she acting like this? I want my real mom back," Emma said, trying to compose herself.

"I know, darlin'. I miss her too, and I really haven't known her very long. Although I should have. That is all my fault. Your mom is dealing with a lot, and I don't think she knows how to feel or react either. Your dad and Marissa went back to work. You went back to school. Your Grandma and I come and go as we please, but your mom is locked up inside that broken body and she can't go anywhere."

"I never thought about it like that," Emma said, sniffing.

"Just know your mom loves you a lot. She is just trying to figure out how to find her way back to herself too. I keep telling your grandma that too. It is hard on us, but not like it is Charlotte. Hang in there, kiddo, and know we are all here for you too. You can come to us anytime you need to. I will talk to your Grandma when we get home. You can eat in your room if you like. I am sure she and your dad will understand," Charles said, smiling, and winked at Emma.

He always made her feel better. She was so grateful he was in their lives now.

Things Have Changed

Charlotte was amazed by the changes in her family while she was in the hospital. It was such a dramatic change and what she had been praying for all of her life. She found it hard to absorb it was real, to just wake up and everyone is one big happy family. They are all happy and content, and life is great for all of them—all but her own life. It seemed to be in shambles.

It was surreal to see her parents not only in the same room, but getting along as though they had never been apart, to see her father and sister interacting so well and to see Marissa in such a happy mood and talking about the Lord and praying and to see her light up around Dan was remarkable. It was all so overwhelming. She felt like she had woke up in some parallel universe, but she knew that was silly; she just didn't know how else to explain it to her own mind.

Her headaches were easing up in frequency, but they still could shut down her world when one hit her. She slept a lot on her bad days, and the room had to be cool, pitch-black, and quiet.

On her good days she was gaining strength and getting pretty good at getting around the house in her motorized wheelchair. She couldn't ask for a more devoted family. Elliott and Emma were always at her side and willing to do anything she asked. She realized how scary it must have been for them to see her like that and wonder if she was going to pull through.

Her parents and sister were there to fill in anytime needed that Elliott and Emma were away. School had started back for Emma, Elliott and Marissa were working again, and life seemed to be picking up its own new routine for everyone but Charlotte. She had her physical therapy sessions and doctors' appointments of course, but it wasn't the same.

Larry, her boss at the family restaurant, had visited her and brought her flowers. He was kind, but she could tell he had something to tell her. He had hired a new waitress to fill her spot. He assured her that when she was ready to work again to call him and if he had a spot or even a few hours here or there, he would give them to her. He also promised if he didn't, he would give her the best references. Charlotte understood. Life went on for everyone else but her.

There was just this nagging feeling of irritation or jealousy or something. She still had to fight so hard to do anything and felt so helpless. She just wanted to be back to her old self. Everyone was being so overwhelmingly patient and helpful that that seemed to irritate her too. She tried hard to hide it but sometimes she got snippy with them. No one ever complained or showed any offense. Charlotte would apologize, and they would assure her it was fine, but that seemed to annoy her more.

She felt so ungrateful and so frustrated but felt she had to keep this smile on and be the happy good little Charlotte she had always been. She was tired of it, tired of living up to everyone's expectations of her and tired of feeling so guilty for the feelings she was having.

Everyone's life seemed to be all perfect and tied up neatly with a bow on top. Everyone's life but Charlotte's. She felt resentful toward her family. She had all this anger and ugly feelings swirling inside of her. On top of the anger was guilt and more anger at herself for everything. Her gift of just pushing things down and just making everything right again seemed lost to her now. She was trying desperately to regain it but didn't know how.

"Charlotte," Elliott said softly, seeing she was deep in thought.

Charlotte looked up, surprised. She hadn't heard Elliott come in. She was sitting in her wheelchair facing out the window of their bedroom.

"Are you okay?"

"Yes. I am sorry. I have been a little moody today. Or more than today, huh?" Charlotte smiled guiltily. Elliott smiled kindly.

"Maybe a little, but…," Elliott said and he started to continue but Charlotte put her hand up in protest and closed her eyes.

"Please, don't make excuses for me. Don't tell me it is fine or that is understandable. I might just scream," Charlotte said pleadingly. Elliott stayed quiet.

"I don't know what is wrong with me and I am so mad at myself. Everyone is being so kind and it is making me more frustrated. I just don't know how to feel or how to turn it around anymore. I just can't push it down anymore." Tears streamed down Charlotte's face.

"Well…good," Elliott said enthusiastically. Charlotte looked up, surprised. "I never understood how you did it. At some point it makes sense that you couldn't do it anymore. This major life change you have gone through maybe jolted you into facing it. Not to mention that it can't be easy waking up and all of a sudden your entire family are like different people than you have known your whole life. It has to be weird or unsettling, to say the least. I don't know how to process it all myself, and I watched it happen. I didn't just wake up to it." Elliott smiled softly.

Charlotte smiled. "You always said I was the perfect one, but I think it is you, Elliott Wingate, who is perfect," Charlotte said with a sigh. His words helped some. He always understood her better than she could understand herself.

"Ha ha! I wouldn't say that, but thank you. Fine. I won't tell you it is understandable. I will tell you to figure it out and let us help you any way we can," Elliott said.

Charlotte nodded and wiped the tears from her cheeks, laughing. "Thank you. I prefer that over being babied and coddled. Makes me feel more helpless than I already am," Charlotte admitted.

Elliott nodded. "Have you thought about talking to Lewis? He has really helped all of us. You seemed to like him too. I will be honest, Marissa and I have talked. She and I noticed your struggle with your emotions, and seeing you frustrated and angry is new to us. We talked together and to Lewis and he said it was…not surprising to him. He said he could help you if you wanted him to, and if you would rather talk to someone else who doesn't know your family, that is…"

"You are trying so hard to not say the word 'understandable,' aren't you?" Charlotte said, laughing.

Elliott nodded, smiling from ear to ear. "Guilty," Elliott said, walking toward her and kissing her forehead. "Hungry? Your mom made dinner," Elliott asked as he started to push her wheelchair toward the doorway.

"I guess you aren't waiting for me to turn you down like I have been," Charlotte said, laughing.

"Nope. I am not going to be so understandable anymore, at your request. I am going to start pushing you more," Elliott said then laughed. "No pun intended!"

"Good. Maybe that is what I need. I am tired of being asked and encouraged and doted on. It leaves me in a sulk," Charlotte said.

"Just remember if you get mad at me for this, it was your idea," Elliott added.

"That is understandable!" Charlotte said, laughing harder. "And Elliott…"

"Yes, Charlotte?" Elliott stopped pushing the wheelchair; he sensed her seriousness.

"Thank you." Charlotte reached back and put her hand on his hand on the wheelchair handle.

"You are welcome," Elliott said sincerely.

"Elliott, I think I would like to talk to Lewis, alone," Charlotte said, biting her lip.

"I will let him know." Elliott was relieved this had gone well. He had been so lost on how to help her. This had been the first real conversation they had had. This felt like the relationship he knew and loved.

"Thank you." Charlotte was relieved he understood and thought just maybe this was what she needed to find more healing, not just the physical but emotional.

She was so relieved he wasn't upset or insulted. Things had changed, but now maybe it could come full circle.

Delores had made vegetable soup, some fresh-baked bread, and a salad. She knew Charlotte's appetite was still light, so she wanted to fill her up easily and nothing too heavy. Charlotte had been in a touchy mood since she got home from the rehab center. She was trying not to take Charlotte's sharp tones and short answers to heart.

Charles was there to reassure her that they were doing their best and they needed to give Charlotte room to go through her recovery how she needed to. They took care of her physical needs, and Delores cooked and cleaned up the kitchen as Charles kept up on the house cleaning to help out Elliott and Emma too.

"Mom, what smells so good?" Charlotte asked, realizing she hadn't been the kindest to her mother in the last few weeks.

"I made vegetable soup, bread, and a salad. Are you hungry?" Delores was encouraged by Charlotte's demeanor.

"Yes, I think I am. Thank you, Mom. I do appreciate all you and Dad have been doing. I am sorry I have been so irritable. I am not quite sure how to deal with all of this, and I don't mean to take it out on anyone," Charlotte admitted, embarrassed.

"Charlotte, thank you. I have tried to put it that way in my mind, but it helps to hear you say it. I thought maybe you were just angry with me," Delores said, smiling weakly.

"Oh, I am sorry. No, it is all me. I just don't know what to think or feel, and it seems I am making it hard on everyone," Charlotte said honestly, wiping a tear from her eye. "Where is Emma?"

"She was going to eat in her room," Charles said softly. He and Delores looked at each other.

"Is she hiding from me?" Charlotte asked, realizing how angry she really has been lately.

"Yes," Elliott said softly. Charlotte felt horrible. She burst into tears.

"Charlotte, this has been a very emotional and challenging time for everyone, especially you. We are all just trying to figure this out as we go along. I will go talk to her," Elliott said, gripping Charlotte's shoulders.

"No. I want to talk to her," Charlotte said, wiping the tears from her eyes. She wheeled herself toward Emma's room, thankful her chair had electric capabilities since she had a broken arm. The door was shut, and she could hear her radio on. Charlotte took a deep breath and knocked on the door.

"Yes?" Emma called. She figured it was her dad checking in on her.

"Emma, it's Mom," Charlotte said. There was no response. Charlotte knocked again.

Emma opened the door; she looked a little uncomfortable. Charlotte's heart sank.

"Hi there. Can I come in?" Charlotte tried to sound cheerful. The look of bewilderment on Emma's face broke her heart.

Emma stood back and opened the door wider. Charlotte wheeled in. Emma's dinner was on a tray on her bed. Her homework was strewn across the bed as well.

"Is the soup good?" Charlotte asked cheerfully.

"Yeah," Emma said cautiously.

"Oh, Em, I am so sorry. I have been a bear since I have come home, and I am so sorry. I have all these emotions and stuff going on inside me, and I don't know how to deal with it or how to react to all the changes, but in my frustration, I never meant to take it out on any of you. You all took such good care of me in the hospital and in the rehab center and since I have been home, and I have been so selfish and a real jerk. I am so sorry," Charlotte gushed and sobbed.

Emma just took it all in, tears streaming down her own face. This was her mom. This is who she was waiting on to return. She just jumped onto her mom's lap and held onto her. Charlotte wrapped her right arm around her as well and they just sobbed together.

"It is okay, Mom. I understand. I have really just missed *you*," Emma sobbed.

Charlotte and Emma clung to each other and sobbed. When they gathered themselves, they wiped each other's tears away and laughed. They looked up to see Elliott, Charles, and Delores in the doorway crying too.

"Well, we better stop crying or we are going to make our bread soggy," Charles said, sniffing and wiping his eyes. They all laughed.

"Em, will you please eat with us at the table? I promise to be nice," Charlotte said softly. Emma grinned from ear to ear. She hugged her mom and grabbed her tray.

"Let's go!" Emma said and led the way. Elliott pushed Charlotte back to the dining room.

Charlotte smiled and talked kindly all through dinner. They all relaxed and laughed. Charlotte still felt all her emotions swirling around, but she pushed through them for tonight. She knew she had to face them and she had a lot more to go through, but tonight they all just needed a break. She saw Elliott looking at her softly and she smiled at him.

"This was really good. Thank you again, Mom. I love you all, but I am very tired," Charlotte admitted.

"Does your head hurt?" Elliott asked; he could see it in her eyes. She nodded.

"Let me get you to bed. Emma, can you get your mom's pain pills and some water?" Elliott asked. Emma jumped up to go get them.

"Elliott, we will clean this up and head home. We will see you in the morning," Delores said softly as Elliott pushed Charlotte toward the bedroom.

"Thank you," Elliott mouthed back quietly. Charlotte waved but her head was really starting to throb and she couldn't even open her eyes. When would this get better?

* * * * *

"What is bothering you?" Dan asked Marissa as he watched her poke her fork at her dinner.

She looked up, blushing. "I'm sorry. I guess I haven't been very good company tonight," Marissa said apologetically.

"No apology needed. I just wondered what you are thinking about and you really should share with the whole class," Dan said, smiling.

Marissa laughed. "Well, I was thinking about how Charlotte just hasn't been herself since the accident. I am worried. Is it just part of the recovery and eventually she will be back to herself, or has this accident changed her forever?" Marissa had been afraid to say it out loud but felt better getting it out.

"Well, maybe a little of both. I think she will probably end up more like the Charlotte you remember, but she may be a little different. She has been through a lot emotionally and physically. That was quite a head injury she had. She is still in a lot of pain and frustrated by her limitations. I think that is the biggest part. I see things like this in my line of work to a point, with other officers who have been injured or just working with the public and talking with people. You should really talk to my dad. He can help you with this more than I can. His line of work really deals with this a lot. I think he could really help Charlotte too, especially since he is just meeting her and he doesn't have expectations of who she used to be. It might be easier for her to open up to him. And he is good at what he does," Dan offered.

"You are right. We are expecting too much too fast. That has to add to her frustration. Even if we try to hide it from her, it has to be obvious to her, not to mention how much has changed while she was unconscious. Talk about everything being turned upside down." Marissa sighed. Her heart went out to her little sister.

Lewis

"Hello?" Lewis answered his phone at his desk in his office at the hospital.

"Hi, Lewis, this is Marissa Medlock. Is this a good time?" Marissa asked nervously.

"Hello, Marissa! It is. What is on your mind?" Lewis asked, smiling.

"Well, it is Charlotte. I have been worried about her. Elliott and I were concerned before she went home, but I haven't talked to him since. Dan made some good points about her head injury and all she is going through with the pain and limitations causing her frustrations. I hadn't thought about that, but my fear is that she won't ever be who she used to be again. Dan said I should talk to you," Marissa gushed, wiping a tear from her eye.

"My son is wise. Yes, she is going through a lot and her emotions are all over the place. It is too early to judge how things will go in the future, but I think you have nothing to fear. I think it will be fine. She is doing remarkably well, even if it doesn't seem that way to her and even the rest of the family. Being patient isn't easy. Keep praying and trusting God. I know you are. I actually met Elliott for coffee last week and we talked about this as well. Elliott called me last night. He talked with Charlotte and she said she would like to meet with me alone. I am going to pay Charlotte a visit and see if she is open to my help or if she isn't ready," Lewis explained.

"Oh, that is great news! Elliott needs to talk things out too, and I think you could really help Charlotte. You have been a big help to me. I am so thankful for you." Marissa let out a deep sigh.

"Thank you, Marissa. Hang in there and you can call me anytime," Lewis said honestly.

They said their goodbye and hung up. Lewis got up and grabbed his keys. He stood there for a minute and let out a deep breath. He knew that Charlotte could be open to his visit or angry that he was there so soon to her agreeing to see him.

"Dear God, please guide me in my words and give me wisdom to be a help to Charlotte. Touch her, Lord. In Jesus's name I pray. Amen," Lewis prayed and headed out the door.

* * * * *

The house was quiet. Elliott and Emma had already left for work and school. Charlotte was in her bedroom sitting in her wheelchair, staring out the window, watching the birds at the bird feeder. It was a sunny warm day, the kind of day she loved. She wasn't feeling the way she usually would on a day like this. It might as well be cloudy and stormy outside. That is how she felt on the inside. She would love to shake this feeling of gloom and doom; she just didn't know how.

"Lord, I feel so lost and broken. I am so angry and I don't know how to be me anymore. I don't want to be like this. I don't want to be hurtful and spiteful, especially to those who are just trying to love me and help me. I have been so caught up in feeling sorry for myself. I haven't been talking to you about it, and I haven't been reading my Bible. That might help, huh?" Charlotte let out a deep sigh.

"Charlotte, honey, you have a visitor," Charles said at the doorway. She looked up, surprised by the interruption of being alone and at the news of a visitor. She felt a little embarrassed that her dad might have heard her too.

"Oh, thank you, Dad. Who is it?" Charlotte asked, choosing to believe he didn't hear her prayer.

"Lewis. Do you remember him? You have met him briefly a few times. He came to visit you at the hospital early on when you woke up, but you were so groggy back then, you might not remember that. He is the hospital chaplain who was with us every day while you were in your coma. He is Dan's father," Charles explained, pretending he hadn't overheard her prayer.

Charles didn't want to embarrass her, and he was so glad she was praying.

"Oh, okay. I remember him vaguely. I do remember he is Dan's dad. Elliott talked to me yesterday about meeting with Lewis, but I wasn't expecting him so soon." Charlotte wished Elliott were here. She knew he had become good friends with Lewis; they all seemed very attached to him too. She tried not to get irritated that once again, everyone else had this new person in their life and she was left out.

"He cares about you but really hasn't had the chance to meet you. He has wanted to give you time to heal. He is someone who is easy to talk to and he is a minister and counselor. Maybe he could be of help to you…" Charles wished he could retract that last statement. He saw her stiffen.

"Oh." Charlotte suddenly felt very uncomfortable about talking to Lewis.

"Charlotte, I am sure he just wants to check on you and get to know you better. I shouldn't have said the other part."

"You are probably right though… I wish Elliott were here. Maybe you should tell him it isn't a good time." Charlotte sighed deeply.

"Charlotte, I don't want to step on your toes or anything, but I did hear your prayer. I didn't mean to, but I did. Maybe this is an answer to that prayer? It wouldn't hurt to talk to him." Charles was really hoping this boldness and tug of his heart was God and not just him.

"Oh, that is okay. I guess you are right," Charlotte said, realizing she was feeling inside a push to talk to Lewis. She nodded. "Dad, I think you're right. Can you push me out there?"

"I would love to." Charles felt relieved and hurried over to push her out to the living room where Lewis sat talking with Delores.

"Hello, Charlotte." Lewis stood to greet her. He put out his hand to her. "I am Lewis, and I know we have met briefly before, but I have been looking forward to really getting the chance to meet you."

"Hello, Lewis. It is nice to meet you. I have heard wonderful things about you, and it is a pleasure to meet you," Charlotte said on her best behavior. Lewis smiled warmly, and Charlotte felt herself relax.

"We will be in the kitchen if you need us," Charles said and waved for Delores to follow him. She started to protest but realized, suddenly, that Charles was right. She smiled and followed Charles to the kitchen.

Lewis sat down on the couch, near Charlotte, but not too close. He didn't want her to feel crowded or backed into a corner.

"How are you feeling, Charlotte?" Lewis asked genuinely.

"Physically, emotionally, or both?" Charlotte asked honestly; she was trying hard not to get agitated. She wasn't in the mood for a lecture or to be probed with a bunch of questions that might bring on a headache.

"All of the above, or whatever you feel like sharing. I am not trying to make you feel cornered or uncomfortable. I want to be your friend, and I also was hoping I could maybe be someone you could feel comfortable talking to who you don't have to worry about offending or apologize to for hurting my feelings. I have worked with a lot of people post severe trauma and I have been friends with them, I have been someone they can yell at, and I have been someone who has given some advice, but overall, I am a good listener and this visit can be as long or as short as you want it to be. You are in complete control. I can leave now if you want, but I hope you don't want that," Lewis said sincerely.

"I can see why you and Elliott hit it off so well," Charlotte said sincerely, softening to the idea of this visit.

"Elliott is quite a guy. I am glad he is my friend, but I am very sorry for how we met."

"I believe you mean that. I expected you to be different. I am glad I was wrong."

"I take that as a compliment," Lewis said, smiling.

"So I guess I haven't answered your question. For some reason I do feel like I can talk to you," Charlotte said and then let out a deep sigh. "So physically, I hurt a lot. These headaches come and go and it is getting a little better, but they are horrible. I hate being dependent on everyone as much as I am. I am angry at myself for the accident. I am angry at myself for putting my family through this emotionally and financially. I am angry that I have lost my job, but I understand that Larry needed help and it broke his heart to do so. At least he came out to tell me in person. I am angry that everyone's life kept going on and so much changed while I was in a coma. I am angry that I am that petty because wonderful things happened in my family while I was in a coma. I am angry that everyone's life is still going on and I feel like I am on pause. I want to scream and cry, but that would cause me to have a headache. I haven't been praying like I should and I have been hiding in my pain and licking my wounds and only hurting everyone around me, and I don't know how to get back to who I was and I am scared I never will," Charlotte gushed as tears rolled down her cheeks.

Lewis sat listening intently. He took in everything and let her say all that came rushing out of her. She hadn't meant to say so much, but once she started and she knew she didn't have to try and protect his feelings from what she said, it just all came out. It even surprised her. They sat in silence for a full minute. Charlotte took in a deep breath and let it out.

"Good. Deep breaths help us so much. Keep doing that when you feel upset or don't know what else to do," Lewis said with a smile on his face. He also took in a deep breath and let it out.

"Charlotte, thank you. Thank you for entrusting me with all of that. Everything you said is completely understandable and you have every reason to feel all of those emotions," Lewis said supportively and paused.

"It can't be easy to go through what you are physically, and keeping all of that bottled up emotionally is even harder. You don't want to hurt your family."

"But I am. I have been so ugly. I even overheard Elliott apologizing for me to a nurse once at the rehabilitation center after I bit the poor woman's head off for no reason. I have become this horrible monster and I don't like all this ugliness that is coming out of me, but I don't know how to stop it." Charlotte sobbed.

"You have to let it out. You have been in very limited ability to let it out any other way. The medical staff at the rehabilitation center understand that. Your family loves you no matter what, and they aren't going to abandon you. We need to find ways to help you deal with all of this in a way so you don't have it all bottled up. We can talk as much as you need to, and we can work to find other outlets for you as well," Lewis said and paused again.

"Charlotte, your body is going to heal. You will be back to your past physical abilities in time. You also have to give yourself grace to heal emotionally as well. You understand that the physical healing is going to take time, but you have to embrace that the emotional healing will take time as well. Accepting that is a huge big step in the right direction." Lewis smiled at Charlotte, and she returned his smile with one of her own.

"I guess that makes sense." She couldn't help but feel so relaxed talking with him. She was so grateful he had been at her family's side at the hospital, and she was especially glad he was there for Elliott who she knew was holding strong for everyone else.

"I am not going to be ugly like this forever?" Charlotte asked, needing to hear there was hope for her.

"No, Charlotte. You will be happy again. You will forever be changed by all of this, but you will be stronger," Lewis said pointedly. Charlotte took another deep breath and let it out slowly.

"I have felt so selfish for these feelings," Charlotte admitted, "and that somehow has made me angrier."

"You have great insight of yourself, and that is very helpful in your healing as well. You have a right to every emotion you are feeling. You are human, Charlotte Wingate. You are used to carrying the burdens of others and making everything right for everyone else. Let them help you now."

"Well, that human thing isn't all it's cracked up to be," Charlotte said, laughing.

"You can say that again, but we have a heavenly Father who never leaves us," Lewis reassured her. She nodded. Her face was so much more relaxed and brighter than when she first came in the room. He was feeling so grateful she was open to talk to him. God was good, all the time.

"Yes, we certainly do," Charlotte said, wiping a fresh tear from her eye. "Lewis, I am so grateful God brought you into our lives. I am so grateful you were there for my family, especially Elliott."

"You are very welcome. You have an amazing family. And you are okay too," Lewis said, smiling.

"You sure about that?" Charlotte laughed.

"Absolutely positive," Lewis said, beaming. He got up and walked over to Charlotte. He kneeled down in front of her to be at eye level. "I have really looked forward to getting to know you, Charlotte. I thank God that I got this chance. I am so glad you are recovering. It is a long journey on, but you are going to make it, I promise, one day at a time, one hour at a time, but you will make it."

"Thank you," Charlotte said quietly.

Lewis embraced her in a hug then stood up. "I should be going now. I don't want to exhaust you. Here is my business card. It has my office phone and cell phone on it. You can call me any time, day or night, to talk. I have some ideas of things I would like to bring over and for us to do to work through some things for you. If you are okay with that?"

"Thank you. Yes, I would be open to whatever you think would be good for me."

"Good, but feel free to tell me if you don't like an idea I suggest. You have complete control of what you want and don't want to do. I want you to own that. You do have control. You aren't at the whim of everyone else. Your feelings matter. You don't have a lot of control in a lot of areas of your physical body, and that can be frustrating enough. You need to feel control in all the ways you can. Does that make sense?" Lewis asked.

"Yes. Thank you! I need that." Charlotte was beaming.

Lewis nodded. "Would you like me to let your parents know I am leaving or to wheel you anywhere?" Lewis asked.

"No, thank you. I think I just want to sit here for a bit and think. I can wheel myself or call for them and they respond quickly. I really am blessed," Charlotte said, realizing how true it was.

Lewis nodded, smiling, and left.

It was amazing how much just being validated and heard can mean to a person. God was definitely moving here too. He also knew there was a lot of hard days ahead still, both physically and emotionally for Charlotte. He was just grateful she was open to it. That was God and he also felt he was getting a peak at the Charlotte that she used to be. She would soon discover she was still more herself than she realized. She had a lot going on inside of her, and she was afraid to let it out. She didn't want to hurt anyone, and she was ashamed of how she felt. That much bottled up can really torture the soul and change you. Then there was the physical pain added in. Prayer and patience and a lot of hard work would carry her through.

* * * * *

Charlotte sat in the living room thinking about all she had said to Lewis and what he had said to her. She was kind of surprised at all she had said. She had been working so hard on keeping it all in, she didn't realize all that was upsetting her. She wheeled herself in to the kitchen and found her parents sipping coffee and smiling at each other. This was all so strange. She tried not to bristle and took a deep breath. They realized she was there.

"Is Lewis gone?" Delores asked.

"Yes. I like him. I see why you all are so fond of him," Charlotte said honestly.

"He has been a help to all of us," Delores said, nodding. "How are you feeling?"

"Tired. I think I need a nap," Charlotte admitted.

Charles jumped up to wheel her back to her room and help her into bed.

"Dad, can I ask you something?" Charlotte asked as he helped her with her pillows.

"Anything, dear," Charles said, smiling.

"Are you and Mom…together again?" Charlotte asked timidly.

"We have decided to begin dating, to reconnect, and see what happens. We are a lot older and wiser now and we both know the Lord now. That changes everything. So we are starting again… How do you feel about that?"

"I don't know. I mean, you don't need my permission or anything. It just seems so strange and yet it is nice. The whole world changed and turned on its axis while I was in that hospital bed, it seems. I don't know how to process it all," Charlotte admitted.

"I understand. In ways it did, didn't it?" Charles said, nodding in agreement.

"Rest, my dear. I love you." Charles kissed her forehead and headed for the door.

"Thank you, and I love you too." Charlotte watched him shut the door and felt a tear run down her cheek.

She wasn't sure what she was feeling, but out of place in this new family was definitely part of it.

* * * * *

Charlotte took a long nap and actually slept through lunch. Her meeting with Lewis took a lot out of her. She woke up and it was dinnertime. Elliott was sitting in a chair next to their bed, watching her.

"Oh, hello…" Charlotte was coming out of a deep sleep and was a little disoriented.

"Hello," Elliott sat up smiling; he looked relieved.

"I'm okay. I met Lewis today and we had a good conversation, but I think it wore me out. I am okay. You can relax," Charlotte said, smiling at Elliott. She could read his mind just as easily as she always could. He chuckled and went to help her sit up.

"Hungry?" Elliott asked as he waited for her cue to help her into the wheelchair.

"Now that you mention it, yes, I am starving! Mom will like that!" Charlotte mused.

"Yes, she will. I think we all will." Elliott let out a deep breath and pushed her to the dining room. Her parents and Emma were setting the table, and Marissa and Dan were there setting out the food and drinks.

"Well, look who woke up to join the party!" Elliott announced.

They all beamed at her. Charlotte felt a little uncomfortable with all the attention.

They took a seat at the table. The food smelled delicious, and they all looked at Elliott for the prayer.

"Can I say the prayer?" Charlotte asked. They all smiled.

"Please do," Elliott said, beaming at her.

"Dear Jesus, thank you so much for this meal before us. Thank you for all the care my family has given me and for bringing us all together. This is something I never dreamed I could have. I thank you for it. Help me to continue to heal and to be the Charlotte I once was. Carry my family through this time as well. In Jesus's name I pray. Amen." Charlotte raised her head. Through her tears she saw the tears in their eyes too, even Dan.

"Well, let's eat," Charlotte said, wiping her tears away and laughing nervously.

They all ate and had a nice dinner. Charlotte felt better than she had been feeling but couldn't get past this feeling of being an outsider in this group of people who all seemed so comfortable together. She ate quietly and listened to all the conversation and laughter. She smiled but felt so lost. She felt like someone was watching her, and she glanced at Elliott, but it wasn't him. Then she looked across at everyone and realized it was Emma. She looked concerned and sad. Charlotte winked at her and smiled. Emma returned the smile, but her eyes looked sad still.

After dinner, Marissa and Dan insisted on cleaning up, and Charles and Delores headed out early.

"Charlotte, where do you want to go?" Elliott asked.

"Emma's room," Charlotte said.

Emma looked up, surprised, and a genuine smile crossed her face.

"You got it!" Elliott pushed her into Emma's room, and Emma came in and plopped onto her bed.

"I am getting the feeling this is Mother-Daughter time and I am not needed," Elliott said, smiling. He left, closing the door behind him.

"Emma, are you okay? I saw you watching me at dinner." Charlotte decided not to dance around what was on her mind.

"Sorry if I made you uncomfortable. I just thought you looked sad. You were smiling but your eyes were sad," Emma said softly.

"Oh honey, you are fine. You didn't make me uncomfortable at all. I just realized I wasn't fooling you," Charlotte said honestly.

"What was bothering you?"

"Everything in my life was one way. The next thing I know, I wake up in a hospital and everything is different. In a good way, but I feel so out of place or disconnected. I want to be happy and I feel uncomfortable. I feel like an outsider, like I don't belong. I don't know how to fix it," Charlotte answered honestly.

Emma nodded and looked thoughtful. Then she got a big smile on her face. "I got it! You feel out of place because you weren't a part of it. The only way that you can change that is to become a part of it!" Emma squealed as she jumped up and down on her bed.

Charlotte was confused at Emma's excitement. How would she do that? "How do I become a part of it?" Charlotte asked.

"You need one-on-one time with everyone. You need to have some time with each one and talk about the changes and reconnect that relationship. You haven't had that chance," Emma explained as she jumped off the bed to stand before her mother.

Charlotte took in what Emma said, and a smile spread across her face. "Emma! You are a genius!" Charlotte said, laughing. Out of the mouth of babes!

"You both okay in there?" Elliott asked through the door. They were laughing and crying when he peeked in. Women.

"Is Marissa still here?" Charlotte asked.

"Yes, she and Dan are in the kitchen. I couldn't talk them out of doing the dishes, so I was supervising until we heard all the commotion back here," Elliott said, smiling.

"Please take me to Marissa," Charlotte said, beaming. Emma was jumping up and down, laughing. Elliott had no idea what the two of them were up to, but he wheeled Charlotte to the kitchen and Emma bounced along too.

"Marissa, could you and I do brunch on Saturday? Just you and I?" Charlotte asked.

Marissa was drying a bowl and looked at Charlotte, surprised at the request, but smiled.

"I would love to do brunch with you. Is something up?" Marissa was confused.

"Yes, everything. We need to talk about everything. I want to hear about how you came to know Jesus as your Savior. I want to hear about how you met Dan, and how this has all began. I mean, I know you met him at the hospital, but I don't know *the story*. I know you love me, and our relationship is definitely different than it has ever been or at least since we were very young. I want to know how you and Dad connected and began your relationship again. I need to be a part of that healing. I want to be a part of your life. I think Emma is right. I feel so disconnected from everyone because I missed being a part of all the changes. I need to have my time with each of you to become a part of it all. I need to have some time with Mom too and Dad and after time with you, I need to meet Dan again, with you like it was a normal situation and a normal sister introducing me to her boyfriend scenario. I need to talk with Elliott and Emma one-on-one too about that time and catch up on how they truly were and are. I need to get my time back that I lost," Charlotte said through tears, but her smile was genuine.

"I can't be a part of this family until I become a part of it, each family member, each relationship," Charlotte announced confidently. Then she looked at Emma. "My sweet girl, you have no idea what you have helped me find in me. I can't ever thank you enough!' Charlotte cried.

Emma jumped onto her lap and wrapped her arms around her. She held her mom close and felt like this was the beginning to everything she had been hoping and praying for. This was the beginning of her mom really waking up.

CHAPTER 5

Born Sisters, Finally Friends

Marissa sat nervously at the booth at Oliver's waiting on Charlotte to arrive. She wasn't quite sure why she was so nervous, but she had a feeling it was because it was time to make true amends with Charlotte over the past and truly begin a real sister's relationship with Charlotte. She wanted it so much, but facing who she used to be and all she had said and done to Charlotte wasn't pleasant. She shuddered at how she had talked to her and treated her. Dan had told her to relax and just trust the Lord to guide her.

Elliott pushed Charlotte into the restaurant and to the table where Marissa was sitting at, waving at them. Once he had her settled at the table, he said his goodbyes and left. This was a sister's only brunch. Charlotte had been so happy and excited for this brunch and her spirits seemed high. It was good to see the woman he loved acting more like herself.

"I don't think I have ever been here before," Charlotte said, smiling at Marissa and looking at the menu.

"I have only been here a few times, but there is a special reason why I wanted us to meet here. I'll explain that later," Marissa said, smiling. Charlotte nodded, accepting that as enough for now.

"Pancakes sound really good this morning. Smothered in strawberry syrup and real strawberries and whip cream!" Marissa said as she looked over the menu.

"That does sound good!" Charlotte added. "Works for me!"

They placed their orders, and when the waitress walked away, they locked eyes.

"I will start," Charlotte said, seeing Marissa's nervousness. "We have had a rocky relationship over the years, and I think that was just a product of our dysfunctional family. I think had Mom and Dad handled things differently, our lives and our relationship could have been so different. I don't blame them because they were young and they were really just trying to figure it all out. I don't blame you either, Marissa. I want you to know that."

"How do you do that? How do you always see everything out of love and compassion? Aren't you angry at me at all?" Marissa asked. She was grateful for Charlotte's words, but she wanted to be sure they were really facing everything now.

"No. I have only ever wanted was to be your sister. I took it personally at times, but I prayed about it, and God showed me how you were reacting out of your pain. You have painful memories from our past that I was too young to remember. You have carried a burden I didn't. I didn't remember Dad, so he was more of a character I never knew. He wasn't real to me, his absence was, but it wasn't anything I really ever knew or felt I lost. It was my normal to have him not there. That wasn't how it was for you."

Tears streamed down Marissa's face, and she offered a weak smile to Charlotte, nodding. "I knew you didn't remember, and that it wasn't the same for you in that way. That is part of the reason why I think I resented you so much. You were just living your life as you knew it. I knew a different family and I ached to have it back. I hated that you didn't feel that too. I had to blame someone and I couldn't blame them. I loved Dad too much, and Mom was all I had and I was afraid she would leave too. So you became my target for blame. It wasn't fair. You were the most innocent besides me, but Mom seemed to do the same thing, so it seemed right. It was dead wrong. I am so sorry, Charlotte. It was one thing when I was a child, but at some point I should have changed and corrected matters."

"Marissa, thank you. It does feel good to hear your apology. I accept it. I hope you can forgive yourself. That point is now. It has come. The only one who really needs forgiven is you from yourself. There is no point in punishing yourself. It is the enemy's way of keeping you in pain, isolated, and keeping a wall between us. If he can't hurt you one way, he will in another way," Charlotte said, looking to see if Marissa was taking her seriously.

"Thank you so much, Charlotte. I was so afraid I wouldn't get the chance to have this conversation with you. When I got the call from Elliott, I was in shock and then I was terrified. I didn't want anything to happen to you. I suddenly realized just how much I loved you and how much I needed you. Even if I had told you I never wanted to see you again. Deep down I knew you would always be there. I needed you. The thought of losing you for real…," Marissa said, wiping more tears away.

"Wow. You really felt that way?" Charlotte was honestly surprised.

"Yes, I did. I took you for granted, and I just assumed you would always be there trying to love me and I could always be nasty to you, and it would go on that way forever. Then the realization that I could really lose you hit hard. I ran to pick up Mom, and she reacted the same way. We rushed to the hospital. It seemed so unreal. We were both so scared for selfish reasons. We needed you and we realized that and we realized that we had a lot of apologizing to do and a lot to make up. Elliott and Emma were in shock and terrified, but yet they had a calmness to them that we didn't and that we didn't understand. Then later Dad showed up."

"Oh wow! I can just imagine the shock of that to both of you! Did Mom know I had even met him yet?" Charlotte gasped and sat back in her wheelchair, taking in what that must have been like.

"No. It was uncomfortable. I was hit with all these emotions and so was Mom. Oh my goodness. Lewis was a godsend! He picked up on what was going on and he was there for both of us. He helped us so much. I was reeling and hit with those emotions I had when Dad left. It all rushed back, not that I hadn't relived it over and over in my head all these years…"

"I know," Charlotte said softly.

Marissa looked up from the pattern in the tablecloth she had been staring at in confusion.

"How would you know that?" Marissa asked skeptically. She never had talked about him.

"You cried in your sleep sometimes, calling out for him, begging him not to leave," Charlotte said gently. Tears rolled down her cheeks. "I would go over to your bed and watch you toss and turn and sob and cry out for him to come back and begging him not to leave. Even as a teenager you sounded like a little girl as you cried out for him."

"You're kidding!" Marissa felt embarrassed and exposed.

"I didn't know what to do. I would stand next to your bed, wanting to reach out to you or to comfort you, but I was afraid you would wake up and be mad or embarrassed. I would just stand there shaking and praying for you quietly. I didn't know what else to do. It was always late at night or in the early morning."

"How often?" Marissa whispered; she was in shock.

"Maybe three times a month I guess. More around the holidays, your birthday, and Father's Day," Charlotte said quietly.

"Oh my…you never said a word…" Marissa was in shock.

"I knew that wouldn't go over well, and I didn't want to cause you more pain. I could see how deeply you were hurting, and I didn't want to cause you more. I could forgive you because I knew how you were hurting. I recognized I didn't have that pain like you did. If lashing out at me helped you at all, I could take it. It was my only way of helping you."

"Does Mom know?"

"Not that I know of. She was never there. We shared a room all those years, and I never told anyone. This is the first time I have spoken of it. I only prayed about it," Charlotte said.

"Wow…. Every time I think I have you figured out, you blow me away. You never teased me or threw it in my face to hurt me back. You just prayed for me and loved me… You are absolutely amazing, Charlotte." Marissa was blown away.

"I have Jesus in my heart and leading me. I accepted Jesus as my Lord and Savior at Vacation Bible School. I never let go. I needed him and I found peace and love in him. That is how I made it through, and that is how I could see you and Mom and even Dad with eyes of love and forgiveness. I have been forgiven and I prayed to see with His eyes. I wanted to have a heart for people like He does."

"You certainly do. I am so grateful. I used to find your faith so trivial and weak. I thought you were crazy. I thought it was funny. I made fun of you so much for that, but through your faith, you were praying and loving me. Wow, I am the biggest heel in the world."

"Oh, Marissa, you were a kid who was hurting so much. You didn't know how to deal with it, and you didn't know Jesus. You were just trying to make sense of everything and I knew that. I prayed about that too," Charlotte said, laughing at the end.

Marissa started to laugh too. She reached for Charlotte's hand. "Thank you, Charlotte. Thank you for not hating me. Thank you for loving me and never giving up on me. I am truly sorry for all the pain I have ever caused you. I wish I could take it all back."

"I told you I forgive you, Marissa. You have to forgive yourself now. Let God help you do that."

"I will try. Thank you." Marissa smiled weakly.

Their plates of piled high pancakes and strawberry topping and whipped cream towered over it.

"Oh that looks good!" Charlotte said, grinning from ear to ear.

"Yes it does!" Marissa smiled, grabbing her fork to dive in. "You know, Dad did try to contact us and Mom sent back everything he sent and kept telling him to stay away. That is how she knew where he was living to tell you."

"He explained that to me. I just didn't want to rush in telling you more than you were ready to hear," Charlotte said, nodding.

"Thank you for always looking out for me. It is supposed to be the other way around, but you have always been the one to take care of me," Marissa said, sighing softly.

"How did you find that out?" Charlotte asked, assuming their dad had told her.

"Mom told me," Marissa said, and Charlotte started to choke on her bite of pancakes.

"What?" Charlotte couldn't believe it.

"Yes, the day you were in the accident. We had been at the hospital all day, and we left to go have dinner and get some rest. I decided to stay with Mom that night so we could get up and make breakfast to take to everyone in the morning. We all felt so helpless and we wanted to do something. Mom confessed to me at dinner. I was in shock and it unlocked something in me... I just realized that he did look back! Not that day, but he did and he wanted to be in our lives. It broke something in me or fixed something in me. I don't know how to explain it..."

"Mom confessed... That must have been a long, emotional day. Seeing Dad too...it probably brought everything back to her. She probably realized you were about to find out, and she wanted to be the one to tell you. I am so sorry for all you went through that day, especially—"

"Aw, Charlotte, you had the worst of it, but it is like you to worry about everyone else instead of yourself. It isn't exactly like you were vacationing in the Caribbean or anything at the time."

"No, unless I was in my head and I don't remember it. I remember weird dreams and running lost through a thick fog, my legs and my left arm hurting, and horrible headaches. In the distance, I could hear familiar voices, but I couldn't make out who they were or how to find them at first. Then I recognized the voices but was sure it was a dream, especially hearing you, Mom, and Dad and that you and Mom were saved and Mom and Dad were talking to me at the same time. It was scary and frustrating," Charlotte said.

Marissa just stared at her. She had had no idea. "I thought you were just sleeping," Marissa confessed. "We talked to you, but I thought it was just for us. I didn't know you could hear us..."

"You are the first person I have told that to," Charlotte said, locking eyes with Marissa. "I guess some things you can only tell your sister."

"I really want that kind of relationship with you," Marissa said and reached for Charlotte's hand. "I can't make up for the past, but I can start right here, right now, and *be the sister* you always deserved and get to know the sister *you have always been.*" Marissa felt a tear slide down her cheek.

"Marissa… I never dreamed this day would come, but I am so glad it did. I have caused so much needless pain to everyone and myself, but maybe if something good can come from it, then maybe I can forgive myself," Charlotte said, swallowing hard.

"Charlotte, it was an accident. You can't blame yourself," Marissa said. She hadn't realized Charlotte was feeling this way.

"But it was an accident I caused by running a red light. I could have hurt or killed someone with my foolishness. If I had been late one time, it would not have been a big deal. My boss was great, and as long as it wasn't routine, he understood. I had never been late in all the years I worked there, so he would have just been glad I was okay when I got there. I am just grateful no one else was seriously hurt."

"My wise little sister told me once that the only person left to be forgiven was me forgiving myself."

Charlotte burst into tears. It felt good to get that out, but it really had bothered her so much, and now saying it out loud just released a tidal wave of tears. Marissa got up and came to her side and just wrapped her arms around her sister and let her cry.

A few people looked over to see what was going on, but Marissa didn't care. She was glad Charlotte was letting this out and opening up to her. This was a big part of the healing Charlotte needed as well as the physical healing.

"Oh good grief, I am a mess and making a scene. I am sorry!" Charlotte said, trying to gain control. She knew Marissa didn't like attention drawn to her.

"Who cares? If there is one thing I have learned through all this is that being in the present and people are what are important, not what others think or what it looks like. I am so grateful you shared this with me, but I am more relieved you are letting this out and dealing with it," Marissa shared honestly.

"Who are you?" Charlotte said, laughing through her tears. Marissa laughed too. They realized people were really staring now and they just laughed harder. Marissa gave Charlotte a big hug then sat back down.

"I am a woman who finally woke up to what really matters in life. Becoming a Christian unveiled everything in life to me in a new

FOR THE LOVE OF FAMILY

way. It was like I was blinded to things, and suddenly I could see beyond myself. God touched my life. Jesus saved me and healed my heart. I had this refreshing awakening! It was indescribable!" Marissa gushed.

Charlotte sat smiling at her with so much excitement and love. "I am so glad you did, not to mention you met an amazing man to boot!" Charlotte grinned.

"Yes! A man who loves Jesus and is teaching me more about God every day in our talks and in who he is." Marissa beamed, thinking about Dan. "Again, all of this happened in the aftermath of your horrible accident. I feel a little guilty in that. You were lying there in a coma, having nightmares and having multiple surgeries and you have all this healing to do, and my life is falling into place, and I feel like my life became a fairy tale and yours a nightmare."

"Oh, but look what I am gaining too? Both my parents are a real part of my life, my sister is really my sister now, and we are one big happy family. It is mind-blowing. I have felt overwhelmed by all of that, as well as jealous and angry that I am kind of on the outside looking in at all of you. It was a weird feeling, and a kind of rage was building in me."

"I noticed. I didn't know why, but I knew it wasn't you, and I didn't know how to help you. We have all been worried, but we can't imagine what it feels like to face all you are going through. I don't think we ever thought about the rest. It makes sense. We had naively thought you would just be so happy." Marissa sat back in her seat, pursing her lips together in deep thought.

"I didn't know how to process it or explain it or what to do to get beyond it. When I spoke with Lewis the other day, I just let it all out. I learned a lot as it all came spewing out. He is so kind and I can see why he and Elliott bonded so quickly. Then I got to talking to Emma about it a little bit. Well, she drew it out of me, and she made the connection of how to deal with it. She is so remarkable."

"Lewis is great, and Emma is definitely remarkable. She is so grown up, but she was so scared and worried about you. She was like a very vulnerable little girl at the same time. It was a lot for everyone to wrap our minds around. She is definitely your daughter." Marissa beamed. She was so proud of her niece. "She was amazing. Here she was terrified, and yet she always was taking care of all of us as well as anyone in the waiting rooms or that had shown us kindness. She didn't want anyone feeling alone or not being fed. She touched so many lives in that hospital."

"She did all of that? I am so proud of her." Charlotte was amazed by how much Emma was really growing up. "I can't take all the credit. She has a lot of Elliott in her and quite an individual in her own right," Charlotte said, shaking her head gently.

"I had been worried about her. She had been so moody and angry all the time. The whole fight to be seen as not a little girl anymore, and I wasn't ready to really see that. We worked through it and I let her grow up a little. I gave her what she needed, and she blossomed right before our eyes. Then the accident happened. I wasn't able to give her the thirteenth birthday party we had talked about. I feel bad about that." Charlotte sighed.

"More anger at yourself, huh?" Marissa asked gently.

Charlotte nodded and wiped a tear from her eye.

"Charlotte, you give everyone so much grace and understanding and love but yourself."

"What?" Charlotte was confused.

"You hold yourself to this unreachable standard, and you can see the absolute best in everyone else. When is Charlotte going to get a little grace? When are you going to let yourself be human and forgive and love yourself?" Marissa asked pointedly, leaning forward and staring Charlotte in the eye.

"I, uh, I guess I never thought about it." Charlotte looked down, thinking about Marissa's words carefully. "I guess I need to do some thinking on that," Charlotte said, smiling softly.

"And some praying too. Give it to God and let go," Marissa added, squeezing Charlotte's hand.

"Look at you! What a good big sister you are!" Charlotte said, laughing.

Marissa chuckled and looked at Charlotte seriously. "Please do think on that. Pray about it. We can talk more about it if you want to, later."

"I would like that," Charlotte said, smiling. "I think I am going to like this sister thing a lot."

"Me too." Marissa smiled warmly and took her last bite of her pancakes. "That was so good!"

"Yes, it was!" Charlotte said, finishing hers as well. Her heart felt so much lighter. "I can't believe I ate the whole thing!"

"We have a lot more to cover, like I want to know all about how you and Dan got together and you and Dad reconnecting and how you came to the point where you accepted Jesus as your Savior, but I am full and getting tired. I am afraid if I don't lay down soon, I will get a headache."

"No problem. We have forever to talk about everything, but let's get you home and resting."

Marissa waved the waiter over to pay the bill. She promised Elliott she wouldn't let Charlotte overdo it and they were getting close to that point. "Let's get this bill paid and get you home. I don't want Elliott mad at me!" Marissa teased. "I will tell you one more thing before we go, why I wanted to eat here…"

Charlotte sensed Marissa growing serious and she strained to focus.

"I was saved right here in this restaurant, that large table over there. I was waiting for everyone to meet here for dinner. Elliott went to the restroom and I was alone. I was trying to figure out how to pray so I could pray for you. A sweet older lady named Mary Ann came over to me and said God sent her over to talk to me. She hesitated but finally followed God's leading. We began to talk and I confessed I was trying to pray and I didn't know how. The next thing I know, she asked me if I believed Jesus was my Savior and if I wanted to ask him into my heart and I said yes. She prayed with me right then and there."

"Oh, Marissa…that is beautiful. God works in such miraculous ways!" Charlotte felt so much peace and joy in her heart. It certainly felt better than the rage and frustration that had been there. "The whole family was able to share in that with you here that night, and you brought me here to help me be a part of that too. Thank you, Marissa."

Feels Like Home Again

Elliott peeked in to see if Charlotte was still sleeping. She had been asleep for a few hours since Marissa had brought her home. He had hoped the venture out wouldn't be too much for her. The look of peace and happiness on her face when she came in, even though she was obviously tired, was a good sight to see. Marissa also had looked so happy and relieved. She had given him a big hug and told him all was going to be fine. He was dying to know about their talk, but he would wait to hear from Charlotte what she wanted to share.

He sat in the chair in the corner of the room, watching her sleep. She seemed so peaceful; it wasn't always like that since the accident. There had been a lot of restless sleep and headaches that she would wake up screaming from. It broke his heart. To watch her sleeping peacefully was a comfort.

He had sent Emma off to the mall with Tracey. It had almost felt normal. Emma out with Tracey, Charlotte off doing her own thing, and he was milling around, enjoying a quiet Saturday morning in the house with nothing to do but relax and watch his shows that the women in his life felt were boring.

Charlotte began to stir and realized he was in the room and watching her. She smiled at him. "Been here long?"

"Just a few minutes. You have been sleeping a few hours. I was wondering if you were going to wake up soon."

"Wow, really? I guess I was tired, but it was a good tired. I had a great time with Marissa. We have never been like that before. It felt nice. I am excited for our new relationship. She is too, and it's a lot to take in for both of us," Charlotte said, smiling.

"You feeling better about that?" Elliott asked honestly.

"Yes. Yes, I do. I feel like I am a part of it and not on the outside looking in. I know I keep saying that, but I don't know how else to describe it. She told me all about getting saved there at Oliver's and Mary Ann. I know you all celebrated that together. You were all there, and by taking me there to share it with me, it was like I was reconnected to the family by one piece," Charlotte said thoughtfully, turning on her side to face Elliott.

He nodded. "We just never thought about it. We were so excited to tell you about all the changes and see how excited you would be about it all, and we never took into consideration what it would feel like for you. It makes perfect sense. I am sorry for the feeling of being locked up inside and like an outsider. That is the last thing anyone wanted. Piece by piece, you will become connected to everyone and can fully move forward in healing and all the future has in store for all of us," Elliott said softly.

"I know. I always knew that. I just didn't know how to explain it, how to understand it even myself, and I definitely didn't know what to do about it. I felt so ashamed of feeling that way too. All of a sudden, I was the negative force fighting against everyone. I didn't understand why or how to change it even though I hated myself for it. I am so thankful that talking to Lewis helped me start to face what was going on inside me and leave it to Emma to figure out how to address it." Charlotte smiled proudly.

"I am really not surprised." Elliott said, chuckling. "She is growing into quite the young lady."

"Marissa was telling me all about that too. Where is she?" Charlotte said, realizing it was Saturday.

"I told her to go to the mall with Tracey. Tracey called and said her mom was willing to drop them off for a while. They wanted to shop, have some lunch at the food court, and see a movie."

"Good. She needs to be a kid again, not just waiting on me hand and foot," Charlotte said, sighing.

"So it will be awhile before she is back. I hate to admit it, but I am feeling kind of hungry." Charlotte laughed. "I ate this huge plate of strawberry pancakes and then slept and now I am so hungry! Good grief!"

"Hey, you are still regaining your strength, and all physical and emotional exertion is very taxing on you right now. What sounds good to you?" Elliott smiled. It was good to feel like he was finally getting his wife back.

"Pizza, with lots of cheese and pepperoni and sausage and breadsticks and cheese!" Charlotte gushed.

Elliott laughed. "You got it. Are we going out or ordering in?"

"Ordering in. I don't think I am ready for two outings in one day just yet," Charlotte said honestly.

"Sounds great to me. Do you want to stay in here or go to the living room?"

"Living room. I am tired of being in bed all the time," Charlotte announced.

Elliott helped Charlotte into her wheelchair and pushed her to the living room. He got her comfortable on the couch.

"You pick out something to watch on TV, and I will call in the order." Elliott handed her the remote control and then called in their order.

They spent the afternoon watching TV, movies, eating pizza and breadsticks, and talking and laughing. It was the first time since the accident that they had had time together like this, no doctors or nurses, no other family hovering around and watching her. Charlotte felt so relaxed and connected to Elliott again it was amazing. She wasn't Charlotte the fragile or Charlotte the patient. She was just Elliott's wife, Charlotte.

"This is nice," Elliott said, smiling at her.

"Yes, it is. It feels like home again," Charlotte said, smiling.

Elliott took her hand. "Yes, it does," he said warmly.

"*Hey!*" Emma said, bursting through the doorway. "I wondered where you guys were."

"Hey, Em, how was the mall and movie?" Elliott asked cheerfully.

"The mall was amazing. There is a new store that just opened up that sells only girls' stuff like jewelry, hair stuff, purses, and perfumes. They pierce your ears too! Tracey and I want to get our ears pierced. What do you think? They have tons of really cute earrings."

"Well, that sounds like something a thirteen-year-old should be able to do. Don't you think, Elliott?"

"Um, well... I guess I am outnumbered, so I think that what your mom said was right." Elliott held up his hands in surrender, knowing he was going to be ganged up on if he answered any other way.

"*Yes!*" Emma jumped up and down and hugged her parents. "I gotta go call Tracey!"

"Didn't you just spend most of the day with her?" Elliott asked.

Emma stopped and stared at him in confusion. "Uh, yeah, but now I have news to tell her that I didn't know before." Emma really didn't get why her dad was always so lost on this stuff.

"Hey, we ate pizza at the mall!" Emma said, pointing at their pizza box.

"I could go for some ice cream," Charlotte said, smiling at Elliott.

"Oooh, yes! Sundaes!" Emma said.

"Okay, I know when I am outnumbered, and when it comes to ice cream, I am definitely in too!" Elliott said, getting up and heading to the kitchen.

"I will go call Tracey and then we can make sundaes. I think we have everything we need," Emma said as she ran for the phone. "The movie was great. I will tell you all about it!"

"I will get the ice cream and bowls out," Elliott said, laughing.

Charlotte watched them both leave the room and a tear spilled out of her eye. She took a deep breath and looked up.

"Thank you, Jesus, for another chance at life and all that you are bringing together. Thank you for healing me and my family. I need you. Every day, I need you," Charlotte whispered. She felt so overjoyed. "Thank you for your peace in my heart. I have been missing it, and I wasn't sure why. I needed to let go of this pain and anger and open up to my family. I needed to forgive myself. Thank you for your guidance and your grace. I think I have been a little mad at you too. I am not sure why, but I ask you to forgive me and to help me to continue to heal and learn through this. Maybe I can use this to help others. I want all the good to come out of it that can. I love you, Lord."

Emma returned momentarily, squealing and excited because Tracey said her parents agreed to let her get her ears pierced too. They were trying to figure out when they could do it. She was gushing about their plans and the movie and who was at the mall and who wasn't at the mall and she chattered on all evening long. Elliott and Charlotte ate their ice cream sundaes quietly, taking in all Emma had to tell them and smiling at each other. It was good to be home again.

Surprise!

Marissa had taken Charlotte home and said goodbye. Her heart was singing from their talk and new beginning as real sisters. There was so much promise to their relationship, and to see Charlotte be more of her old self was such a relief.

It was completely understandable, especially as she had opened up to Marissa about what she had been going through. No wonder she had been so angry and distant toward everyone.

Marissa couldn't take the smile off her face as she cleaned her house and listened to the radio station Dan had told her about. It was all she wanted to listen to anymore. She never dreamed she would be listening to Christian Contemporary radio station of her own free will. She giggled to herself.

She glanced at the time. Dan would be there soon to take her out to dinner. Those pancakes had filled her up, but now she was getting really hungry.

She took a look at her hair and decided to wash it and style it before he got there. She had put it up in a ponytail all day and had a comfy sweatshirt and jeans on. She changed into a deep purple sweater and dark jeans. She slipped on some purple flats and put on some makeup. She really wasn't sure what the plans were tonight, but she couldn't wait to tell him about her brunch with Charlotte.

Dan had worked all day and was planning on heading home to clean up and then he would be by to pick her up. She didn't care what they did or where they went; she was just looking forward to seeing him.

Just as Marissa finished getting ready, she heard the doorbell. She couldn't help but feel giddy and giggle. She hurried off to the door and threw it open. Dan stood smiling at her. He had a dark gray sweater and jeans on. He smelled nice too.

"Hey there, you ready?" Dan asked.

"Sure, let me grab my purse." Marissa smiled. He was in a hurry. Usually he came in and they talked for a bit then decided where to go.

"So where would you like to go?" Dan asked; he seemed a little different.

"Are you okay? You seem...nervous," Marissa said. She was starting to feel nervous all of the sudden.

"I'm sorry. I had a surprise for you, but then I started to think maybe it was a bad idea," Dan admitted.

Marissa gave him a serious stare. "What?" Marissa wasn't so sure she was hungry if he was about to spring on her what she thought he was about to spring on her.

"I was thinking we could have dinner with my parents. You know my dad, but you haven't met my mom yet. She thought having dinner out would be nice. She suggested I make it a surprise, so you wouldn't worry too much in advance about it. The guys at work told me today that I messed up. I should have asked you if you were ready to meet her and give you more notice, but then it was too late. I wasn't able to call you on my shift. There were some crazy calls today, and I never got the chance. I am sorry, Marissa. I wasn't thinking. I can cancel on them, and we can do it another time."

"Wait, but she is expecting to meet me tonight, right?"

"Yes. She is really excited. I promise she isn't scary at all."

"I don't want to make a bad impression by canceling... Some warning would have been nice, but maybe it is better this way. I didn't have time to be nervous or overthink it, and now there is no time for that. Your mom was right about that. Where are we going?" Marissa put on a weak smile.

"She said since we were giving you this surprise, we should let you pick. I'm sorry." Dan looked genuinely remorseful.

Marissa smiled half-heartedly. "Don't feel bad. We will just go with it. Let's call it an adventure," Marissa said, biting her lip, trying to convince both of them. "It will go well or not, but it will be over, right? The first meeting. Like a bandage pulled off fast." Marissa tried to sound lighthearted, but her stomach was turning in knots.

"Yeah, and she is excited, and Dad will be there. Where do you want to go?" Dan was trying to put a good spin on it but felt he was losing.

"Where does she like to go?" Marissa wanted all to be in her favor tonight; picking her favorite place had to be a good choice.

"Barney's Grill is her favorite," Dan offered.

"Barney's Grill it is," Marissa said, exhaling slowly.

"Relax. It will be fine. She is a very nice lady," Dan said, smiling genuinely.

"I have no doubts, but I hope she likes me." Marissa smiled tensely.

Dan winked at her as he pulled his cell phone out of his pocket to call his dad to tell him where to meet them.

* * * * *

Lewis hung up with Dan and smiled at Beth.

"She chose wherever my favorite restaurant is, didn't she? We are going to Barney's Grill?" Beth asked, smiling.

"Yes. So she passed your first test, right?" Lewis said bitingly. "Now I want you to be nice to her, Beth." Lewis was feeling annoyed.

"I don't know what you mean by '*my first test*,'" Beth exclaimed in her best attempt at shock and innocence.

Lewis knew her too well. "She is a lovely woman, and she is a very good match for Dan," Lewis said, giving her a hard stare. "Have you ever seen Dan so happy, confident, and at ease? Marissa brings out the best in him. I think he does that for her as well."

"I know you have said that she is lovely, and if she has my Danny so smitten, she must be. And to answer your question, no, I haven't ever seen him like this before. It gives me a lot of mixed emotions," Beth said honestly. "I understand the unfortunate circumstances on how they met and how you know her so well, but to be honest, I feel like I am on the outside looking in. You both have this relationship with this woman and I have never laid eyes on her. I always envisioned us on equal footing, meeting some lovely young woman he brings home at the same time," Beth sputtered. "Just like when Grace brought David home."

"So you are jealous? Is that why you planned this ambush on Marissa?" Lewis asked accusingly.

"Ambush? She knows she is coming to dinner with us. She even picked the place!" Beth said defensively, putting on her jacket to leave.

"Yes, ambush! You cooked up this idea and proposed it to Dan, and the poor unschooled boy on how women behave thought it was a great idea. I am sure you spun it well. He had no idea this was unfair to Marissa until he told her. I bet he figured out real quick by her shock and nervousness that this wasn't the best way to meet his mother. You don't just plan a surprise like that on someone, not having her meet his mother with no advance warning," Lewis said loudly.

"You think she threw a fit?" Beth asked, raising her eyebrows.

"Marissa probably handled it with grace and as calmly as possible. She is a very poised woman, but on the inside she is probably a bundle of nerves. This is an ambush to see how she passes all your tests."

"I think you are being unfair to me! You make me sound like a monster. I don't think I deserve that." Beth was so angry she could cry.

"No, you are not a monster. You are the woman I love, but when it comes to your little boy…well, that changes you from Beth the amazing woman I share my life with to Beth the lioness, protecting her cub. But your cub is a grown man, and he has met his future wife, in my opinion, and I don't want you to act in a way that will cause any harm to their relationship or yours and Dan's either. Do you really want to start out a relationship with the woman who is most likely going to be your daughter-in-law, a part of this family, like this? Sneaky and grilling her and making her feel uncomfortable around you? Making her jump through hoops for you? First impressions mean a lot..."

"Exactly! First impressions do mean a lot, and I want to make mine! They have been dating for a while now, and I have yet to meet her." Beth was feeling very attacked and angry with Lewis.

"And this will be her first impression of you! It goes both ways, Beth. Think on that," Lewis warned, softening his tone.

He wasn't detoured by Beth's growing anger with him. He wanted to get her to see she could be causing undue stress and a bad start to a relationship that could be very promising between her and Marissa.

"Your little boy is a grown man, a police officer. He is a good man and a quiet man. He needs someone, and I believe God has matched him with Marissa Medlock. She is a lovely woman, successful in her career, a new Christian, and devoted to her family. She hasn't had the easiest of lives by way of her family, and she is healing from that. Marissa is everything you have prayed for in a mate for Dan all of his life. Do you really want to go against all those years of prayers and trust in God by acting spiteful or ugly to the answer to those prayers? Do you trust Dan's instinct? Do you trust mine? Do you trust God?"

Beth winced, and Lewis began to worry he had been too rough on Beth. She exhaled heavily and had tears in her eyes. "Lewis, you are right," Beth said quietly. "I was being petty and childish and trying to gain the upper hand and let her know whose boss. That is mean, spiteful, and beneath me." Beth smiled at Lewis softly. "Thank you for seeing through me to protect me from myself. I don't want to hurt Dan or start off on the wrong foot. I do trust Dan's instinct. He has always been a great judge in character and he has a good discernment in situations and people. It helps to make him a good police officer. I trust you, Lewis. You love our son just as much as I do, and if you feel this strongly about her, that she is *the one for our Dan...*

and I do trust the Lord. I have prayed since he was growing under my heart for his future, his salvation, and for his life mate. I can't doubt God now." Beth's tears were rolling down her face.

Lewis walked over to her and embraced her. "It is okay, Beth. You just want to protect the only son you have left. I just don't want you to do anything you will regret or cause a rift between you and Dan or you and Marissa. You don't want Dan to feel like he has to choose between Marissa and his mother," Lewis said gently. "That wouldn't be fair, and asking a man to choose between his mate and his mother just might put you on the losing end. Then everyone loses."

Beth nodded, pulled back, and went to the bathroom to wash her face quickly. "Let's go. I will pull my claws back in and be as sweet as sugar," Beth said, batting her eyes.

They both laughed and headed to the car. Beth wasn't sure what she had been thinking, but she was glad Lewis had given her a reality check. She needed to do some quick thinking and praying on how to proceed with this evening. Her plan of tests to make Marissa jump through hoops was silly and childish. She was better than that.

* * * * *

Dan and Marissa got to Barney's Grill first. They were seated and placed their drink order when Lewis and Beth arrived. Marissa had been praying all the way that God would help her. She felt this was going to be a long dinner full of tests and she really wanted to pass them all.

Dan and Marissa both stood as they approached the table. Lewis smiled reassuringly and winked at Marissa. Beth smiled warmly and went straight to Marissa and gave her a quick hug.

"Marissa, it is wonderful to finally meet you," Beth said genuinely.

"It is nice to meet you as well. I mean, it is wonderful to meet you, I mean…" Marissa was fumbling all over herself already. This wasn't going to go well.

Beth reached out and took Marissa's hands in hers and smiled warmly at her. "Marissa, I am so sorry to do this to you," Beth said honestly. She took a deep breath and continued. It was time to come clean and make things right before she ruined it all. "I was feeling left out. I was hearing from Dan all about this amazing woman in his life and Lewis knew you and they would talk about you as if they had known you for years. I felt jealous and out of the loop," Beth paused, trying not to cry.

"I talked Dan into this surprise, and I had a list of tests for you. I wanted to see for myself if you were right for my Dan. Lewis called me on it right before we left. He made a lot of sense, and I was very wrong. I want to apologize for meeting you in this way. And I want you to know my plans have changed. I don't want to play any games but to get to know you as a new friend. I hope you can forgive me and we can start fresh, no games, no tests, just honesty," Beth gushed.

Dan looked shocked. How could his mom do this to Marissa? How did he not see through this? He felt angry and used and so horrible for what he had walked Marissa into. What kind of policeman was he? He shouldn't have to check his own mother's motives. This was ridiculous.

"What? Are you serious?" Dan raged. "Mom, I have never known you to be like this! I can't believe I was so stupid. Marissa, I am so sorry. We should leave." Dan grabbed his jacket angrily.

"Wait, Dan. It's okay. Don't you see? She is being very honest and vulnerable here," Marissa said as she grabbed ahold of Dan's arm to slow him down. "We are all human and make mistakes. Any mistake your mom made was out of love for you. Trust me, you don't want to start a rift in your family. Small things lead to bigger things, and those valleys are hard to cross back over once they divide. You forget how it ever started, but then it doesn't matter. It's too late. Pride and anger destroy everything. She realized her mistake, and she is trying to be honest and make it right. That is very commendable, and she deserves forgiveness, not anger."

"This isn't the same as your family. Your parents had their issues and things got out of control. My mom was trying to be mean and nasty. She had intended to put you through a horrible night. For what reason? To hurt you? To try and show dominance as some kind of alpha female or something? I won't stand for it," Dan sneered, glaring at his mother who had tears streaming down her face.

"Dan, calm down," Lewis said. "Let's not make a huge scene or lose our cool here."

"Dan, I am so sorry," Beth whispered hoarsely. What had she done?

"Marissa, you really are a jewel. You are being so kind. I love my son very much, but it was more selfish on my part than out of love. I am very ashamed. Dan is right. I was being ridiculous." Beth was shaking. "God forgive me."

"It takes a strong woman to realize when she was wrong and own up to it. You could have just come in here and acted like everything was fine. You went out of your way to be honest and set things right. I admire that and appreciate your honesty and sincerity. I can definitely forgive that, and I think we will be good friends. Thank you," Marissa said, turning back to Beth.

They embraced tightly. Lewis smiled at them. They had a lot in common, and they would be very close in years to come. He just knew it. He had known it as soon as he realized the chemistry between Dan and Marissa.

Dan was dumbfounded and looked from his dad to Marissa and his mother hugging and both crying. This made no sense to him, but he didn't know what to do or think, so he just sat down.

"Don't be so bewildered, Dan." Lewis chuckled. "To have women in your life is quite the adventure. It is worth every minute of it, but it is a ride. You will understand more as the years go by."

Beth and Marissa looked at Dan and both laughed.

Beth went to Dan and looked down into his eyes and put her hand gently on his shoulder.

"Danny, I am truly sorry. Please forgive me," Beth pleaded.

Dan sighed. "If Marissa wants to stay, we will, but if you give her a hard time..."

"I won't, I promise," Beth vowed. Dan nodded and smiled. He stood up and hugged his mother.

"Well, now that all the drama is out of the way, shall we stop being a spectacle and have some dinner?" Lewis said, grinning, and sat down.

They all laughed and took their seats. Dan still felt a little irritated that his mother had planned on being so cruel to Marissa and how she had used him to do it. He felt like a fool. He knew he had to forgive her and he would. He would just have to pray about it. He felt betrayed, but forgiveness wasn't a feeling; it was a decision. He knew that. And he would make the right decision.

Marissa smiled kindly at him and held his hand. Her kindness and loving heart had won him over even more, if possible. There was no way he was going to let anyone come between them. This was the woman for him, without a doubt.

"Hopefully, we haven't scared the waitress off from our table. I am starving," Lewis said, trying to lighten the mood.

Marissa giggled. Dan and Beth smiled, uneasily.

"Marissa, Dan told me you played basketball in high school. I have always loved basketball. It is my favorite sport," Beth began.

"Mine too." Marissa grinned "I don't really play anymore, but I coach a girls' basketball team. I started it because of the love of the game, but I keep doing it for my love of those girls."

"I can understand that. I would love to come and watch a game. You are so lovely. I see exactly why Dan and you are such a good match," Beth said genuinely.

She had been stupid, and Marissa was the answer to all her prayers. She was so glad she didn't ruin it all.

Beth had planned on surprising Marissa, but the surprise was really on her. She learned her lesson and was grateful she hadn't caused irreparable damage. God was good; he was always faithful.

CHAPTER 8

All We Have Is Today

The week was filled with spending days at Elliott and Charlotte's house, taking care of Charlotte and their home and meals. Evenings, Charles and Delores would go for ice cream or coffee and pie. They would talk a lot about their daughters, the men in their lives, and their amazing granddaughter. On Saturdays they genuinely stayed at their own homes and relaxed. Charles would pick Delores up for church on Sunday and they would have lunch together and spend the afternoon together and back to evening church.

Charles stared out the window from his kitchen table. Saturdays seemed so long. He missed Delores more each passing week. He had thought his life would be a quiet one, spent alone. It had been for years, too many years. He never longed for a new love interest. He could never look at another woman as someone his heart could yearn for. He had one love. It hadn't worked out. He didn't talk to anyone about it over the years. When someone wanted to fix him up with a lady, he politely declined. He said he had had his chance at love and he couldn't love another. He could offer no more explanation.

He was still her husband, even if she didn't want one. He had wondered if one day he would be sought by a letter requesting a divorce so she could move on. He found peace when it never arrived. He had loved Delores since they were children. He had always loved her and couldn't love another.

Showing up at the hospital after Charlotte's accident was hard; he didn't know how Delores and Marissa would react, but he had to face them to keep his promise to Charlotte. His heart wasn't sure it could take another verbal assault from Delores, but it was time to be a man and a father. Delores had been shocked and angry to see him, but she had held her tongue. As the days went on, she softened, and they formed a truce. Then a friendship. Now they were dating.

It was like how it was in the good days, but different. They weren't young kids anymore. You just see things better in your older years. Somehow being with Delores seemed right and comfortable. In ways it felt like all that time apart never happened. He wished more than anything he could go back and correct it all. He knew it was too late for that. All he had was today. They both had a boatload of regrets but had agreed to forgive themselves and each other and move on. He couldn't help but wonder if she felt the same way he did about her. Did she still love him? Could they reunite as a married couple after all these years? Or was this is as good as it got?

Charles leaned back in his chair and sighed deeply. "Charles, you old fool, you are acting like a teenager wanting to ask her out for the first time. You are 'dating,' so you can call her on Saturday morning. What could it hurt? You know you miss her."

He went to the phone and picked it up to dial and hung up. He did that seven more times before he dialed each number and willed himself to not hang up. He was about to put the receiver down after the second ring when she answered.

"Hello?" Delores said, smiling. She saw Charles's name on the caller ID and felt as giddy as a school girl. Her heart began to race. Saturdays were so long without him.

"Hi, uh, Delores…" Charles didn't know what to say. He felt his face blushing.

"I missed you too," Delores said knowingly. They both chuckled.

"I didn't mind the alone time on Saturday's at first, but now…," Charles said.

"I know," Delores said, grateful he felt the same way.

"What are you doing today?" Charles asked.

"I have the sudden urge to go skating," Delores said, beaming.

"Oh…really? Did you want to invite Emma?" Charles said, smiling.

"No. I mean, I adore our granddaughter, but I want to just be with you." Delores felt her cheeks redden. Her boldness surprised herself.

"Oh, well then… I think they open in an hour. I will pick you up in a half hour. We can be the first ones in the door." Charles beamed.

"Won't they be surprised?" Delores giggled. She hung up and ran to the bathroom to check her hair. What would she wear? She couldn't believe how she felt. Was she sixteen or sixty-one?

She had been so shocked when Charles had walked into the hospital waiting room. She had no warning, had no idea Charlotte had reconnected with him. She was angry and scared, but for some reason she just stayed quiet. She wanted to jump up and demand he leave, tell him to never come back. She just couldn't. She didn't know if it was the Lord intervening, even if she didn't really know God yet, or if something in her, in the fear of losing Charlotte, needed him as much as she didn't want to admit it. Whatever the reason, she did no more harm. She had done enough of that.

She remembered the day he left, Marissa chasing him out, begging him to stay. Charlotte was so young; she really didn't understand. Delores was shut up in her room angry, scared, and hurting. She wanted to stop him, she hoped he would call her bluff and refuse to leave, but she heard the car door and then the car start. She knew, it was over. When the cards and gifts came for the girls she was angry. If he didn't want her, he couldn't have them. That was so wrong. The crazy thing was he did want her too, but she had pushed him away. She never could heal the hurt in her heart from her parents' deaths. She thought marrying Charles and having children would heal it. It didn't. She thought it was the fact they didn't have more money. Surely that would fix it for good. She was sure if she could have a boy, then it would all feel right, and when she found out there would be no more children, it felt irrevocably over.

She knew now, the only thing that could fix it was God. She had wanted no part of a God that took her parents from her at six years old, a God that would deny her a son. If there was a God who let that happen, she wanted no part of him. She realized now, God had loved her and had never left her side. Looking back it was so clear. She had rejected him and pushed him away just like she did Charles. Even her daughters, she had pushed them away too. No one was going to hurt her again. She could only depend on herself.

That hadn't worked out too well in the long run either. Now she had found God. She was learning so much and healing little by little. Just like her relationship with Charles was healing and growing little by little. Life was good. Charlotte was recovering. She felt like she had a full life full of love and family, and she was no longer the hurting orphan girl she once was. God was good. He loved her. Her life could have been so different. She couldn't change that now. She only had today. Did Charles love her like she still loved him? His call today encouraged her that he just might.

"Oh Jesus, help me in my walk with you and in my relationship with Charles. I don't know how to make it all right again. I know you can. Guide me and help me find peace and happiness in whatever your plan is for me and Charles. I want to walk in your will, not mine. I have tried mine and it doesn't work. I want you to lead me. Amen." Delores opened her eyes and felt complete peace, the peace that passes all understanding. God was so good. Why had she not understood that before?

* * * * *

Charles picked up Delores and they talked and laughed all the way to the skating rink. They were the only ones there for the first hour then a few families streamed in for a birthday party. They had so much fun together.

"We should have brought the girls here and taught them to skate. I never took them skating. I think they went with friends a few times each, but I don't think they really learned," Delores said.

"So many regrets. We have to learn to let them go," Charles said kindly.

"I know, it is just so hard. So many wasted years," Delores said.

Charles squeezed her hand. "I could skate longer, but since we are just getting back into this, we better pace ourselves."

"Oh Charles, we've been here two hours!" Delores gasped, looking at the clock on the wall.

"Yep, you hungry? We could share some nachos and sodas here or go somewhere else."

"Nachos sound really good," Delores said. They went to the snack bar and then found a small table near the fireplace.

"So the girls were going out for brunch this morning. I don't think they have ever done that, ever," Delores said. "That is my fault too. I turned Marissa against Charlotte. We both were hurting and Charlotte was too young to understand. She wasn't hurting like we were. It was easier to blame her." Delores had tears in her eyes. "I was so focused on having a boy that I didn't see God gave me two angels who were all that I ever needed and could ask for. I failed them both in so many ways."

"We both did. We made big mistakes to our own lives and to theirs. They are amazing women, so you did something right. I can't take credit for that. That is all you," Charles said gently.

"Well, I see you in them. Both of them have your qualities, I hated it and was glad of it too," Delores said, chuckling.

"I can see how that was hard for you. A lot was hard for you. I copped out on you. You did it all. You were always good at surviving. You just never learned how to partner, I guess, how to trust." Charles hoped he wasn't ruining everything.

"Thank you. They are both remarkable women, but I don't know how much credit I deserve. You are right about the other part. I am learning now," Delores said softly.

"All we have is today," they said at the same time.

Their eyes locked and they smiled. Charles reached and took her hand.

"I hope I am not ruining what we have been carefully building here, but I miss you, Delores. I really miss you and I love you," Charles said honestly.

"I miss and love you too, Charles. Do you think we can really make this work this time? What if we mess it up?" Delores was relieved and scared all at the same time.

"It isn't just us this time. This time God is in this. We are not alone," Charles said, feeling more confident than before.

"You are right." Delores nodded and felt more reassured as well.

"So what is next? If we weren't married, we could run off and elope," Charles said, grinning.

"But it feels wrong to just move in together. We need some kind of fresh start or something to mark the beginning of the rest of our life together," Delores said, laughing but serious.

"A wedding. We need to plan and have a wedding. We eloped last time. We have savings now. We can have whatever type of wedding your heart desires," Charles said, feeling like a teenager plotting something crazy.

"A wedding! You mean, renew our vows?" Delores was surprised and excited all at the same time. Why hadn't she thought of that?

"Yeah! What do you think?" Charles said, beaming.

"I think it sounds perfect. But..." Delores grew serious and Charles nodded in understanding.

"Charlotte," Charles said.

"Yes, she is dealing with so much and adjusting to all the changes that has happened while she was in the coma. She is just starting to come around and heal emotionally as well as physically," Delores said thoughtfully.

"Okay, so we don't run out and renew our vows today. A wedding takes planning anyway. Charlotte wants a chance to reconnect with everyone and take things slowly. Not to mention the way Dan and Marissa are constantly staring into each other's eyes, they might be getting married soon too," Charles said, beaming again.

"I don't want to take away from them either. Good point. We put ourselves and our feelings first long enough. This time around we put our daughters first," Delores said, determined.

"Agreed. But we know where we stand with each other, and when we feel the timing is right for the girls, we will talk to them about planning our wedding," Charles said, nodding. "That doesn't mean we can't talk about it or begin planning what you want. It can be our secret."

"What we want, you mean. I am done putting myself first. This time it is going to be different," Delores said, taking his hand in hers again.

They smiled, and he leaned in and kissed her.

CHAPTER 9

Nice to Meet You

"Good morning!" Charlotte greeted as she wheeled herself into the kitchen Monday morning. Charles and Delores had just come in and were talking to Elliott and Emma who were about to leave for school and work.

"Bye, love." Elliott kissed her and waved to Charles and Delores, a huge smile on his face, and he gave them a quick wink.

"Have a good day, Mom," Emma said, hugging Charlotte.

"You too, sweetie. Don't worry about that Algebra test. You are ready." Charlotte beamed.

"Thanks, same for you and your physical therapy today. You got this, Mom!" Emma squeezed her mom's hand. She hugged her grandparents goodbye and followed her dad to the car.

Charles and Delores couldn't help but stare at Charlotte in amazement. They had noticed Charlotte had been less quiet and smiling and happier in church on Sunday, but to see her same light, cheerful demeanor on Monday really stunned them. They exchanged looks of surprise and delight.

"I have been that bad, huh?" Charlotte said, noticing. Her parents immediately seemed apologetic, but Charlotte laughed. "No, it's okay. I have been. That is going to change. I am no longer going to see myself as a victim. No more *poor little Charlotte*. I am blessed to be alive and to know that in time, I will be able to walk and live a normal life. I didn't die and I need to act like it. I have had a big chip on my shoulder and feeling very sorry for myself." Charlotte sighed deeply. "I am so sorry. You both have done so much for us, for me every day.

"I was mad that everyone's life was better and had gone on while I was in a coma. I was feeling left out and I was pouting. I was taking my anger out on everyone around me, everyone who was devoting their time to take care of me, and it was very wrong. I am so sorry. I owe you both an apology. You come over every weekday and take care of me, my house, and my family. You take me to physical therapy and doctor's appointments. You grocery shop and cook and clean up after us, five days a week. You have never once complained about my attitude or treatment of you. I have acted so ungrateful and ugly, and I am so sorry. I want to make things right from this moment on. Please forgive me." Charlotte had tears in her eyes.

"Oh Charlotte, we never blamed you. We were concerned about you, and we can't imagine what this whole thing has been like for you. You don't owe us an apology. Especially us, we haven't exactly been the best parents, but we want to make that up to you," Delores gushed.

"Charlotte, God gave us a second chance to have a relationship with you and we plan on being anything and everything you need us to be. We both have made mistakes, and we understand more than anyone what it is like to try and figure out what is going on and how you are going to continue when your life is turned upside down. We are so happy to see the real you starting to shine through again. It… it's almost like you really just woke up from that coma," Charles said, wiping a tear from his eye.

"You both are so gracious. Thank you. I love you both so much. God has given us all a second chance. I am not going to mess this up with letting my emotions and my flesh rule me. If that is how I am going to live my life, what use was it to wake up?" Charlotte said, pursing her lips together. "I want to live my life giving God all the glory. I can't exactly do that and treat everyone so horribly and be moping around. I see that now. God has been talking to me, but I hadn't been listening. So he spoke to me through Lewis and Emma, and I finally saw what God was trying to get through to me. I understand how to heal emotionally, and that had to begin with a change of my mindset and an attitude adjustment," Charlotte said, smiling.

"Oh Charlotte, I am so glad you are healing." Delores rushed over to give her daughter a hug.

"I was really feeling hopeful for our relationship from our last phone call before the accident, Mom. Now we have that chance to reconnect on a new level, not only as mother and daughter, but as sisters in Christ. I really am so happy you had an encounter with Jesus Christ. I am so glad you are saved."

Tears streamed down all their faces. Charlotte began to laugh and Delores and Charles exchanged confused looks again.

"Well, here I was trying to figure out how to tell you I found Dad and now that is one thing I don't have to do." Charlotte laughed.

"Yes, that was a surprise. I am not sure how I would have taken it had you told me. I am surprised I handled it as well as I did when he walked into that hospital waiting room. I was shocked and angry but somehow for the first time in my life, held my tongue. It had to be God."

They all laughed harder.

"Dad, that had to be so hard to walk in there. I am so glad you did, but I would have understood if you hadn't come. That took so much courage to face Mom and Marissa," Charlotte said honestly.

"Well, I struggled and I went over every scenario, but in the end I couldn't get away from I made you a promise to always be there for you from now on, and I couldn't break that promise. I wasn't sure how they would react, but maybe Marissa needed to see me keep that promise to you. Maybe not, but I had to do what was right and face whatever the consequences were. It was time to grow up," Charles said, half smiling as he thought back. "Best decision I have made since accepting Jesus as my Lord and Savior." Charles nodded.

"Thank you. I do appreciate it," Charlotte said sincerely. "Well, I guess it is time to go to physical therapy," Charlotte said, glancing at the clock. "On the way, can you fill me in on how you two found each other again? How did you go from that awkward, upsetting meeting at the hospital to the relationship you have now? I didn't get to watch it unfold like everyone else. Can you fill me in?"

"Let's go," Charles said, wheeling her out to the car. Delores followed. This was usually an unpleasant experience. Charlotte hated physical therapy and was usually extra moody and angry on these days, but today was different. They both shared how they had felt upon seeing each other again and how they slowly made peace with each other's presence, to Charles giving Delores the Bible and how he helped her cope with the tragedy of Charlotte's accident and the old pain it brought back from losing her parents in a car accident as a child. Charlotte took it all in and shed a few quiet tears, realizing what it had been like for both of them, especially her mother. Oh how she had suffered so much in her life, and this accident opened up old wounds. She felt so guilty.

"Charlotte, it did bring up a lot of painful memories, but it really didn't rip off the scabs on those old wounds because they never stopped bleeding. I just kept wrapping them up in more bandages. This helped me face things, and finding God had helped me find healing for the first time in my life. God used this to help wake me up and show me who he was," Delores said softly as she noticed Charlotte becoming overwhelmed with guilt.

Charlotte took a deep breath and nodded as she wiped her tears away. Charles parked the car and wiped away a tear in his eye as he squeezed Delores's hand in support and gave her a loving smile. Charlotte swallowed hard, more pieces fitting together of her family and her heart. She was in such awe of how God moved in the lives of her family members. So much was going on. There were a lot more surgeries happening in that hospital than just on her—heart surgeries by the Lord.

Charles wheeled Charlotte into the rehabilitation center and Delores went to the desk to check Charlotte in. Charlotte spotted her physical therapist Joel from across the room. He saw her and headed over to her.

He stopped halfway and just stared at her for a moment. Something was different today. It was what he had been hoping to see for a long time. Some of his patients got there, and others never did. He began to laugh and ran over to her.

"Charlotte Wingate, is that a smile on your face?" Joel asked, laughing. It wasn't only the first time he had ever seen this woman smile; it was that her whole continence was different. Her face was lit up and she seemed peaceful. It was a mindset change, and now, if this was truly what had happened to Charlotte, now the real work could begin. She would start to make strides in recovery and her whole life would be different.

"Yeah, it was about time I got my head in gear, right? You have given me enough pep talks and heart to hearts, but I was so angry at the world I wouldn't listen. You have been trying to help me on more than just a physical level. I have been a huge pain, but today, that changes," Charlotte said.

Joel bent down on one knee to look Charlotte in the eye. He smiled big and waited a moment before he said anything.

"Today, Charlotte, the real work begins. The recovery begins. This is what we have been waiting on. We have been waiting on *you* to show up. Welcome! Let's do this." Joel gave Charlotte a hug and then he jumped up.

"*Woo wee! Let's do this!*" Joel jumped up in the air and pumped his fist in the air. They all laughed. Joel grabbed the handles to the wheelchair and pushed her over to their workout area. Charles and Delores took a seat near the desk; they held hands as they watched Joel and Charlotte begin to work. This time was different. Instead of looking like enemies fighting against each other, they were working together.

They had watched Joel and Charlotte in the past battle against each other. He tried to get the best out of her and she fought him on every level. He would be tough on her, but not too tough. He tried to reach her emotionally, but she had been too shut off. He never lost his temper with her, he just kept trying. He stayed consistent and so had she. They hadn't gotten very far.

Today was different, just as Joel had said. They jumped right into the exercises, and this time Charlotte gave it her all. Joel was so excited and encouraging. They laughed and she worked hard. He was right there with her.

"That is enough for today," Joel said.

"What? We usually work longer." Charlotte was confused, looking at the clock.

"No, we usually fight harder, but against each other. Today, you gave it your all. You let me work with you. You made more improvements in less time. You did well. I am so proud of you. And I knew it. I knew I was going to like you if I ever got to meet the real you. You are strong and I mean on the inside. You just had to get there. That is enough for today. You are going to be seeing your strength come back more and more. You are going to have less headaches, and you will be walking before you know it. Keep this new mindset and you can move mountains, Charlotte. I promise you." Joel spoke pointedly.

Charlotte nodded and began to cry. Why had she been so difficult? Why had she been her own worst enemy? Why had she treated everyone so horribly?

Joel got down on his knee again and took her hands in his. He looked her right in the eyes.

"Charlotte, everyone who has been through this type of physical trauma has their demons to overcome. Everyone faces it in their own way and unfortunately some never win. You, Charlotte Wingate, are a winner. Don't beat yourself up over where you have been or how you have got there. Just take every day, every moment for what it is now. Work hard and give yourself grace. Love and experience life and all it has to offer you. You have this second chance at life, and you are going to make the best of it. Let the past go. Live in the now, it is all we have." Joel spoke from his heart.

"Thank you." Charlotte managed to find her voice. She licked her lips and she felt herself shaking. "Thank you for today, all you have said…thank you for all the fighting for me you have done. Thank you. I will follow your advice. I will live in the now. I promise."

"I can tell Charlotte Wingate is a woman of her word," Joel said, beaming. They hugged and he wheeled her back to her parents.

"She did great today and we are going to stop before we tire her out too much. Get a good nap in, Charlotte, and soak in the tub later. Your muscles got a good workout today," Joel instructed.

He put out his hand and smiled big. Charlotte smiled and shook his hand.

"Nice to meet you, Charlotte. I look forward to working with you." Joel winked at her and headed back to the workout area whistling.

Charlotte smiled all the way home. It felt good to be happy. She wondered what exactly God had in store for her future. That wasn't something she had thought of until now. This was truly a new beginning, not an ending.

Dinner for Two

Marissa pounded away at her keyboard. She was in such deep concentration that her phone ringing made her jump out of her chair. She laughed and reached for the phone.

"Hello?" Marissa answered, almost laughing.

"Hello, Marissa, this is your dad. Am I calling at a bad time?" Charles was nervous.

"Oh, not at all. I was so engrossed in my work when the phone rang I jumped. It isn't a bad time at all."

"Oh, good. Um, well I was wondering if you have some time available in the near future for dinner with me. We have all been focusing on Charlotte so much, and now that she seems to be starting to do so well... We haven't really had a chance to sit down and talk and I would like that. Whenever your schedule is open of course." Charles felt like a teenager asking a girl out on a first date.

"We haven't, have we? That sounds like a great idea. Are you free tonight? Dan had a department meeting this evening and was just going to grab a bite with some of his work buddies afterward. I was going to just pop in a frozen pizza and watch some television, but dinner with you sounds great."

"Good, good...um, where would you like to go? My treat?" Charles said, smiling. He hadn't been sure what to expect.

"Well, does pizza sound good to you? I get off work at five. If you want to be at my house at five thirty, we can order in and have it delivered. Then we can relax and have a nice visit," Marissa asked.

"You know, it does. I'll pay for the pizza. You order whatever you want. I am not picky, and I like everything. If you want any breadsticks, order those too. Can I bring anything else?" Charles was beaming. He couldn't believe he had a relationship with both his daughters. It was something he had been too afraid to ever dream of for all those years.

"Nope. I have sodas and some ice cream for dessert," Marissa said, feeling excited to have some one-on-one time with her dad. "I am really looking forward to this."

"Me too, Marissa, more than you will ever know…" Charles said goodbye and wiped a tear from his eyes.

Delores was sitting next to him, holding his hand. She also had tears in her eyes. She swallowed hard.

"I did it. She said yes! Ordering pizza in at her house. Dan had a work meeting and is going out with his buddies for dinner after. This was perfect timing. I can't believe this is happening. I can't believe I have my family back." Charles was excited and overwhelmed.

"I am so sorry I took everything away from you. I stole from all of us," Delores said, ashamed of her younger self.

"No, no…it is not all your fault. I could have demanded to be a part of their lives. I could have taken it to court if you refused. I just ran off and hid all these years. I really should have fought for our marriage, and all this mess would have been avoided. *I won't let you blame yourself, Delores.* We made horrible mistakes, but God is good and He has given us so much mercy and grace and a second chance," Charles said sincerely. Delores nodded and sniffed back her tears.

"I am so thankful," Delores said, nodding. Charles squeezed her hand.

"I am too," Charles said, smiling.

* * * * *

The day went slowly after Marissa's call from her dad. She couldn't wait to spend some one-on-one time with him. She had accepted him back into her life, and she had started dating Dan, Charlotte had woken up from her coma and a lot of focus was on helping her, and her parents seemed to be reconnecting on a serious level too. Charlotte had shared with her a little about her visits with their dad and getting a lot of answers to her questions, but she hadn't had that chance yet. So much had been going on at once that she hadn't thought about that they really hadn't had any time to really talk and connect. She was so glad he had asked, and she couldn't wait to spend some time and really talk about the past, present, and the promising future ahead of all of them.

Marissa wasn't angry anymore. She had come to understand that it was a combination of mistakes, emotions, and things going on that she just never knew about. It was enough to let her know she had never been unloved and really rejected, as she thought most of her life. It would be good to let him know that and fill in the blanks of their lives with each other.

She had called Dan right after she hung up with her dad to tell him, and he was so happy for her. He was a good man, and she was definitely falling in love with him. Her life was really coming together, and she felt like a new person with Jesus in her heart and Dan and her dad in her life. She also felt guilty about how everything was falling in place for her and her sister was going through so much. Charlotte had made it clear to her that feeling guilty didn't help anyone.

"Dear Jesus, thank you for everything," Marissa prayed out loud. She was so overwhelmed and she felt so much, it was hard to say it all. She knew the Lord knew her heart, and that was all she had to say. She wiped her tears and let out a deep breath.

"Help me concentrate on my work today and bless my time with my dad tonight. I thank you for it, in Jesus's name. Amen." Marissa wiped away her tears and tried to put her focus back on her computer screen. Her eyes kept switching over to the clock the rest of the day, and she found herself giggling as the time slowly ticked away.

It was four fifty-five, and Marissa was logging out of everything and straightening up her desk to leave. She had her coat on at four fifty-nine with her purse and keys in hand.

"Big date tonight?" a coworker, Rachael, called out, laughing as she saw her almost running for the door.

"Yes I do!" Marissa said smiling back at her.

"Tell Dan we all said hello!" Rachael cooed.

"I will, but I am not seeing him tonight. I have a date with my dad!" Marissa said, beaming.

"Oh wow, enjoy, Marissa. I am so happy for you!" Rachael said sincerely. She had worked with Marissa for a long time and understood what this meant to her.

Marissa straightened up her house quickly and then ran to change into some jeans and a sweatshirt. She grabbed a couple of glasses and filled them with ice and put them in the freezer to chill. She double-checked her ice cream stash and was satisfied she had enough for them both.

She picked up the phone to order the pizza and breadsticks and just hung up the phone when she heard her doorbell. She opened the door and found her dad standing before her with a bouquet of pink and yellow roses with lots of baby's breath. She gasped in surprise.

"Your mom told me your favorite flowers were pink and yellow roses. Charlotte told me not to skimp out on the baby's breath either," Charles said nervously. Marissa threw her arms around his neck and hugged him tightly.

The tears poured hard for both of them. After a few minutes Marissa started to giggle. "You better come in before my neighbors start to wonder what is wrong with us both!" Marissa pulled back and ran to grab them both tissues. She handed one to her Dad and cleaned up her own face.

She grabbed a vase and filled it with the flowers and water. She thought they were the most beautiful flowers she had ever seen. Charles was taken aback by her response, but it helped him to know it was going to be a good night and not awkward.

"Let's sit in the living room. I just called the order in. I ordered veggie supreme pizza and breadsticks and cheese," Marissa gushed.

"Sounds great! I am getting hungry. I had a bowl of soup for lunch but that has worn off." Charles chuckled.

They sat across from each other and just smiled at each other for a few minutes, both drinking in the fact that they were together.

"This reminds me of when Charlotte first came to my house." Charles laughed, breaking the silence. Marissa felt good to know that this is what it was like for Charlotte too.

"Tell me about that. I know Elliott found you online from Mom telling Charlotte that you might be in Carsonville, and then she connected with you, but I don't know anything else. I would love to hear how it all happened," Marissa said excitedly.

"Oh yes, I guess that is a great place to start. Well, I guess she was milling over the phone call she had had with your mom and she had shared more information about me than Charlotte knew, and she was just struck by it, and all of a sudden couldn't stop thinking about it and all these questions she had never had before. She told Elliott about it after Emma went on her vacation with Tracey's family. Then at work her three regulars, Bob, Mel, and Ned, were talking about their past jobs, and Bob talked about owning Abbott Foundry. It hit Charlotte that Bob knew me. He was a link to all the questions she had. It overwhelmed her so much, she fainted, and they all were so worried they called Elliott and made her sit down and eat. Charlotte explained to Bob what was wrong, and Bob filled her in on the past and about me. Elliott took her home, and he looked me up online and found me. The next day they had a mission. They headed to Carsonville to find me. They didn't know what they would do, but they decided to find me and then decide whether to meet me or gather more information. They had no idea what to do."

"*Oh my goodness! How that snowballed fast!* That is so unlike Charlotte to just be so bold. It had to be eating at her. All the information at the tip of her fingers, all coming together. No wonder she had to find you. She had never seemed that interested before. I was so surprised she had found you, but that all makes so much sense. It all just fell into place... What happened next? She obviously found you," Marissa gushed, thinking how overwhelmed Charlotte must have been.

"Yes, exactly! They found my house and pulled up a few houses away just to take a look and see what they wanted to do from there. It just so happened, well, I don't believe in coincidences. I believe in God's perfect timing, but at that moment I came out to walk to the end of the driveway to my mailbox. Elliott said she just jumped out of the car as I turned to walk back to the house, he didn't know what she was doing or what to do himself, but he followed her after the initial shock of her reacting so boldly. I remember hearing someone yelling my name. I thought it was a neighbor saying hello walking down the road until I turned, and she was running up to me. She just stood in front of me and was out of breath, looked in a panic, and it all came out so fast. She told me her name was Charlotte and she thinks she might be my daughter..." Charles stopped, overwhelmed with the emotion of the memory. The moment his life changed for the better. The complete turnaround he was always too afraid to pray about or ever dream possible.

"Oh wow! That is like in a movie or something...what did you say?" Marissa was hanging onto every word, picturing the whole scene in her mind.

"I was shocked, and I just kept staring at her, and I could see her as that little, tiny, sweet baby girl I remembered..." Charles stopped for a minute to regain his composure, and the doorbell rang.

"Saved by the bell," Marissa teased, trying to lighten the moment. Charles laughed and got up to follow Marissa to the door.

"Medlock?" the pizza delivery guy asked.

"Yes," Charles and Marissa said in unison and smiled at each other. Marissa took the pizza box and breadsticks bag from the young man. Charles handed him the cash and told him to keep the change.

"Really? You sure, sir? All of it?" the pizza delivery guy asked in surprise. He was appreciative of his tips but didn't want to take advantage of anyone.

"Yes, son. All of it. Have a good night," Charles said, patting him on the back, laughing. The pizza delivery guy smiled big and thanked him and headed on his way.

Marissa was dishing up the pizza slices and adding the breadsticks and some cheese sauce on each plate. Charles joined her at the kitchen table. Marissa pulled out a two liter of soda and asked if it was okay. He nodded, beaming at his daughter. He still could see that five-year-old spit fire she was, yet always wanting to please everyone, in her today. He was a lucky man.

They sat down at the table and Marissa reached for his hand.

"Dear Jesus, thank you so much for your goodness and blessings. Thank you for bringing us back together and for letting Charlotte heal and stay with us. We do not deserve your goodness, but we are so thankful for it. Bless this food before us, in Jesus's name we pray. Amen." Marissa opened her eyes to see Charles beaming at her.

"Just think, it wasn't that long ago you didn't know how to pray," Charles said proudly. Marissa laughed.

"I know, right?" Marissa said jokingly. They both laughed. They needed to lighten the mood a little. "Can you tell me more about meeting Charlotte?"

"Oh yes, Elliott was right there and I met him too. I invited them in, and we talked for a little bit. She explained how they found me and what Bob had told her and how things had been for the three of you after I left... I am so sorry for the turmoil both of you girls went through. You both deserved better."

"I know. Charlotte and I agree wholeheartedly that the past is what it is and we understand so much more now. We both forgive you and Mom, and Charlotte has forgiven me too."

"I told Charlotte what I am about to tell you. You can ask me anything you want, what can I answer, fill in, or help you with. Nothing is off limits, and don't hold back on me. I can take it," Charles said pointedly.

"Oh, Dad... What I struggled with the most was when you left. I begged you to stay. I pleaded with you. You pulled me off of you and told me you loved me and ran...you ran out and got in your car and never looked back." Marissa paused. "That hurt me more than you being gone all those years. How could you do that? How could you just leave and not look back? I know now that you did reach out, and everything you sent to us Mom sent back to you unopened. That gave me a lot of healing, to know you did still love us and you tried.

It is still that day that is clear as a bell and so painful to me," Marissa answered slowly and honestly.

"It was so hard. I knew I had to leave as quickly as I could, or I wouldn't be able to do so. I couldn't look back, Marissa. My heart was breaking too and the tears were flowing. I drove around the block and pulled over. I was crying so hard I couldn't see to drive. I sobbed and sobbed. I have had nightmares of that night for years. I could hear you crying out to me and begging me to stay. I have hated myself for that. I was afraid if I pushed your mother and came back that she might disappear with the two of you as she threatened to do. I didn't want to make your life harder with constantly moving around. I wanted you to have as much stability as you could have. I was so wrong. I should have come back. I don't think your mom would have taken you anywhere. I think it was her trying to see if I would come back, if I would fight for all of you. She needed to know that people you love don't always leave. I failed her and you girls. I failed." Charles sobbed and pushed away from the table. He got up and went to the couch and sat down.

Marissa took in all he had said; she listened hard. She pictured what it was like for him and all he was sorting out that as a small five-year-old girl she didn't understand. She could understand what her mom was doing with the past she came from and how her dad was trying to do the best he could by all of them. He just didn't know what was best and what was wrong. It was out of love and concern. It wasn't that he was running from them or trying to forget about them. He had nightmares too...

Marissa understood and felt so much compassion for both her parents. She went over and sat by Charles, putting her hand on his back and rubbing it softly.

"I am so sorry, Marissa. I am so sorry..." Charles sobbed.

"I know, Daddy. I know... It is okay. Tonight you have given me the answers I needed. You have let me understand that none of this was because you didn't care or that you didn't love me. I understand now. Thank you," Marissa said, the tears flowed freely. Her heart felt so much lighter.

Charles looked up at her. He wrapped his arms around her, and they both held onto each other tightly and sobbed. They both had to get it out. They felt a release and layers of pain lifted off of them, one by one.

When they composed themselves, Marissa excused herself to the bathroom to freshen up. Her face was red and blotchy and tear-stained. Her eyes were puffy and red too, but her smile was as wide as the Grand Canyon. She felt free, validated, and loved. It was what she had needed for thirty-eight years. She splashed some water on her face and blotted it on the hand towel.

She came out to see her dad at the kitchen sink splashing water on his face and reaching for a paper towel. He turned to see her by his side.

"It is good now. We are good now," Marissa said, beaming. Charles let out a deep sigh and hugged her tightly.

They returned to the kitchen table and finished their pizza, not saying much. They were just smiling at each other and letting their emotions settle back down. When they finished, they put the leftovers in containers and put them in the fridge and went back to the couch.

"So you went to Carsonville and lived with your brother, right?" Marissa asked.

"Yes, William and Janet. I lived with them a year then bought that little house I was living in that Charlotte and Elliott found me in. Janet was a schoolteacher and had gotten a job there. That is how they ended up there. I found a job right away at a grocery store. I worked my way up through all the jobs to manager. I retired last year. I had been invited to church by a coworker years ago. I went at first just to escape the loneliness of the house on Sundays and Wednesday nights. It didn't take long, and I asked Jesus into my heart," Charles said, smiling.

"Did you ever date or think about having another family?" Marissa asked softly, not sure if she wanted to know.

"No. I couldn't ever be with another lady or have more children. I had a wife and two beautiful, perfect daughters already. I had messed that up. I always waited for that letter requesting a divorce to come from your mother but was relieved it never came," Charles said honestly.

"Mom never dated either. She just worked and took care of us. I had a full ride scholarships and Charlotte never went to college. Mom had managed to make a good savings for us in case, but I helped her invest it, and she was able to quit working a few years ago and live off of her savings and pension. She still gave piano lessons but didn't have to work outside of the home anymore," Marissa said proudly.

"That is wonderful, Marissa. I am so proud of all your accomplishments and how you have taken care of your mother," Charles said. What fine girls he had indeed. Delores did well.

"So I have one more question to ask you and then I am done." Marissa smiled big.

"Go for it," Charles said, smiling. He was sure they had covered all the hard stuff already.

"So what is exactly going on between you and Mom? Is it serious? Will you end up back together officially?" Marissa asked, smiling from ear to ear.

"Well, that is more than one question!" Charles laughed. "But to be completely honest, yes, it is serious, and we are back together. We see our future, and it is definitely together again."

"That is what I was hoping to hear! Why are you still living apart then? You are married." Marissa was confused.

"Well, after all these years, it feels like we need to make it more official than just moving in together just because legally we have always been married. Then there is the matter of you girls…"

"What? Us? I understand what you mean about making it more official. Do you plan on having a wedding to renew your vows? What do we have to do with it?" Marissa was puzzled.

"Well, first we didn't want to push or upset Charlotte. There has been so much change already for her to adjust to, and we didn't feel it was fair to add to her plate," Charles said.

"That makes sense. She is taking great strides now, but I understand the easing her into more." Marissa nodded but then grew serious. "But what about me? You implied you were holding off because of both of us?"

"Well, we thought you and Dan might be moving toward a wedding of your own in the near future, and we didn't want to steal your thunder by any means," Charles said nervously.

"You are both so precious," Marissa gushed. She jumped up and hugged her dad again. "I love you both so much." Then she sat back. "We have talked about it a little bit, we both know we feel that we are moving that direction in the future, but we really want to enjoy the journey to get there. I don't know when it will feel like the right time, maybe sooner or later. We both would want you to not wait on us. I do appreciate your thoughtfulness," Marissa said, beaming. Thinking of marrying Dan was an exciting thought, but they weren't ready just yet.

"I love you, Marissa. I am so glad we had this chance tonight to work through all of this."

"Me too. Thank you, Dad. I really needed it, and I know we are good now," Marissa said honestly. "How about some ice cream now? I have chocolate brownie bits ice cream and butter pecan."

"I'll take a scoop of each!" Charles announced. Marissa laughed and decided to do the same.

They had a great night together. Marissa told Charles about her job and moving up in positions at the bank. She told him about how she got into coaching and about the girls on her team that she adored, and of course they talked about Dan. They all had been so wrapped up in concentrating on Charlotte, Elliott, and Emma. It was nice to have him interested in just her tonight. They were getting to know each other and growing their relationship.

"Thank you for suggesting this, Dad. I really have had the best time with you," Marissa said.

"Me too. It was your mom's idea. We were talking about you girls, and I was talking about I felt so blessed that Charlotte found me and that you had forgiven me too. She asked about Charlotte finding me and then asked if I had had that chance with you to just sit down and really talk and connect. I realized we hadn't and I wanted it very much. It was a wonderful idea, but it was your mother's."

"She is a better mom than she ever gave herself credit for," Marissa said, feeling touched by her mother's thoughtfulness. "And since Charlotte's accident and accepting Jesus into her heart, she has become even better."

"We all have, haven't we?" Charles asked and Marissa agreed. Charles helped Marissa wash their few dishes and he said goodnight. Marissa watched him leave. He stopped at the car as he reached for the door handle and turned. He locked eyes with her then ran back to her. She came running out. They embraced and they both began to sob.

"I promise to get it right from now on. I will never not look back again," Charles managed to say. They finally composed themselves, and she went back inside and shut the door. He then got in the car.

"God, you are too good to me. Thank you for your healing touch to all our lives and hearts. Thank you." Charles cried and praised God all the way home.

* * * * *

Marissa went inside and got ready for bed. She crawled into bed with a smile on her face. "He looked back. He came back. He really came back," she whispered over and over as she drifted off to sleep peacefully.

CHAPTER 11

I Love It When a Plan Comes Together

Elliott whistled as he drove home from work. Life was really good with Charlotte seeming more like her old self. They all were more relaxed. Even Charlotte's strength was gaining and her headaches were easing up and happening less and less. He found her up in her wheelchair most nights now when he got home, smiling and laughing.

After dinner, Delores and Charles were getting ready to leave. Elliott and Emma were getting the dishwasher loaded up. Charlotte was watching them smiling extra big this evening, Elliott thought to himself. She was up to something; he just wasn't sure what. She had been almost giddy since he got home from work, and he knew his wife well enough to know she had something up her sleeve.

As soon as Charles and Delores left, Charlotte sat up straight, listening for their car doors to shut and the car to turn on and pull out of their driveway. She began to giggle and picked her phone up off her lap and began to dial. Emma and Elliott exchanged looks. Emma was starting to pick up on it too.

"They just left. How far away are you? Great. See you in a minute." Charlotte sounded like she was a spy and then broke out into giggles before she hung up the phone. Emma ran to her mother's side. Something was going on and she was dying to know what it was.

"Charlotte Wingate, what are you up to?" Elliott asked accusingly with a smile on his face.

"Who was that? What is going on?" Emma gasped in excitement.

"Marissa and Dan are on their way. They had dinner nearby so they could get her faster then parked two roads over waiting for my call. I hadn't thought of that, but I guess it was Dan's idea. It really helps having a police officer in on your schemes!" Charlotte giggled.

"*Schemes*? What are you all plotting, and why are we not in on it? Why did you wait on your parents to leave? Is this about them?" Elliot asked, crossing his arms over his chest and looking down at her like he was scolding her. That only made Charlotte giggle more.

"They will be here any minute and we will explain. Emma, grab five bowls, spoons, and Elliott, grab the ice cream. We have some serious business to attend to!" Charlotte directed. Emma sprang into action, and Elliott followed her orders but he kept his eye on her and she winked at him.

They heard the car turn into the drive, and Marissa and Dan came bursting through, both beaming like Charlotte. Marissa and Charlotte locked eyes and burst into a fresh fit of giggles.

"Dan, what is going on? What are these two up to and how did they drag a nice police officer like you into it?" Elliott pleaded. Dan laughed and helped Emma take the bowls, spoons, and ice cream scoop to the kitchen table. Elliott handed him the ice cream and Dan began to scoop it.

"I will let Marissa and Charlotte explain," Dan said proudly.

"Okay, so you know Dad came over to have dinner with me last night, right?" Marissa asked Emma and Elliott. They nodded.

"Yes, he was so excited and nervous," Emma gushed.

"Me too," Marissa said, smiling at her. "Well, we got through all the tough stuff, and then were just talking about our lives, filling in all the missing parts for each other. Then I asked him about him and Mom."

"Oh, that sounds interesting. I have been watching them for a while now myself," Elliott said, smiling.

"Yes, well I asked him if they were officially together now and what happens for them now," Marissa explained. "He told me they were officially back together and planning to be. They are still married, but after all that has happened and being apart so many years, they decided they need to make it official. They want to have a wedding to renew their vows."

"Oh that is wonderful! How perfect!" Emma gushed. Elliott let out a deep sigh. He was very pleased with what he was hearing but still didn't understand what these two sisters were up to.

"Good to hear, but what is going on here with the two of you?" Elliott asked pointedly. "Or should I say, three of you?" Elliott said, raising an eyebrow at Dan.

"Well, I asked him when they were going to do it, and they said they didn't know. They were wanting to be considerate of me and Charlotte. They didn't want to put more change onto Charlotte before she was ready, and they didn't want to take away from any announcement or plans Dan and I may have in the near future," Marissa said, glancing at Dan. They both were blushing. "I was touched by their wanting to look out for us first. I called Charlotte this morning and spoke with her. I wanted to tell her about our conversation and I eased into this part to see how she was taking it," Marissa explained.

"I was so excited! I so appreciate their care and concern. It would probably have been too much for me before, but not anymore. I have had a chance to sit down and talk with Marissa over brunch. I have had time to talk to Mom and Dad, and spending time with both of them, I feel connected again. I don't feel like an outsider anymore. I see them together and I would love for them to be officially together again. This is exciting!" Charlotte gushed.

"Okay, so I am following so far, but what else is going on? What are the two of you up to? All the secrecy and hiding out and the giggles..." Elliott pushed as he looked back between Charlotte, Marissa, and Dan.

"Yeah, what is going on?" Emma asked, standing next to her dad with her hands on her hips.

"We are wanting to figure out how to let them know that it is the right time now. How do we help them get the show on the road?" Marissa exclaimed.

Emma squealed and started jumping up and down and clapping her hands.

"Dan, how did you get dragged into all this?" Elliott asked, smiling at Dan.

"I fell in love with a Medlock sister," Dan said, grinning.

"Fair enough, my brother. I have fallen into that same fate," Elliott said, laughing.

"*So* are we talking a double wedding?" Emma squealed.

"No, no we aren't," Marissa said, laughing. "We have talked about this at dinner and we are on the same page. We are enjoying this journey, and we both agree we see this ending up in marriage, but there is no reason to rush. Everyone is in a hurry these days, and we know this is forever, so why push it? Let's just get to know each other more and enjoy this part of our relationship. When we feel it is right, we will make plans for the next step. This is Mom and Dad's time," Marissa explained, looking at Dan most of the time but back to Emma for her last statement.

"I understand. That is so romantic!" Emma giggled. They all laughed.

"I am not ready for you to be thinking about anything romantic, little girl," Elliott warned.

"Don't worry, Elliott. I am an officer of the law, and we will make a great team looking out for Emma," Dan said with his hands sternly on his hips. Emma ran over to hug him.

"Okay, so now that we are all on the same page, now what?" Elliott asked, sitting down to eat the ice cream Dan had passed to him.

"Well, I have been thinking about that. Do you ladies have any plans this weekend?" Marissa asked, looking from Charlotte to Emma. They both shook their heads no. "Well, I was thinking we can talk to them tomorrow and give them our blessing. Let them start discussing plans, and I thought this Saturday we could go to a bridal store and do some shopping for her dress!" Marissa shared.

All three of the ladies began squealing and clapping. Elliott and Dan laughed.

"What if they want to wait a little bit or for their anniversary? Do you know when they originally got married?" Elliott asked.

"Well, I believe it was right after Mom graduated high school. She would have had to leave the orphanage, so I think they got married the next day and moved in with Dad's family. I am guessing late May or early June? So that gives us around nine months, but finding the right dress usually isn't done in one day. It can be done, but it has to be the right dress," Charlotte explained.

"Well, let's see…," Elliott said, and he left to go sit at his computer and do some investigating.

Dan followed him. "It shouldn't be too hard to find out."

"I wouldn't think so, not with today's internet capabilities," Dan agreed.

"Aha, here it is. You were right, Charlotte," Elliott announced.

Dan came around and took a look at the screen, and they looked at each other and began laughing. Dan slapped Elliott on the back.

"You found it, Elliott. June 1, 1975."

"It is September now. If they want to wait and plan something more formal since they just eloped originally, they have plenty of time. Or if they realize we are all on board, they may want to do it really soon. Can we plan a wedding in a few weeks if needed?" Marissa said, biting her lip in deep thought.

"We can do it," Charlotte and Emma said together.

"Yes, we can!" Marissa said back.

"So how are we going to approach them tomorrow?" Charlotte asked. "They come over in the morning before Emma and Elliott leave."

"Well, we will have to be here then too," Dan said. Marissa smiled at him. She was touched he was so on board with all of this. "Nothing like getting right to it, and I don't think Charlotte can go another full day without bursting."

"I really don't think I could! Today was torture." Charlotte let out a deep sigh and they all laughed.

* * * * *

Charles and Delores arrived right at their normal time that Friday morning. They found Emma loading up the breakfast dishes into the dishwasher and Elliott and Charlotte at the kitchen table. They exchanged looks. Usually the morning was a big rush for Emma and Elliott and Charlotte was moving a little slower. Today they all seemed ready for the day and just waiting on them.

"Good morning!" Emma beamed and hugged them both.

"Good morning. You all are up and around a little earlier this morning, it seems," Delores said. Something felt off but she wasn't sure what it was.

"Just ready for the day, I guess," Elliott said, trying a little too hard to act normal. Charles and Delores exchanged looks.

"Good morning, everyone," Dan announced as he and Marissa came in beaming.

"Okay, what is going on? Elliott and Charlotte have these big smiles, and they seem to just be waiting on us to get here or something and you two are here. What is it?" Delores was starting to get annoyed. She was not a big fan of surprises.

"Well, we had a family meeting last night, and it was about the two of you," Emma admitted.

"What?" Delores and Charles exclaimed together.

"Dad told me, when I asked the other night, that the two of you were back together and were wanting to take it slow because you wanted to put Charlotte and I first this time," Marissa offered.

"Yes, and we completely appreciate it. A few weeks ago, it might have been too much for me, but not now. Marissa called me yesterday morning to tell me how wonderful your visit was with her, Dad. Then she brought up the last thing she asked you about and we discussed it."

"Charlotte is fully onboard for the two of you to make it official and live the lives together you both deserve. As far as Dan and I go, we want to take it slow. There is no hurry, and we want to enjoy every stage of our relationship. We will know when we are ready to move onto the next step," Marissa said proudly. Dan at her side, with his arm around her, they locked eyes and smiled.

"So we had a meeting to let Elliott and Emma in on the details. I talked to Dan over dinner last night. We all agreed we want to help you and support you in this next step," Marissa added.

"So we want you both to talk and plan out what exactly you want to do and when, and we will get to work on making it happen," Charlotte explained.

"Starting tomorrow!" Emma gushed.

"Tomorrow?" Delores and Charles asked in surprise. They had tears in their eyes and were holding hands as they took in all their daughters had to say.

"Well, yes. No matter big or small, you will need the perfect dress. That could take more than one shopping trip. We thought that we four girls could go dress shopping for you," Marissa said, a tear falling from her eye. She quickly wiped it away.

"Wow, I don't know what to say... I am so touched by you all and your support. Charlotte, you sure you are okay with this?" Delores felt a little overwhelmed.

"Yes, definitely." Charlotte nodded vigorously, her smile wide.

"Marissa, you are sure—" Delores looked at her other daughter.

"Yes! Yes! Yes!" Marissa gushed.

Charles beamed at Delores through his tears threatening to spill out of his eyes and cleared his throat to try and find his voice and took a deep breath.

"Delores, I think it is time." Charles turned toward her and went down on one knee. "Delores Ann Norton Medlock, will you marry me? For better or worse, and with no more thirty-eight-year or thirty-eight-minute breaks in between until death do us part?" Charles asked.

"I will," Delores whispered and began to sob. Charles stood and embraced her.

"I love you, and I am here to stay," Charles whispered to her.

On a Mission

Marissa picked up Delores first then headed to get Charlotte and Emma. They went out for breakfast and looked over some bride's magazines that Emma had bought after school the day before.

"I can't believe we are doing this, but I am so happy we are," Delores said, blushing as she looked at her two daughters and her granddaughter. "I am so thankful for all three of you."

"We feel the same way," Charlotte said, taking her mother's hand. "God brings the dreams we are too afraid to dream for ourselves to reality when we trust in him."

"So what did you wear when you eloped, Grandma?" Emma asked.

"Well, we really didn't have any money and we had to move fast. I had just graduated high school and the orphanage rules were clear. I had to move right away. So your dad talked to his parents and they agreed to let us live with them until we got on our feet. My head mistress gave me a gift of a silk white blouse and a blue and white plaid skirt, an old silk handkerchief of hers to keep as a reminder of her, and she let me borrow her pearl necklace. So I had something old, new, borrowed, and blue. The outfit was something nice to get married in but would be practical to wear again. She even gave me some white dress, shoes, and a small blue clutch purse. She was good to me. I loved her and she loved me." Delores remembered fondly. She wiped a tear from her eye.

The others were quiet. They really took for granted how good their life had been and not fully realizing all that Delores had endured and didn't have that they did. It really did explain so much. For all she went through, she was a remarkable woman.

"That sounds very pretty," Emma said sincerely. Delores snapped back to the present and smiled at Emma. She leaned forward and kissed the girl's forehead.

"What are you thinking for this wedding?" Marissa asked quietly.

"Well, I am not really sure. I don't want to try and dress like I am a young woman. I was thinking something more mother of the bride like, but in white. All white this time. I really like lace and silk…"

"That sounds beautiful," Emma said dreamily. They all laughed.

"I was wondering if you girls would be in the wedding. I talked to your dad, and we would like you two to be my bridesmaids and junior bridesmaid, Emma," Delores asked excitedly.

"*Oh yes, yes!*" Emma gushed.

Marissa and Charlotte exchanged looks and big smiles. They had never thought about that.

"That would be a true honor," Marissa managed to get out.

"Thank you. That would be so special," Charlotte said quietly. She loved the idea, but she shuttered to think of being in a wheelchair at the wedding.

"Your dad wants to ask Elliott, Dan, and Bob to be his groomsmen. We thought that Marissa and Dan could walk down the aisle, then Elliott and Charlotte could come next and Bob and Emma before me," Delores said, looking at Charlotte. She and Charles had thought about how to make it easier and as comfortable as possible for Charlotte.

"That is a great idea," Charlotte said genuinely. She felt better not going down the aisle alone.

"You seem to have a lot of plans thought out already, Mom. You and Dad have been talking and planning for a while, haven't you?"

Marissa asked knowingly. Bless their hearts, they were waiting but still planning for their one day, whenever it would be.

"Yes." Delores giggled. "We have done a lot of planning. It filled our time of waiting."

"Awe, that is precious," Emma said, wiping a tear from her eye. They all laughed.

"Well, I think it is time we pay the bill and head to the stores. We have a lot of dresses to look at," Marissa said, smiling.

"Yes, let's keep an eye out for what you ladies like as well," Delores added. They all giggled.

"Do you have a color scheme picked out?" Charlotte asked.

"Yes we have. Blue and yellow. We were thinking yellow sunflowers, white roses, and some kind of blue flowers too," Delores said excitedly. "We thought we would have the wedding on our original wedding day, June 1."

"Mom, that sounds beautiful..." Charlotte sighed. She looked at Marissa and they locked eyes. This was starting to feel real, wonderfully real.

"Let's go!" Emma squealed.

* * * * *

They spent the day all trying on dresses and making notes in a notebook on their favorites. It was a fun day, and Charlotte kept up pretty well. They decided not to make any decisions just yet.

"Thank you, girls. I had so much fun today, but it is more than that. Thank you for being there for me and your dad and for being okay with this," Delores said, trying so hard to keep from bawling.

"We love you, Mom," Charlotte said, smiling.

"Life wasn't perfect, but you took great care of us and always made sure what was important to us was made a priority. We want to do the same for you," Marissa said then pursed her lips together to keep from crying.

"Thank you," Delores managed. Emma just smiled and rested her head on her grandma's shoulder in the back seat of Marissa's car as they headed home. Delores patted Emma's cheek and held her hand.

CHAPTER 13

More Plans

It had been a full day, and after Marissa took Charlotte and Emma home, she looked at her mom and smiled.

"Where to? Do you want me to take you home or to Dad's apartment?" Marissa asked.

"How about your Dad's apartment? He was going to come over and pick me up to go out to dinner. Let's just save him the trip." Delores giggled. Marissa beamed as she headed to Charles's apartment.

She headed home after and lied down on the couch, exhausted but happy. Her phone rang.

"Feel up to company or are you too tired?" Dan asked. Marissa smiled.

"I am hungry, and I am never too tired to see you," Marissa answered.

"I was hoping you would say that. Eat out or in?" Dan asked.

"Let's go out," Marissa said, sitting up, suddenly feeling more energetic.

"I am on my way," Dan said, hanging up. He was at Marissa's house in about ten minutes. She came bouncing out to his car, all smiles. She told him all about the day and all her mother had shared about her first wedding and their ideas for the wedding.

"I am honored they want me in the wedding," Dan said, smiling.

"Maybe I shouldn't have ruined the surprise," Marissa said, feeling guilty.

"You didn't," Dan said, still smiling. Marissa looked at him, confused. "This morning your dad called me and asked me to join him and Elliott for breakfast. We met up over at Oliver's, and Bob was there too. He asked us all to be in the wedding. He knew Delores was going to tell you ladies so you could start dress shopping for yourselves too, and he wanted to be the one to ask us each. We all agreed."

"Wow, they are pretty sly themselves." Marissa laughed. Her parents were surprising her a lot these days.

"Yes, I believe they are pretty proud of themselves." Dan laughed as he pulled into the parking lot of the steak house. "I didn't ask what you wanted. Is this okay?"

"Yes." Marissa thought it sounded great, but she was so hungry she would have eaten just about anything. "I never realized shopping could make me so hungry."

They headed in and were seated at a table. They placed their drink orders of sodas and began to look over the menu. Marissa wanted a salad, steak, and a sweet potato. That sounded divine. She suddenly realized Dan was staring at her.

"What's wrong?" Marissa felt nervous. He was staring so intently at her.

"Nothing. I didn't mean to make you uncomfortable. I'm sorry." Dan smiled softly.

"Oh that's okay. What are you thinking?" Marissa relaxed.

"Just about how much I love you and I am so glad I found you. I wish it were under different circumstances, but I am still so glad I found you," Dan said quietly.

"I feel the same way." Marissa blushed.

"How long of an engagement do you want to have?" Dan asked.

"What? Are you serious?" Marissa was stunned.

"I know we are not rushing, but I still was curious. How much time do you think you will need for a wedding? To have the wedding you really want to have, how long will you need? A few months? A year?" Dan asked, smiling big. Marissa was flustered.

"I don't know… I have never thought about it. I guess when we get engaged, I will decide then. I am not a fussy person. I know what I like, and I think I could pull off a wedding of my dreams in a matter of a few months with ease," Marissa said proudly.

Dan laughed. "I am sure you could. I just wondered. I don't want to rush anything here, but I was curious once we do feel the time is right to start planning, how much longer would it take," Dan explained.

"I see," Marissa said, locking eyes with Dan. "Are you real? Is this real?"

"I believe it is. Yes, to both of your questions." Dan grinned. "Emma has her heart on an Uncle Dan, so I don't think we should disappoint her."

"No, we shouldn't," Marissa said, giggling. "On that subject, we spend a lot of time with my family…"

"Well, I think that is understandable. There has been a lot going on with Charlotte and supporting her, Elliott and Emma. Now the planning of your parents' wedding is underway. I really enjoy all of them."

"I know that, and I am very thankful for that. I also think we need to devote some time to your family as well," Marissa said quietly. Dan bristled at her comment.

"I don't know. I am still a little angry at my mom." Dan said bitingly.

"Dan, please forgive her. She meant well, and she did all she could to make it right. I want to get to know her better, and I adore your dad already. Does your sister and her husband get back to the states much?"

"I know. I will. I am amazed you are here defending her and wanting to get to know her. You are quite a lady, Marissa Medlock… What is your middle name? I don't even know your middle name."

"It is Lynn. Marissa Lynn Medlock," Marissa said, laughing. "What is your middle name?"

"Harrold. Daniel Harrold Williams." Dan grimaced and Marissa laughed.

"Well then, Daniel Harrold Williams, I would like for us to spend some more time with your parents. And you didn't answer me about your sister."

"Sorry, I guess I didn't. Grace and David come back twice a year, around the holidays and Mother's Day. They know it is hard on their mothers with them out of the country on the mission field so much, so they try to make it easier with those two visits," Dan explained.

"That is very sweet of them. I look forward to meeting them too," Marissa said, smiling. "That gives us two possible months for our wedding then, doesn't it? May or December." Marissa smiled.

"You are amazing. You are always thinking of others." Dan hadn't even thought about planning his wedding around his sister's visit home.

"Trust me, it is newer for me." Marissa laughed. "A Christmas wedding sounds nice. Everyone in my family has summer weddings. We can be a trendsetter."

"Mine too. A Christmas wedding. I love it." Dan beamed.

"Good. Now let's keep that a secret, or Charlotte and Emma will have us wed this Christmas!" Marissa and Dan laughed. "Would tomorrow after church be a good time to visit your parents? Does your mom need more time?"

"Oh no, she had a surprise for you, didn't she?" Dan said, smiling mischievously. "But I will be more courteous to her." He pulled out his cell phone and called his parents' home. Marissa smiled.

* * * * *

"Hello?" Beth answered the phone next to her. She was sitting on the couch working on a crossword puzzle. "Dan! I am so glad to hear from you."

Beth looked over at Lewis who smiled back at her. They hadn't heard from Dan since the surprise dinner with Marissa a couple weeks before.

"Really? That is wonderful! I would love to have you both here for Sunday dinner! We can have a nice family lunch and visit the rest of the day," Beth gushed. Lewis smiled. This is exactly what Beth needed. She had felt so badly and had cried a lot over how she had tricked Marissa and hurt Dan.

"Thank you so much for this, Dan. I really do love and miss you. I am so sorry... Well, thank you and thank Marissa for me. I can't wait for your visit tomorrow. I will take care of the meal. Can you bring the dessert?"

"Thank you. See you tomorrow after church. I love you, Dan... Goodbye." Beth was standing at this point. She hung up and danced around the living room. Lewis began to laugh. Another answer to prayer.

"Marissa wants to spend more time with us. She wants to get to know me better. She suggested they come for a visit tomorrow. I suggested Sunday dinner after church! I will make the meal, and they will bring the dessert. Oh, he forgives me, Lewis! He still loves me! She is such a sweet girl. She is the one who pushed for this. I am so grateful for her kindness." Beth sat back down and began to sob.

Lewis went over to embrace her. Her heart carried a lot of pain. It is never natural for a parent to lose a child, and Grace was so far away. She had really held onto Dan tighter these past few years especially. She was so afraid she had lost him.

"I told you it would be all right. Have faith in God and your son. I knew Marissa would be the bridge you needed. She is a good woman, and you two are going to love each other," Lewis said softly as he held her. She sobbed on, knowing he was right. Lewis was always right, and that was as comforting as it could be frustrating.

"I know. I am so thankful," Beth sobbed. She had to get a handle on herself and figure out lunch tomorrow. She jumped up and ran to the kitchen. Lewis laughed. He would go help, but she was in her element, so he would let her do what she did so well.

He looked up and smiled. "Thank you, Jesus. She really needed this."

Sunday Dinner

Beth could barely keep her mind and attention on the sermon on Sunday. She was so excited for her guests. She kept feeling the scolding look of Lewis then he would smile. She blushed each time. As soon as service was over, she grabbed Lewis's hand and ran for the car. Lewis laughed all the way.

"I don't know what time their church gets out. I want to get cooking!" Beth said defensively as Lewis chuckled as he put on his seatbelt.

"I know, I know," Lewis said, trying to calm her down.

"He used to come to church with us," Beth added. "He seems to like the church Marissa and her family go to, and I am happy for him. I just miss him coming to church with us," Beth said wistfully.

"Therefore shall a man leave his father and his mother and shall cleave unto his wife…," Lewis began.

"They are not married yet!" Beth added, sighing deeply.

"Just be glad he is going to church with his lady," Lewis countered.

"You are right. I know," Beth said, pouting a little. "Do you think they are planning on getting married soon?"

"I have no idea. I don't make it a habit in guessing what others will do in these matters. I know Dan, and he is not an impulsive man. Marissa likes things in an orderly fashion as well. I don't think they eloped last night, but then again when it is right…maybe they did…," Lewis said, grinning from ear to ear.

"*Stop teasing me!*" Beth was getting irritated with Lewis. She wasn't in the mood for jokes today.

"All right, I will stop." Lewis smiled and reached for her hand. "It is going to be fine. Today will go well, just wait and see," Lewis said gently. Beth squeezed his hand and let out a deep sigh and nodded.

As soon as they got home, Beth ran into the kitchen. Lewis went to get into more comfortable clothes. Lewis headed back to the kitchen to see how Beth was doing. She was glowing; she was so happy. She had chicken frying on the stove, a fresh salad tossed together. She had mashed potatoes ready that she had prepped that morning and some brown gravy in a small pot as well.

"Lewis, can you put the biscuits in the oven and grab a box of macaroni and cheese and some green beans from the pantry for me?" Beth asked as she was looking in the cabinet for more pots.

"Yes, ma'am." Lewis went into action.

"Hello!" Dan said as he came through the kitchen door. Marissa was right behind. Dan had two pies in his hands, and Marissa had a container of Cool Whip and a container of vanilla ice cream.

"Hello, I hope apple pie and chocolate pie are okay?" Marissa looked like she hoped she had made the right decisions.

"They both sound perfect! Thank you, Marissa," Beth said and went over to hug them both.

"This all smells wonderful! Can I help do anything?" Marissa exclaimed.

"No, dear. I have it under control. Just come talk to me. I want to know how you are doing," Beth said genuinely. Dan smiled and hugged his mom again.

"Now this is the mom I know and love." Dan hugged her tight to let her know they were okay.

"Thank you for forgiving me, Danny." Beth wiped a tear from her eye and looked back at Marissa. "Thank you, especially," Beth said warmly to Marissa. "Now tell me, what is new with the two of you?"

"Yes, you didn't elope last night, did you?" Lewis asked teasingly, and Beth threw a dish towel at him. They all laughed.

"No, but Marissa did go dress shopping with her mom, sister, and niece yesterday," Dan announced. Beth and Lewis exchanged looks of surprise.

"For my parents' wedding! Dan, stop teasing them. My parents are officially back together and are planning a wedding to renew their vows," Marissa explained.

"Oh, how wonderful!" Beth exclaimed, excited and relieved.

"Wow...now that has really come full circle. That is so God," Lewis said, so happy for them both. The healing that only the Lord can do, it never ceased to amaze him.

"Yes, there is no other way. He has changed our lives. Mom and I can't believe we were so blind for so many years, but that is in the past, and we are in the here and now," Marissa said, smiling.

"Yes. Marissa found out from talking with her dad about what was going on with them, and he told her they were back together but wanted to have a wedding to start anew since they had been apart for so long. They were waiting to see when it would be a good time for their daughters," Dan added.

"They didn't want to overwhelm Charlotte with her recovery and..." Marissa stopped and blushed. "And they were worried we might be planning a wedding and didn't want to intrude on our time."

"Oh, I see...," Beth said, suddenly wondering herself how soon these two might be getting married.

"We assured them we were in no hurry, and they need not wait for us. Charlotte is doing well and was overjoyed at the news. She said it was fine with her as well. So we approached them and let them know. They decided to have the wedding on their original anniversary date, June 1, so we started to go dress shopping. She also asked us to be in the wedding, so I was trying on dresses yesterday, but bridesmaid dresses," Marissa explained.

"What a lovely gesture you girls made for them. I am sure they were excited. It is exciting news! That does sound like fun," Beth said.

"So since you brought up the subject, are you thinking of a date for yourselves?" Lewis couldn't help but ask, more for Beth's peace of mind than his.

"Well, we have talked about it. We know the time of year we want to be married but not sure on the year just yet," Marissa said, smiling and locking eyes with Dan. They both looked so adorable and so in love. It really touched Beth's heart, and she felt more calm hearing it wasn't any time too soon.

"Well, you will know when you are ready, and we will be here to support you and help in any way we can," Beth said confidently and sincerely. Lewis and Dan exchanged smiles.

"Thank you," Marissa said and wiped a tear from her eye. Beth went to her and hugged her again.

"Ladies, I am getting hungry, and if the two of you are just going to hug, please instruct Dan and me on what to do next," Lewis teased. They all laughed, and Beth threw a pot holder at him.

"Marissa, I would like to assure you that there is generally not this much violence in our home," Lewis teased. They all laughed again.

"Lewis, why don't you set the table? Dan, get the glasses and fill them with ice for us. Marissa, do you like sweet tea? I also have milk, water, and sodas. What would you like?"

"Sweet tea sounds wonderful," Marissa said.

"Got it, four sweet teas," Dan said and went to work as did Lewis.

"What can I do, Mrs. Williams?" Marissa asked.

"Well you can start with calling me Beth. If you call me Mrs. Williams again, I will throw something at you too!" Beth laughed. "Next, if you can grab some serving spoons from the drawer next to the refrigerator, we can get this food on the table."

"Got it, Beth." Marissa and Beth exchanged smiles and they hugged again.

"I love this girl, Daniel!" Beth cried out as she held tightly onto Marissa.

* * * * *

When church let out, Delores and Charles headed back to her house for lunch. She had some chicken and noodles in the crock pot and she whipped up some mashed potatoes. Charles set the table and got two glasses of milk poured and set out some bread and butter.

"So last night at dinner, you were telling me all about the fun time you had with the girls and their dresses. I know you shouldn't tell me about yours, but did you find one you liked?"

"I liked a lot of them, but yes, there was one that felt right. I want to be sure and try on a few more before I decide. Marissa wrote down the dress information, so we have it if I want to get that one."

"Take as much time as you need. I want you to have everything you want," Charles said honestly.

"I already have that," Delores said, smiling at him. "I like that we are having the wedding on our anniversary date."

"I was thinking the same thing. It isn't that long of a wait, and I think planning all the details are fun and time will go quickly," Charles said, chuckling.

"Yes, I agree," Delores asked thoughtfully. Her thoughts went to Charlotte.

"Charlotte seems to really be gaining strength in therapy now. I think her days in that wheelchair are almost behind her." Charles seemed to be reading Delores's thoughts.

"I was thinking that too. She looked a little self-conscious when I brought up them being bridesmaids. She seemed to like the idea of coming down the aisle with Elliott at her side. I don't know how long it will take for her to learn how to walk again. Maybe she will be on a walker or a cane. We could decorate it with flowers if she is so she feels less uncomfortable." Delores smiled big. She liked that idea.

"I bet she would like that. Wow, if she is walking again...so much will be going right for all of us. If I were a betting man, which I am not, but if I were, I would say we might see a diamond on Marissa's hand by then or shortly after," Charles said.

"*Rings...* I hadn't thought about rings. I still have my wedding band in my jewelry box. Do you still have yours?" Delores asked.

"I do. How could I ever throw it away? I stopped wearing it because of people asking about my wife and if I had a family. It was painful to try and offer an explanation, but it was hard to take it off too. I still have it," Charles said softly.

"Same for me," Delores said as tears rolled down her face. Charles went to his coat pocket and took out a small box and brought it back to the table. Delores was trying to compose herself. Charles held out a small square ring box to Delores. She looked confused as she looked at it and back at Charles.

"But...but I just told you, I have my ring...," Delores stammered.

"Yes, you have a wedding band. We can get newer ones if you would like. We didn't spend a lot of money on that first pair because we didn't have any. You never had an engagement ring, Delores, and I think it is high time you did," Charles said, beaming.

"Oh... I... I don't know what to say..." Delores was in shock.

"Open it up," Charles said, laughing. Delores took the box out of his hand and opened it up. It was a beautiful gold band with a large diamond in the center of it and five stones around it.

"It's beautiful... What are these colored gem stones for?" Delores asked, confused.

"They are the birthstones of Marissa, Charlotte, Emma, Elliott, and Dan, our family. I had them design it, so if we need to add more birthstones for any children Marissa and Dan have, we can add them on it," Charles explained.

"Oh Charles, I love it," Delores whispered, and Charles took it out of the box and slid it on her finger. It fit perfectly.

"You are still the same ring size," Charles said, beaming.

"I can't believe you remembered..." Delores couldn't believe what she had thrown away with this man. The life they could have shared all these years...

"All that matters is today and all the days together that is to come," Charles said softly. He could read her mind. Delores nodded but couldn't take her eyes off of her ring. It was gorgeous.

"I chose a triangle cut diamond so that it stands for all three of us in this marriage: you, me, and the Lord. We aren't doing this on our own this time. We are keeping God in this so that we have a solid marriage this time around," Charles said hoarsely.

Delores leaped off her chair and embraced him. They cried, holding each other up. They cried for what was lost, what was found, and what was to come, by the grace of God.

* * * * *

Marissa was having a wonderful time. The meal was delicious and the company, even better. Marissa and Beth discovered they really liked each other a lot. Dan relaxed and Lewis smiled, knowing this was all going to work out well from the beginning.

"Well, I was thinking Dad and I could do the dishes while you ladies head to the living room to talk more, and then we can have some pie and ice cream later." Dan beamed.

"Oh, Dan, that is so wonderful of you. Thank you so much. Come on, Marissa, let's go before Lewis starts to protest!" Beth laughed as she jumped up, grabbed Marissa's hand, and pulled her along with her. Marissa was laughing and trying to keep up. Lewis just sat staring at Dan with mock anger. As soon as the women were gone, they began to laugh.

"All right, are you washing or drying?" Lewis asked, realizing he should really get Beth one of those dishwashers everyone else seemed to already have.

"I'll wash," Dan said, winking at his dad and heading for the sink. "I think this has gone well, don't you?"

"Yes, I knew they would love each other. Thank you for offering the olive branch, Dan. She has been a mess since that night. She really needed you to forgive her and give her a second chance."

"I know. I just was so mad and so shocked. I felt so used and angry at her. Marissa helped me to see it was doing no one any good. How can I be mad very long at the woman who has done everything for me my entire life?"

"I am glad you came around, and I am glad you have Marissa in your life. You complement each other well," Lewis said sincerely.

"I think so too. I can't believe something so amazing could come out of such tragedy." Dan said, feeling guilty.

"I know, but you have to move on from that guilt. Charlotte is well and going to make a full recovery. She is very happy for you. You can't let that eat at you," Lewis advised. Dan nodded.

"So we have been talking about the future, and Marissa was asking me about Grace and David and when could she meet them. I told her they come for Mother's Day and Christmas each year. She said then we know our two possible months for our wedding. Can you believe that? She wants to plan it around when Grace can be here! She thinks of everything. I never would have thought of that…"

"She is an amazing lady. I am touched she thought of that too. Grace and David will be happy to hear that, and your mother…" They laughed.

"Dad, we are really just happy not rushing things, but with knowing when we picked to have the wedding, I am starting to think about when we should become engaged. I don't want to scare her off, but I want to let her know I really mean it. I have an idea of how and when to ask her to marry me, but I am going to need some help from two people. I need to think this through and ask them for help."

"I don't think Marissa plans on going anywhere but into her future with you. Whoever they are, I am sure they will be glad to help," Lewis said confidently.

"I think you are right. I need to talk to them though. I need their help to pull this off the way I want to pull it off," Dan said, beaming. Lewis was intrigued but didn't want to push. He was sure whatever Dan was planning, it would be perfect, and whomever they were, they would be very willing to help.

Once the men had the leftovers put away and the dishes done, they decided they were ready for dessert.

"I'll get the saucers, forks, and ice cream out to soften, if you will cut the pies," Dan offered.

"Sounds good, don't forget the Cool Whip," Lewis said, heading for the pies.

"Should we serve them in the living room or call them to come back and join us?" Dan asked.

"Go ask them, but don't leave me alone with the pies too long. I am not responsible for my actions when pie is involved," Lewis teased.

Dan returned with the ladies who happily took their seats back at the table. Marissa was having the best time and really loved Beth.

"I got there just in time. Mom had just gotten out the photo albums! I told them they were needed in the kitchen for pie," Dan groaned. "I didn't offer to bring the pie to them."

"Aww, you were the cutest thing ever!" Marissa giggled.

Beth beamed. She had to agree. "And you are the loveliest thing ever. Thank you for coming into our lives. I just wish it hadn't been so traumatic to start with," Beth said genuinely.

"Thank you. I feel the same way." Marissa hugged her tightly.

"I knew this was going to happen," Dan said, rolling his eyes. Lewis laughed and slapped his son on the back.

"Trust me, this is better than them hating each other. I have seen some families ripped apart by things like that," Lewis said honestly. Dan nodded in agreement.

"I know. I am grateful." Dan had also seen the ugliest side of families in his line of work.

Hopes and Dreams

Charlotte was working hard in physical therapy and was making great strides in regaining her strength. Joel could see she had something on her mind but was giving her all to everything he asked her to do.

"Charlotte, you are doing great, but you seem to have something bothering you and you are pushing yourself too hard. You don't want to injure yourself by doing the exercises too rough or hard. Is there something you want to talk about?" Joel asked.

"I'm sorry. I just want to give it my all… I wasted so much time with a bad attitude." Charlotte fought back the tears.

"It's okay. You have made up that time now. You are right on schedule for what your doctor and I are expecting and hoping for out of you. What is wrong, Charlotte?" Joel asked honestly.

"My parents split up when I was really little. I found my dad and reconnected with him, right before my accident. That was the first time my parents have been face-to-face in thirty-eight years. They have reconnected and are back together. They are planning to have a wedding to renew their vows to make their reconciliation official. My mom asked my sister, daughter, and I to be bridesmaids. I don't know if I am still going to be in a wheelchair or not, but I really don't want to be," Charlotte said, frustrated and failing to keep the tears at bay any longer.

"Wow… I understand now. That is amazing. I see them bring you in, and I just thought they had always been together." Joel was blown away. You just never know what people are going through and what tragedy can destroy and restore. He saw it all the time: the good, the bad, and the ugly.

"When is the wedding?" Joel asked. He hoped they would have time to get her out of that chair.

"On their original wedding date, June 1. We have some time, but I don't know what to expect or hope for…," Charlotte said, wiping her eyes with the tissue Joel had handed her.

"June 1. That is great. That is plenty of time to get you out of this chair. Depending on how your body reacts, I know you are on board with your effort… I am sure we can get you at the very least on a walker, but hopefully on a cane. How do you feel about that?" Joel asked honestly. He wanted to know her mindset. It meant a big difference on the outcome.

"I would prefer the cane, but at least with a walker, I would be standing. You really think we can do this?" Charlotte asked honestly.

"I do. I need you to do your best work but not push yourself to injury. We don't want a setback. I also need you to be in a positive mindset. We have to be a team. Don't go backward on me," Joel warned.

"I promise," Charlotte said, nodding. Joel smiled.

"Then we got this," Joel said, locking eyes with Charlotte. "I won't let you down. We will make goal."

"Thank you, Joel. I appreciate you so much," Charlotte said, sighing in relief. "Will I spend the rest of my life on either a walker or cane?"

"No. It is too early to know if you might have a slight limp, but I think we can get you off of the cane. It really is too early to know how you will do, but my gut instinct says you will have a complete recovery. I am not giving up on you, so you don't either."

"Agreed." Charlotte smiled. It was good to hear he believed she would be fine. Then she could start seeing a real future for herself, as an independent woman and not an invalid anymore.

"What did you do for a living before the accident?" Joel asked.

"I was a waitress at Larry's Family Dining. They had to fill my position but promised to give me a job if I needed one in the future. I was set on getting back there, but as much as I care about all of them there..."

"Now you feel differently?" Joel asked, smiling. He had seen it before. After trauma and tragedy, sometimes a new life is born out of it and a new career path or life is found for his patients.

"Yes... I want to think on it, but I have been through so much, I wonder if there is something I can do that would help others who are going through something like this. I don't know just yet, but I am thinking," Charlotte said, smiling. "I have never told anyone that before."

"It is so new. You have a lot to focus on and a lot going on in your family, obviously. You have plenty of time," Joel said, smiling. He loved the way she was thinking. It would help her in recovery.

"You have no idea. The sister I have never gotten along with and I have reconciled in all of this as well. Also, the police officer on the scene who was with me and contacted my husband is now dating my sister. We should have another wedding in our future as well. Also, the chaplain who was by my family's side the whole time I was in the coma is the father of the officer. He had called his dad to be with my husband at the hospital. Before he met my sister, that chaplain is also my husband's new best friend. He has been counseling me and helping me with this new mindset. He helped me unlock what was going on inside me so I could move on." Charlotte laughed as Joel's eyes practically popped out of his head.

"*Are you serious?* So you have this life-changing accident, then you wake up, and your family is completely different? No wonder you had such a chip on your shoulder! That is a lot for anyone to absorb and digest. *Woo wee!*" Joel laughed and shook his head. "Charlotte, you are an amazing woman, and I am more proud of you than I can say. We got this. Keep your chin up and bright smile on. Life is only getting brighter."

"Yes it is." Charlotte beamed. "Thank you, Joel. I am so grateful for all you are doing for me and with me. I appreciate it."

"That is why I do what I do, Charlotte. For moments and people like you," Joel said, smiling. "Time is up for today. I will see you next time."

* * * * *

Charlotte was quiet the rest of the day. She took a nap and got some rest, but she spent most of the day deep in thought about what her future might look like. It had started out just wanting to be out of that wheelchair in time for the wedding, but now she had much more on her mind. She had a whole life ahead of her. What did she want to do with it? She had originally hoped to be well enough to get back to work at the restaurant, but now she realized her future could be anything she wanted it to be.

What did she want to do? She picked up her phone and made a call. She thought she knew who she should talk to.

"Hello?" Lewis answered.

"Lewis, this is Charlotte Wingate. Did I catch you at a bad time?" Charlotte asked nervously.

"Not at all. Hello, Charlotte. How are you doing?" Lewis asked, surprised to hear from Charlotte but hoped it was a good sign.

"Well, I have a lot on my mind and I am not sure how to sort it all out or what to think of it, and I don't even know how to bring it up to Elliott. It is all so jumbled in my mind. I wondered if we could meet to talk about it. I know we usually meet on Thursday, so if you don't have time until then, I am okay. It isn't urgent, but I want to talk it out with someone who might be able to help me. I think you are the one. It is heavy on my heart," Charlotte shared.

"I understand. I do have some this afternoon if you are feeling up to it," Lewis offered.

"That sounds great! I will be home all day, so whenever you can stop by." Charlotte giggled.

"I am glad you could pencil me in. I will be over within the hour." Lewis chuckled. He could tell this was definitely Emma's mother. They were a lot alike, just as everyone said.

Charlotte hung up, feeling better. She knew Lewis could help her figure out what was all on her mind to help her begin to find a path and how to talk to Elliott about it. She knew he would support her in anything she wanted to do, but she wanted to have some clarity before she spoke with him.

Charlotte headed to let her parents know Lewis was on his way over. She told them she just needed to talk to Lewis about some things and they didn't pry. She was grateful for that. Before she knew it, Lewis was there.

"I hear congratulations are in order for you both," Lewis said, beaming at Charles and Delores.

"Thank you," they said, blushing.

Lewis chuckled and then spotted Delores's ring. "*Wow, that is beautiful*," Lewis said, pointing toward Delores's hand.

"Thank you," Delores said, beaming and held out her hand so he could take a better look. "He picked a triangle diamond to recognize that there are three of us in this union, the Lord with us. He also put the birthstones of all our kids. Both girls, Emma, Elliott, and Dan," Delores said.

"Wow, that is beautiful and the sentiment is perfect." Lewis felt a tear in his eye. To see how far these two had come and to see that they loved his own son so much moved him. It also made him realize they would be family soon enough themselves. "I guess we will share a son and a daughter," Lewis said, beaming.

"Hello, Lewis," Charlotte said as she wheeled into the room. "I thought I heard your voice."

"Hello, Charlotte. I was just checking out your mom's huge rock!" Lewis said, winking at Charles.

"Yes, it is beautiful, isn't it?" Charlotte gushed.

"Well, do you two want anything to drink or a snack? We don't want to bother you, but if you would like some refreshments, we could get that for you and get out of your way," Delores offered. She didn't want to monopolize their time.

"Some sweet tea sounds nice," Charlotte said, smiling. "Thank you, Mom."

"I will take the same. Thank you very much," Lewis said, smiling.

"Great, I will get it. You two head to the living room and I will bring it to you," Delores instructed. She brought it right away, and Charles had a plate of cookies right behind her.

"Just in case you are hungry. I made some to surprise Emma, but I made plenty. She was so worried about her history test today, I thought she needed a surprise tonight," Delores said proudly.

"They look and smell delicious," Lewis said as he reached for one.

"Thanks, Mom. I know she will be excited when she gets home." Charlotte was touched by her mom's kindness. She had forgotten the times her mother had done things like this for her and Marissa as kids. Things had been so tense the last several years. She had forgotten all the loving touches her mom really did try to do for them.

"You are welcome. We will leave you now," Delores said, pleased, and she led Charles out of the living room.

Lewis turned to Charlotte, and she took a deep breath.

"Okay, Charlotte, what is on your mind?" Lewis asked politely.

"Well, all this excitement about Mom and Dad's wedding, and wow, that still seems wild to say and think about, but it has me thinking about my future as well," Charlotte said, pausing. "At first it was just concern and embarrassment about possibly being a bridesmaid in a wheelchair... I know that sounds shallow, but I don't want to feel like a spectacle. I had never thought about how long I would be in this chair or if it would be forever until Mom asked us to be her bridesmaids. It never once has bothered me since it was some freedom and independence from being stuck in bed all the time, but it made me start to wonder what my future holds..."

"That is perfectly understandable. I am sure there have been many a beautiful bridesmaid in wheelchairs, but I don't think it was the thought of that as much as realizing you don't know how much longer you have to be in that wheelchair. It is the first time you thought beyond today, am I right?" Lewis asked.

Charlotte's face lit up. "*Yes! Exactly!* The chair has never really bothered me at all. I was frustrated with being so helpless before, but not really about the wheelchair itself. I was grateful to have a motorized one so I could have some independence. I just started to wonder what I can expect for the future." Charlotte was so glad he understood. She didn't want to sound like she thought she was better than anyone else in a wheelchair.

"Have you had the chance to ask your doctor or physical therapist what they think or expect?"

"I did, this morning. I was in physical therapy and I was trying so hard to make progress, and I was feeling so stressed to push myself for the wedding. Joel realized I was pushing myself too hard, and he questioned me on it. He was afraid I was going to cause myself an injury. I told him what I was hoping to do: get out of this chair before the wedding. Since they are planning a June 1 wedding, he was confident that it was possible. He wasn't sure if I would be on a walker or a cane, but he was sure we could get me out of the chair." Charlotte beamed.

"I promised to not push harder than he asked and he promised to help me achieve my goals. That got me thinking about what other goals I might want to start thinking about. If I am going to be able bodied again, and he fully thinks I will. He said there is a possibility of a limp, but not necessarily. I started thinking about getting my job back at Larry's, and then I realized I wasn't sure if that is what I want. It kind of surprised me to feel that way, but he isn't holding that position for me. He replaced me. He had to, I understand that. It wasn't fair to the other waitresses or customers for him to be always short staffed. He had his business to run. I started to think about having some hours eventually if I recovered and work my way back into full time when he had a position available. It is the only job I have ever had, and I just didn't think beyond it, until now..."

"I see... If that is all you have known, of course that would be your natural first expectation. To get your life back to the way it was, but now that you are getting better and seeing life differently from this side of the accident, you have realized that it isn't an automatic decision. You can explore new options, look for new opportunities, and dream a new dream. It is kind of exciting, isn't it?" Lewis said, catching her excitement.

"Yes, it is. I have been doing a lot of thinking today, and I don't have to make any decisions today, but I wanted to see if I am getting carried away or if there are things I can explore. I only have a high school diploma," Charlotte said, wondering if she was wasting his time.

"Well, that is the best first place to start. You can go back to school if you need to in order to become whatever you want to do. There are online classes you can take and community college classes if you don't want to tackle a big university. There are so many opportunities you can take advantage of if you want to. What are you thinking about?" Lewis was intrigued, and he didn't want her to talk herself out of it. "There is no hard and fast rule that you have to go to college by twenty-two or it is all over. You might find what you want to do doesn't even require a full four-year degree."

"I guess that is true," Charlotte said, biting her lip. "I want to help people. I want to do something to help people through the worst crisis of their lives. I want to help them to have hope and to realize there is a future. I want to do something that matters. I feel like I was given this wonderful gift of a second chance at life and I want to make the most out of it. I want to really help people like I have never helped them before. I am just not sure how or what yet."

"That makes complete sense. Your whole life has been altered and changed. You are feeling grateful and overwhelmed and you want to help others like yourself or your family through the same thing. I understand more than you think...," Lewis said quietly. "I don't know if you know this or not. Beth and I have three children. Dan, you know, our daughter, Grace, and her husband, David, are missionaries and our son Paul passed away as a child. That is a pain I wish on no one. It changed me. Once I got through the darkest days, I realized I had to do something. I had to help my son have a legacy, to know his life mattered beyond just our little family. I was a schoolteacher. I went back to school and became a minister and took a position as a chaplain at the hospital. It helped me find purpose again and helped me feel like I was doing this for my son as much as for me. He wanted to be a firefighter. He wanted to save people's lives. I found a way to try and help people in his honor. It is because he lived and had a desire to make a difference that I do that every day. Beth felt the same way. She volunteers and works with babies in the NICU and supports families there, especially the ones who do not have a happy ending," Lewis said, the tears in his eyes threatened to spill out.

"Oh Lewis, I had no idea… I am so sorry," Charlotte said, tears flowing down her face as she listened to all he had shared. She suddenly felt like he did completely understand.

"Thank you," Lewis said, smiling. He wiped his tears away and stood to take a quick walk around the room and regain his composure. He sat back down and locked eyes with Charlotte.

"You can do anything you want to do. You have an amazing heart for others and love for people. Pray about it. Let God lead you to your path, your next adventure in life, your journey on. You don't have to make any quick decisions or commitments. I know Elliott and Emma and the rest of the family will cheer you on. Figure out what your calling is now. What every part of your life up to now has laid the groundwork for. It wasn't wasted before. It was groundwork. If you weren't in that job for so long, you never would have met Bob or started on the road to find your dad the way you did. God's timing is perfect. He doesn't cause bad things to happen, but he can turn them around and use them for good," Lewis explained. "Once you know what you want, I would be honored to help you get set up on the path to make it happen any way I can."

"Thank you, Lewis. I… I just wanted to know I wasn't getting ahead of myself or being silly," Charlotte said. "I needed some reassurance before I talked to Elliott or just gave up on it like some pipe dream. Thank you," Charlotte said, reaching for Lewis's hand.

Lewis squeezed her hand back and let out a deep sigh. He couldn't wait to see what the Lord had in store for Charlotte next. They said their goodbyes, and he grabbed a cookie for the road.

Charlotte watched him head for the kitchen to say goodbye to Delores and Charles, and she stayed in her spot, feeling so peaceful and happy.

* * * * *

Delores and Charles never asked or mentioned Lewis's visit to Elliott and Emma. They felt it was Charlotte's place to do that if she wanted to. They enjoyed a nice dinner, and Emma and Elliott cleaned up the kitchen as Delores and Charles left for the night.

"Thank you for not mentioning my visitor today. I wanted to talk to Elliott alone about that," Charlotte whispered to her parents. They looked at each other with concern; this secrecy made them worry something was wrong.

"I promise, nothing is wrong. I wanted to talk to Lewis about some things to help me figure them out first, kind of as a sounding board and get his unbiased opinion before I talked to Elliott about it, and I am not ready to talk about it with Emma or anyone else just yet, not until I have more clarity on this," Charlotte explained. They smiled with relief.

"We won't pry but are glad nothing is wrong. It actually sounds promising, whatever it is," Charles said, understanding.

"Whatever it is that is on your heart, you can do it. God will see you through," Delores said softly.

"Listen to you!" Charlotte said proudly.

They all laughed and Delores and Charlotte hugged. Elliott and Emma were watching them from across the room and exchanged curious looks.

"What are they whispering about?" Emma asked Elliott.

"I don't know," Elliott said. He wasn't sure if he should ask or give her some space. "Let's not ask just yet. I will talk to her later."

"Good idea," Emma said. "I think I will spend the evening in my room so you can talk to Mom alone. Can I call Tracey?"

"Sure, but don't stay on the phone too late." Elliott smiled. He appreciated her maturity so much.

"Night, Mama," Emma said, kissing Charlotte's cheek and hugging her. She grabbed a saucer of cookies and a glass of milk. "Dad said it was okay to call Tracey before bed. Nothing on TV I care about tonight."

Charlotte had a feeling something was up. She watched Emma slip out of the room quickly. She looked at Elliott who was studying her carefully.

"What is going on?" Charlotte asked.

"That is what we were wondering. You were whispering with your parents, and we didn't want to pry, but we didn't know what the secrecy was about. Is everything okay?"

"Yes, but I do want to talk to you. Is Emma hiding out in her room to give us privacy now?"

"Yep, she is really growing up," Elliott said, feeling proud and sad all at the same time.

"What a kid. Not that we can call her a kid much longer," Charlotte said, realizing how true it was. "Have a seat, Elliott. Don't look at me like that. Nothing is wrong, but I do want to talk to you about what I have been thinking about," Charlotte explained.

Elliott relaxed a little and took his seat. Charlotte wheeled up to him so they could be face-to-face. She took a deep breath and smiled at him.

"My parent's wedding had me thinking about this wheelchair and how long I might be in it. I had never really thought about it. So much has been going on, and I have just been trying to put all the pieces of my life together of what I missed from the accident. I have never thought a lot about the future too much. Then when Mom asked us to be bridesmaids, I realized I felt uncomfortable with the idea of being in this chair long term. I was pushing myself too hard in therapy, and Joel slowed me down. He knew something was going on in my head," Charlotte said, smiling. She really liked him. "So he started to ask me what was going on, and I told him about my parents and the wedding and being a bridesmaid in June, and I didn't like the idea of wheeling down the aisle," Charlotte said, grimacing.

"I could tell that was bothering you," Elliott said quietly. "It is the first time you have seemed to mind it. I know you were frustrated feeling helpless, but the chair itself didn't seem to bother you until the wedding plans came up."

"Yes. Joel said with that many months ahead, he is sure I can be up on a walker or on a cane possibly! It just depends on how well my body cooperates with our work, but he did warn me not to push more than he asked me to so I wouldn't get an injury. I promised." Charlotte was glowing in her excitement at a good prognosis. "He said he expects me to make a full recovery, possibly a slight limp, but maybe not.'

"That is wonderful news. I know they have always been cautious about too many expectations and told us to just take it as it comes." Elliott was beaming. He was hoping she could have her independence back but would have been devoted to taking care of her in any way needed for the rest of their lives.

"So after we came home from therapy, I took a nap to regain some strength and then I got to thinking. What else is next? When I am fully recovered from the physical trauma and setbacks from the accident, what do I do next? I had just assumed I would call Larry and see if he could work me into the schedule and take me back..."

"But now you are thinking differently," Elliott said, catching on.

"*Yes!* I had all these thoughts and wondered what was possible, and was I just getting carried away or was this really an open door to do something new? And what could that be?"

"It sounds like a perfect opportunity to reevaluate your life and goals and figure out what you want." Elliott was excited for her.

"I knew you would understand," Charlotte said, trying to hold back her tears. "You always do."

"I try," Elliott said, locking eyes with her. "I am still a little confused. Why is this all a secret?"

"Well, it really wasn't meant to be. I needed to talk to someone and bounce some ideas off of that would be impartial. I called Lewis and asked if he could come over, and he did right then. I really like him. He listened to me and agreed with me. He was so encouraging and let me know it isn't too late for me to change paths, or even go to school to get some type of certification or degree. He shared how he and his wife lost their son Paul, and how that propelled him from leaving his job as a teacher to become a minister and a hospital chaplain. He wanted to fulfill Paul's dream of helping people by doing it for him."

"Yes, I knew Paul had died as a child and that he had wanted to be a firefighter. I didn't know that is what led Lewis to become a chaplain or that he had been a schoolteacher. Wow," Elliott said, impressed and touched by his friend again.

"It helped me to see I am not crazy or silly. This is like a new awakening for me, like I have a new calling or opportunity for myself. I thanked my parents for keeping Lewis's visit a secret for now, letting me talk to you first then I would explain to them and everyone what it was all about."

"So they don't know what the visit was about, just that you called Lewis and spoke with him?"

"Yes. I needed to talk to you first. I was just thanking them for not mentioning Lewis's visit to you and Emma earlier. I assured them nothing was wrong, and I wanted to talk to you about it before anyone else. I just needed an unbiased opinion first," Charlotte said, smiling.

Elliott exhaled. "Well, I am glad it was good news, and this is exciting. Do you have any ideas of what you are thinking about?" Elliott was intrigued.

"Maybe. I have a few ideas, but I am not sure which direction is right for me. I am going to pray about it more and see. I will share more when I know more. This is really so new to even consider. I don't know what to tell you just yet."

"I can appreciate that," Elliott said honestly. "Take your time, and know I am always on your side."

"I know. I appreciate that so much," Charlotte said and leaned forward to kiss Elliott. "I just hope I am not being silly or selfish."

Charlotte let out a deep sigh. Her smile faded, and Elliott was confused. She had been so excited. What was wrong? "Don't lose hope now. What is wrong?" Elliott asked.

"Money. Here I have caused all these medical bills and they aren't done yet...and I am thinking of going back to school. I just thought about that. I need to just get a job and work on this debt before we lose our house. You must be under so much stress." Charlotte hadn't thought about it until this moment. How selfish has she become?

"Oh, Charlotte, you are not selfish at all! I believe God has put this on your heart. Pray and let him guide you," Elliott urged. Then he smiled and sat back in his chair. "I wasn't trying to keep you in the dark about our finances, but you have been going through enough, and you didn't need to think about anything else. We are fine."

"What? How?" Charlotte was confused.

"Well, your dad sold his home, and he kept a small savings from it and about 90 percent of it he paid on your medical bills for us. My parents and even my brothers felt bad that they weren't here to help in person with living so far away. They sent money to help us as well. My parents sold their vacation home and sent us the money. We even received money from members of our church, and my coworkers took up a collection as did Marissa's coworkers. She was so overwhelmed and proud to hand me the money. I cashed in my IRAs as well. Emma's school even did a fundraiser and gave the proceeds to us. Kenneth and Cindy had organized it. We weren't trying to keep any of this from you, but we didn't want to add more to your plate. You were struggling so much emotionally. We didn't think you could take one more thing. We thanked them all, and they just wanted to help. My insurance company covered a huge portion, of course. I am so glad I had the extra insurance policies. Larry felt so bad he didn't offer health insurance on his employees. He had one night a week for a month where a portion of all orders were donated to you. He added to it as well. He now offers health insurance to his employees. He said it was worth it. He never wanted to let anyone down again," Elliott explained as he held Charlotte's hand. The tears flowed from both of them.

Charlotte was so overwhelmed by the kindness of others. She began to sob. How could she never have asked or wondered about this before? How could all these people be showing her so much kindness and she not know anything about it? God was good, and his love was shown to them through so many people.

"Don't be upset, Charlotte. I was going to tell you when you asked or when the time was right. It just hadn't come up. We all really just wanted you to get well and be well. That is all we wanted you to be concerned with."

Charlotte understood but was still so overwhelmed. "No, I understand what you are saying. I just am so blown away by it all,"

Charlotte managed to say. Her throat felt tight with emotion. She was so humbled by the kindness and generosity of so many.

"I know now more than ever, I have to find a way to give back," Charlotte said, determined. Elliott smiled and nodded. He was so grateful he had good news to give Charlotte and that she took it well. He loved the mindset she now had and was relieved he had his wife was back.

CHAPTER 16

Happy Thanksgiving

The next few months went by very quickly. The planning of Charles and Delores's wedding was starting to come together. Charlotte was barely having any headaches anymore, and she was gaining a lot of strength and taking steps in therapy with Joel. Marissa and Dan were spending a lot of time with both their families, and all the wedding planning was starting to get them both thinking and talking more about their own wedding someday. Beth and Lewis had invited Marissa and her entire family for Thanksgiving dinner at their house.

* * * * *

"Lewis, how is the turkey doing?" Beth was nervous. She wanted this to go perfectly. This was the first of what she hoped would be a long tradition on the holidays, having Marissa and her family for Thanksgiving. Having a bigger gathering always made Thanksgiving feel more like it should, so much and so many to be thankful for.

"Looks great. Right on schedule," Lewis soothed. Beth let out a deep sigh. She looked around at all they had made and hoped it was enough.

"It's perfect. Don't forget they are bringing side dishes and desserts too," Lewis tried to reassure her, but he knew when she got into this mode, there was no convincing her until it was over.

"I know. Marissa's mother is making a ham too," Beth added, nodding. Lewis wondered if she even knew he was there or was she too caught up in her own thoughts to realize he was talking to her. He just smiled. It was her way.

"Happy Thanksgiving!" Dan and Marissa sang out as they came in carrying bags and covered dishes. Behind them were Charles and Delores, Emma and Elliott pushing Charlotte in her wheelchair.

"Happy Thanksgiving!" Beth said enthusiastically. She hugged Marissa and Dan then made her way through the group, making introductions and hugging everyone. It was the first time she had met Marissa's family in person even though she had heard so much about them.

"Thank you for having us, Mrs. Williams. We are excited to be here," Emma squealed. Beth laughed and hugged her.

"*Oh, Emma*, I have heard the most amazing things about you, and I can tell they are all very accurate!" Beth was in love with her already. "And please, no one call me Mrs. Williams. I have a rule here. If you eat with us, you are family. If you call me Mrs. Williams again…"

"She will throw a pot holder at you," Dan and Lewis said together. They all laughed.

"That is correct," Beth announced proudly. "Now let's get this food ready to eat! Then we can spend the rest of the day visiting and having fun. Emma, I hear you like board games. It is a Williams's tradition to play board games after Thanksgiving dinner."

"That sounds wonderful! I do love them!" Emma gushed. Beth hugged her again.

Dan and Lewis carved the ham and turkey while Beth, Marissa, Delores, and Emma got the food on the table. They all found a seat and were ready to say grace and enjoy the meal together.

"Lewis, may I say grace?" Emma asked. Beth wiped a tear from her eye.

"That would be perfect. Thank you, Emma," Lewis said genuinely.

"Dear heavenly Father, this year has been the hardest and best year of my life. I thank you for all your blessings, the healing you have done in my mom's body, and in our family relationships. Thank you for bringing Grandpa and Grandma back together. Thank you for bringing Dan and Marissa together, and for our new friends Lewis and Beth. Thank you for helping me find a deeper faith in you. We thank you for holding my dad and I together, and I pray for all those we met in the hospital are doing well, and all who are there now, let them know you are with them and touch them and their loved ones. We have so much to be thankful for, and I am sorry for any of my life I have taken you for granted. Bless this meal and all of us. We have much to be thankful for. May we always remember. In Jesus's name, I pray. Amen."

Emma raised her head as she wiped the tears from her eyes. Everyone was staring at her in amazement, and tears were streaming down their faces.

"And God, thank you for the gift of Emma," Beth whispered hoarsely, to which they all choked out "Amen."

Lewis picked up a bowl and dished out some food and passed it to Elliott who was next to him. They all recovered and passed the food around and began to talk and laugh and enjoy their time together. They all got along well and enjoyed their day. They really did blend well together.

Beth and Lewis led them to the living room where they had small card tables and folding chairs set up around the room and different board games set up at each of them. Emma squealed in excitement.

"We have Aggravation, Life, Scrabble, and for those who dare… Monopoly," Lewis announced. They all laughed.

"You weren't kidding. This is a big thing for you all, isn't it?" Charles asked, laughing.

"*It most certainly is!* We are competitive, but we are loving. No grudges, and respectful bragging rights only!" Beth giggled.

"I'm playing Aggravation!" Emma said, running for her table of choice.

"Count me in!" Charlotte said, wheeling herself after her. Elliott joined them.

"I want Scrabble!" Marissa said, and Dan followed her.

"Life, that sounds like fun. The girls had that game when they were young. They would pick which celebrity crush they had as their husbands." Delores giggled. Charles followed her there.

"Our Grace did the same thing," Beth said, beaming, as she joined them at Life. Lewis headed for the Life game table as well.

It was a wonderful day. Friendships were made, family bonds grew stronger, and they were all thankful.

After they all left, Beth and Lewis snuggled onto the couch, sipping their coffee.

"That was the best Thanksgiving we have ever had. I only wish Grace and David were here," Beth said happily.

"And Paul," they said, looking at each other. They snuggled in closer and shed a few tears. They often wondered if he would have become that firefighter he dreamed of, or if life would have led him down another path. Would he have found someone as perfect for him as Marissa was for Dan and David for Grace? Would he have given them grandchildren?

"I am so thankful for the time we had with him, no matter how short. He will always be a part of us, and we will be reunited one day with no more goodbyes," Beth whispered. Lewis nodded as the tears rolled down his face freely. They held on tighter to each other and shared memories of when their children were very young, and Paul was with them.

* * * * *

Dan took Marissa home and headed toward Delores's house. He had asked them, privately, if he could stop by and talk to them. They were surprised but had a feeling that they knew what it was about.

Charles had taken Delores home and stayed, waiting on Dan to arrive. He was at the door and Delores let him in.

"Come in, Dan. We were having some coffee in the kitchen. Would you like some, or something else?" Delores asked.

"I would like some coffee, thank you," Dan said, suddenly feeling very nervous. Delores nodded and led him to the kitchen where Charles sat at the table, sipping his coffee, trying not to smile.

Once they were seated, they looked at Dan for what he was wanting to talk to them about.

"I asked if I could talk to you both for two reasons. The first, I want to let you know that I am madly in love with your firstborn daughter, Marissa Lynn Medlock. I have been talking with Marissa, and we have been thinking and planning our future together, and I would like to ask your permission to ask for her hand in marriage. We aren't in a hurry to get married, but I would like to make plans and buy her a ring. If that is a pleasing and acceptable idea to the both of you," Dan asked seriously.

"Well...," Charles began slowly.

"I have the most honorable intentions toward your daughter. I want to take care of her and cherish her and work hard to make her happy all the days of her life. I know Charlotte has the most amazing husband in Elliott, and I hope to be as good a husband to Marissa and to make you both very proud," Dan added.

"Dan, I can't imagine a better husband for Marissa in this entire world," Charles said, putting his hand on Dan's arm to calm him.

"You have supported this entire family in our greatest time of need and proven yourself to us in every possible way. It is obvious you love Marissa, and she loves you. We were expecting this was what you wanted to see us about, and you have our full support," Delores added.

Delores and Charles began to laugh, and Dan let out a long, deep sigh, and was smiling so big his face hurt, but he didn't care. He expected to get their blessing, but to actually have it felt great.

"I have been practicing that for weeks," Dan said, laughing. Charles and Delores laughed again and hugged him.

"You said there were two things. What else is it?" Delores asked, remembering.

"Well, I have been pondering on how, when, and where to ask her. We do talk about our future and our wedding plans. We even know the month we plan on getting married, just not the year. Since we have already discussed so much and I know we both have our hearts committed on a future together in marriage, I want the proposal to completely take her by surprise and sweep her off her feet. I had a few ideas, but I wanted to stay away from anything too predictable or expected," Dan explained. "I had one idea, but I wanted to run it past you to see what you thought about it. I am going to need your help for this idea."

"Oh, if we can help in any way, we would love to!" Charles said, beaming at Delores.

"Please tell us your idea!" Delores giggled. Dan went into his elaborate plan and how he thought it might play out. They loved the idea.

"She won't be expecting that. I think that would be absolutely perfect!" Delores had tears in her eyes. Charles took her hand in his.

"Dan, you not only have our blessing in your marrying our daughter. We would be honored to help in this special time of your lives," Charles said, swiping at a tear that spilled out of his eye.

"Thank you so much. I really appreciate your blessing and your help," Dan said, beaming. He had been nervous to approach them with his idea but was relieved they loved the idea. "Please keep this between us. I don't want anyone to accidently ruin the surprise."

"You have our word," Delores said as she gave Dan another hug. Charles slapped him on the back and they laughed.

"We truly have so much to be thankful for," Charles said, hugging Delores.

Chapter 17

David and Grace

December came in quickly, and Christmas had a sweeter meaning to it than it ever had before. Thanksgiving had gone so well that a big Christmas Day gathering was planned at Lewis and Beth's home. They even drew names for a Christmas exchange. Marissa was both excited and nervous to meet Grace and David, but mainly Grace. What if she didn't like her? Dan assured her; if Beth loved her, then Grace would too. That did help Marissa feel a little better.

David and Grace had arrived late Wednesday night, one week before Christmas. They usually would be there through New Years and then head back to Africa. They had been doing missionary work there for three years. Grace was excited to meet Marissa and the rest of her family. Beth had kept her up to date on everything in her letters. David and Grace always spent the first full day at her parents' sleeping and recovering from the long trip. Dan had taken Friday off to spend time with his family. Marissa would be joining them for dinner.

When Dan arrived at his parents' house Friday morning, he found David and Lewis having coffee in the living room. David looked well. He stood and smiled when he saw Dan.

"Hey brother from another mother." David laughed and hugged Dan. "Congratulations on finding the love of your life. That is fantastic! Grace has been so excited and couldn't wait to get home to meet her."

"I'm sure. I can't wait for you both to meet her tonight. You are going to love her." Dan beamed.

"Wow, I have never seen you like this, Dan. This is great!" David laughed. "You weren't lying, Lewis. He is a new man. I have never seen you smile so big. Does your face hurt?"

"A lot of the time, but I don't care," Dan said, laughing.

"I am so happy for them both. I love that Grace and Dan both have made wonderful selections in their spouses. Beth and I couldn't ask for more."

"Danny!" Grace came running in from the kitchen. She jumped up in Dan's arms and hugged him. "Oh it is so good to see you! I can't wait to meet Marissa! I wish we didn't have to wait until tonight."

"Well, I would have asked her to take today off, but I have something I need to do today without her, and I need you and Mom's help. She would have done it in a heartbeat if I had asked, but she figured we wanted some family time to catch up today," Dan said, still beaming. Grace and Beth exchanged looks.

"Danny, are you saying what I think you are saying?" Grace asked.

"I am asking you two if you would come with me to help me pick out an engagement ring for Marissa," Dan announced.

Beth and Grace began to squeal and hug each other. Lewis and David smiled at each other. This really was getting real.

"You really want our help? You waited on me to come home to help?" Grace was so touched she hugged Dan again.

"Of course, I need the two most important women in my life to help me pick out the ring for my wife," Dan said, trying not to cry.

Beth began to sob and hugged Dan. Grace hugged Lewis and then turned to David beaming.

"I am so excited!" she gushed.

"I know," David said laughing and hugged her.

"Well, are you two ready or do I have to wait?" Dan asked, looking at his watch.

"Give me a just a few minutes!" Beth pleaded and ran upstairs. "I didn't know it was such an important day when I got dressed this morning. I need to change my clothes."

"What?" Dan asked, confused. The others laughed.

"Let her be," Grace said, shaking her head and sighing. She knew how much this meant to her and it had to be so much more exciting for her mother.

"Well, Lewis, what are we going to do today?" David asked, grinning ear to ear.

"Well, I haven't played tennis in a while. Do you want to go to the YMCA?" Lewis suggested.

"Sounds like a plan. I better go change. I didn't know I was playing tennis today when I got dressed this morning," David said, trying not to laugh.

"I better do the same," Lewis said, looking down at his sweater and slacks.

* * * * *

Dan took his mother and sister to a few different jewelry stores, but they just weren't finding what he thought felt right.

"Maybe designing your own ring for Marissa would be best. Do you have something in mind?" Grace asked him.

"I didn't think I did, but maybe I do. I don't know. Like look at all these shapes, what one is best?" Dan asked, feeling overwhelmed.

"Well, this is a round diamond cut, a square cut, emerald cut, princess cut, marquis cut...," the saleslady explained, pointing to the different diamond cuts on an information sheet.

"Princess cut...which one is that?" Dan interrupted. He smiled. He hadn't known there was such a thing. The sales lady smiled and pointed to it on the page.

"I like that. I like that a lot. Marissa is a strong woman. She had to grow up fast and always felt like she was on her own. I want her to always know she isn't alone anymore. She will always have me to be her partner in life and to protect her. She is my princess," Dan said pointedly. All three women had tears in their eyes.

"Okay…do you want the band to be yellow gold, white gold, rose gold, or platinum?" The sales lady tried very hard to keep her composure and be professional. This man was touching her heart.

"I have no idea…" Dan looked overwhelmed again.

"I have seen Marissa wear more silver jewelry. It suits her dark eyes and hair. So I would choose the white gold, silver, or platinum," Beth offered.

"That is true, but that doesn't make it clear which one," Dan said nervously. He looked at Grace for help.

"What about the rose gold? That is very pretty, and you don't see that very often. It is so soft and pretty," Grace offered.

"I do like that…okay, rose gold it is." Dan's hands were sweating.

"I like that. Is that the infinity symbol on both sides?" Dan asked, pointing to a band style.

"Yes, it is called a vintage infinity band. It has very tiny diamonds through the infinity symbol on both sides, and then you can pick what size princess cut style you want."

"I like that, infinity. I will love her with no end," Dan said pointedly.

Beth and Grace smiled proudly, both with tears in their eyes. They had never seen Dan like this but were so happy to see him so in love.

The saleslady typed into the computer his choices and showed them the ring.

Beth and Grace gasped. It was beautiful, delicate, but detailed. It was definitely princess quality, but it had a sophistication about it too that seemed to suit Marissa perfectly. Dan was beaming. He couldn't wait to see it on her finger.

"*That is it*! That is perfect. That is Marissa's ring," Dan said confidently.

"Dan, you have made such a beautiful choice," Grace said proudly.

"Yes, this is very beautiful," the saleslady agreed. "Do you know her ring size?"

"Yes, her mother told me it was a size five."

They finished up the process of ordering the ring, then Dan took them out to lunch as a thank you at Barney's Grill. They had called Lewis and David to invite them to come join them.

"Dan, when are you going to give it to her? You won't have it in time for Christmas," Grace said sadly.

"That is right. She said it would take a few weeks," Beth said, sighing.

"That's okay. I have it all planned out, and it wasn't intended to be a Christmas gift. I just wanted to go shop for it when I could take you both with me," Dan said, smiling.

"Oh...well good. When are you doing it?" Beth asked.

"You will just have to wait and see. It is meant to be a surprise," Dan said, laughing as the two ladies looked at each other, flustered with his secrecy. He had to have some fun with them. "Not meaning any insult to you or anyone else, but the less people who know, the better chance I have of making this perfect for her. Marissa deserves only the best."

"Well, when you put it that way, we will respect your privacy," Beth said, smiling.

"Thank you, both," Dan said, feeling giddy. The women laughed. This was not the quiet, serious Dan they were used to seeing.

Lewis and David arrived, both looking a little worn out and hungry.

"That was great. It has been too long," David said.

"Well, was the mission a success?" Lewis asked.

"Yes! Dan wasn't finding what he liked, so we looked at options, and he designed a ring for her," Grace gushed.

"Really?" Lewis was impressed how his son was a completely different man than he had ever been since Marissa had come into his life. He was a good man, but the changes were just making him even better.

"Yes, I was overwhelmed, but step-by-step we figured it out. Rose gold, princess cut diamond, vintage infinity band...when she showed it to us on the computer...it was perfect," Dan said, still in disbelief. "I didn't know what I wanted, but we weren't finding anything that felt right. Grace asked if I had an idea, and I didn't know, but when we looked at each option, it just came together."

"Wow. Great job, Dan," David said genuinely. "That was a great idea to take Beth and Grace with you. I am sure they helped, but it meant more to them than you will ever know."

"Well, I couldn't have done it without them, and I wouldn't have wanted to," Dan said sincerely. "Which is why I am paying for their lunch. You two are on your own."

"What?" Lewis and David said in mock shock.

"Well, since you are home for a visit I will pay," Lewis said, laughing.

"Thanks. I thought maybe you would offer since I beat you two out of three matches," David teased.

"Or I could let you pay for your own..." Lewis teased.

"I will take the welcome home offer, thank you, Lewis," David said with mock humility. They all laughed.

"What is the plan for dinner?" Grace asked. "Is Marissa coming over or are we all going out?"

"We thought you might still be tired, so we thought dinner in would be good. I thought I would make a salad, lasagna, garlic bread, and a chocolate cake for dessert," Beth offered.

"*I love your lasagna, Mom*!" Grace squealed. "That sounds perfect."

"I dream about your chocolate cake, Beth...," David said, smiling.

"I know. I try to cover all your favorites when you are here." Beth laughed.

"Dan, what are you going to tell Marissa when she asks what you did today?" Grace asked.

"I'm going to tell her I spent the day with the two of you catching up and we met Lewis and David for lunch after their tennis match—the truth. I just am not going to offer anything about our shopping trip. I will tell her after I have given her the ring," Dan explained.

"To Marissa!" David said, lifting his tea glass in the air.

"To Marissa!" they all said, clinking glasses.

"Dan, do you mind if I order dessert, or do you want Daddy to pay for my dessert?" Grace asked, giggling. They all laughed.

"Your daddy can pay for it," Dan teased and then shook his head no. "I got ya, sis."

"Thank you. Do you see the waiter? I really want a slice of that lemon crème cake with vanilla ice cream!" Grace said, stretching to look around. They all looked at her and laughed.

* * * * *

Marissa had a hard time making it through the day. She was so excited and nervous. She was surprised when Dan said he was taking the day off to spend with his family that he didn't ask her if she could take the day off. She was sure it was good for them to spend time together as a family, but she still was a little surprised not to be included. They weren't married yet, so she really shouldn't expect to be included like a wife would be. She didn't worry about it too much. She had to figure out what to wear. Suddenly she was very grateful for the surprise visit in meeting Beth. That would have been even more stressful than this was turning out to be.

She called Charlotte for advice, and she suggested her royal blue sweater, some jeans, and her sapphire earrings. She thought that sounded like a good idea. She rushed home after work and got changed, put her earrings on, and touched up her makeup, and pulled her hair up into a messy bun. That would show off the earrings more, she thought as she pulled down a few wisps of hair to frame her face.

She heard the doorbell and let out a deep sigh. Dan was here.

He smiled big when she opened the door. "You look more breathtaking every time I see you," Dan said, grinning from ear to ear.

"Thank you, Officer Dan," Marissa said, beaming.

"Grace is so excited to meet you. She can't stand it," Dan said, laughing as he drove toward his parents' house.

"Oh good, I have been excited and nervous myself," Marissa said, smiling, trying to ignore the butterflies in her stomach.

"Relax. You are not on trial here. She scolded Mom too about how your first meeting with her started. She has been her bubbly self, eating all day and napping too. The jet lag this time must have really gotten to her," Dan said, laughing. "She is excited because Mom is making her lasagna tonight and that is Grace's favorite. Mom made David's favorite too, chocolate cake. So relax. They are excited to meet you, but they might be more excited about dinner." They laughed.

They found Lewis and David setting the table when they came into the kitchen. Grace was carrying the platter of garlic bread to the table, and Beth was cutting the lasagna into serving sized pieces.

Grace squealed when she saw Marissa and ran over to her. She took both her hands in hers and just smiled at her, taking her in.

"You are so exquisite! You are as beautiful on the outside as Dan describes you on the inside. It is so nice to meet you, Marissa. I'm Grace," Grace gushed and pulled Marissa into a hug.

"And there they go," Dan said, sighing. They all laughed.

"A pleasure to meet you, Marissa," David said, holding out his hand. They both seemed so nice, and Marissa felt comfortable with them right away. This was more amazing than she could have dreamed of. Was this really happening? Was she really a part of two families?

They sat down to eat, and Grace and David told Marissa all about their work in the mission field in Africa. Grace helped in the clinic, helping to give medical care to the villagers. Marissa hadn't realized she was an LPN. David helped the men build houses and taught Bible studies every week. You could tell they loved what they did.

"The work you do must be so rewarding, both the physical work and the spiritual," Marissa said sincerely.

"It really is, and we have loved it. We knew when we started on this journey, it wasn't going to be forever. We have done a lot of talking and praying, and the Lord has answered our prayers and gave us the sign we needed to know it was time for a new chapter in our lives," David said, locking eyes with Grace the entire time. He nodded toward her.

"Yes, we have decided it was time to move back home," Grace announced.

Beth and Lewis gasped.

"Really? You are really coming home for good?" Beth asked, too excited and afraid to really believe it just yet.

"Yes, but we wanted to make sure we had your lasagna and chocolate cake before we told you, so you wouldn't make something else," David teased.

"Well, you haven't had the chocolate cake yet." Dan laughed.

"True, but I think we can seal that deal," David said, looking back at Grace.

She had tears in her eyes as she stood up and cradled her belly. "We are having a baby this summer," Grace said softly. They all erupted in cheers, tears, and jumped up to hug Grace and David.

"*That is why you have been so excited about food!*" Beth giggled, holding tightly to her girl. "I wondered but wasn't sure. *Oh Gracie, my baby is having a baby.*" Beth broke down into sobs.

"Are you back for good now? Are you going back to Africa at all?" Lewis asked.

"We are back for good. We didn't have much to bring back with us. You live lightly on the mission field," David explained.

"We were hoping it was okay if we stayed here while we find jobs and a home. We promise not to stay too long," Grace said. "We want to get settled in before the baby comes."

"That is wonderful news, and there is no rush. You know that," Lewis said sincerely.

"Well, I think we need some chocolate cake on that one!" Dan said excitedly.

"Let us clean up the kitchen, and you four, go relax in the living room and talk. We will get the cake served up after," Marissa offered enthusiastically.

"Marissa, that isn't fair," Beth tried to protest.

"No, it is fine. Our pleasure," Marissa said emphatically. Beth and Grace hugged her.

"That sounds wonderful, but let's just sit here in the kitchen so Dan and Marissa can be included," Grace insisted.

"Perfect idea," David said.

"David was going to contact his former employer and see if there is an opening there, and we thought we would check into the housing situation around here. We have some savings, and I was hoping to stay home until the baby is born or wait and see if we can afford me to be able to stay home with the baby. I could take a PRN position and work a day or two a week just to keep my nursing skills strong and keep a work history up, and when the baby is in school, I can work more hours. We are used to living lightly, so we don't need a lot," Grace explained.

"Well, if you wanted to work more, you know you don't have to pay for childcare. I can work my volunteer schedule at the hospital to accommodate your needs, but I want you to be able to be home with your baby as much as you can," Beth gushed. "I know I treasure the memories of being home with my babies. I was fortunate, and I want you to be as well."

"Thank you, Mom. That means a lot," Grace said, smiling. "It is so good to be home. I am so glad we had that time in Africa. It was life-changing for us, but we are ready for the next chapter."

"Yes, we were talking about it and trying to decide what we were wanting to do, and when Grace realized she was pregnant, we knew it was the answer to our prayers. Was this the right time to go home and start a family, or did the Lord want us to be in Africa? We always wanted to come home to raise a family, so when we realized the baby was coming, we knew it was time and we felt complete peace," David added.

Dan and Marissa listened intently as they put away the leftovers, washed the dishes, and then got the cake out. It was an exciting end to an exciting day for Dan and his family. Marissa didn't know the half of it, but one day there would be no more secrets between them. He was so amazed by the goodness of God and his perfect timing.

As Dan drove Marissa home that night, he had a realization.

"So since David and Grace are moving home, we don't have to necessarily have a Christmas wedding," Dan offered.

"Yeah, I was just thinking about that, but it sounds so nice. I really like the idea. Decorating with poinsettias, holly berries, and gold touches. I am in love with the idea," Marissa gushed.

"Then the plan stays the same. A Christmas wedding," Dan said, smiling.

Seasons Come and Seasons Change

Christmas came and went. Marissa was so pleased with how well her family and Dan's family got along. Grace and Charlotte bonded as quickly as Marissa and Grace had. Grace giggled and said she felt like she had two sisters now. Beth and Delores really seemed to hit it off as well. It meant a lot to Delores because she had never really had any friends in her life beyond classmates and coworkers, no one that she talked to on the weekends or after she went home other than her girls.

The weeks went by quickly with plans for Charles and Delores's wedding taking shape. David and Grace found a very nice little two-bedroom home in town that was perfect for a beginning family. They said as small as it was, it was bigger than their home in Africa. Grace got in with her former doctor and began prenatal care right away. David did get a job with his former employer, and they were so happy to realize they could make a good living on his salary alone. Grace did get a job PRN at the hospital where she just worked one or two days a week. She was used to being busy and was bored being at home alone. Nursing gave her the caring for others outlet she longed to have again. She thought the one or two days a week would still work out nicely when the baby came. It would give her mom some one-on-one time with the baby too.

* * * * *

"Charlotte, you have been doing great on taking steps with the bars. I was thinking we would try something new today," Joel said, smiling at Charlotte.

"If you think I am ready, then yes. I am ready," Charlotte said excitedly

Joel ran over to the corner of the room and came back with a walker. Charlotte looked at it and gasped.

"Really?" Charlotte was so excited.

"Really...with a few disclaimers. This does not mean you are done with your wheelchair. This means, you are gaining strength and can use the walker some, with someone right beside you for now, and work on your endurance. You still will mostly be using the wheelchair for a bit longer, but it is a baby steps process. You have to crawl before you can walk, and you have to walk before you can run," Joel said seriously.

"I understand. I will follow your rules. I don't want to go backward," Charlotte promised. Joel relaxed and began smiling again.

Across the room, Charles and Delores held hands as they watched Charlotte. She had been working so hard, and watching her start to take steps and now seeing Joel bring out that walker and to see how excited she was, they had tears in their eyes.

"This is harder and more exciting than when she learned to walk the first time," Charles said.

"It is, but at least that is a memory we both share," Delores said, squeezing his hand and offering a soft smile.

"Yes it is," Charles said, nodding.

Joel allowed Charlotte to take the walker home but made her promise to stick to the list of rules he sent with her. She promised she would be a very good patient. She was so excited she could take it home and practice some every day on the walker. She knew that would help her build up her strength faster, not that she would push herself more than allowed. She really didn't want to go backward. This was a whole new season of change for her, for all her family really. Her mind went to the book of Ecclesiastes 3:1–8:

> For everything there is a season, and a time for every matter under heaven: a time to be born, and a time to die; a time to plant, and a time to pluck up what is planted; a time to kill, and a time to heal; a time to break down, and a time to build up; a time to weep, and a time to laugh; a time to mourn, and a time to dance, a time to cast away stones, and a time to gather stones together; a time to embrace, and a time to refrain from embracing; a time to seek, and a time to lose; a time to keep and a time to cast away; a time to tear and a time to sew; a time to keep silence, and a time to speak; a time to love, and a time to hate; a time for war and a time for peace.

Charlotte recited to herself on the drive home.

She had always saw the beauty in the passage, but they really came to life for her after the accident. She was so grateful her time here was not over. She looked forward to being in heaven one day and setting her eyes on Jesus Christ.

For now, she had a family to love and a daughter to raise. She was so glad she had another chance at everything. She looked at the walker next to her in the back seat, her new friend. She felt confident that by her parents' wedding in June, she would be on that cane, at least with Elliott at her side, for the walk down the aisle.

CHAPTER 19

Wedding Bells Are Ringing

Spring blooms blossomed into their full ripe beauty. Delores found herself as giddy as a school girl as the wedding approached. They had decided on a church wedding and a reception at a wedding venue that offered the shelter of beautiful old barns beautifully decorated with heavy silk fabrics, white twinkle lights, chandeliers, and candles with the room and airiness to be able to move easily inside or outside, weather dependent.

They were all at the final dress fitting before the wedding. Delores stood on the small stool looking at herself in the mirror, tears in her eyes. She couldn't believe this was really happening and that this was really herself in the mirror. Her dress was white silk, knee-length, with sleeves almost to her elbows, and covered in lace. It was actually a mother of the bride dress ordered in white; it just felt right. Delores wanted something that felt bridal but age appropriate. This dress made her feel like a bride, but not silly. She loved it.

"Mom, that is so beautiful on you. I thought it was pretty when you pulled it off the rack, but ordered in white and seeing it on you, there is no doubt that it is made just for you," Marissa said honestly.

"I agree. I love it," Charlotte said, reaching for Marissa's hand. They smiled at each other.

"Grandma, you are gorgeous! You are going to have Grandpa bawling like a baby when he sees you! Then he is going to think, *'There is my woman,'*" Emma exclaimed and they all laughed.

The seamstress smiled as she checked everything and nodded.

"I love working with brides, but stories like yours make me so honored to have a small part in it." The seamstress sighed deeply, stepping back to take in Delores.

"Thank you," Delores said, wiping her eyes. "Now it is you girls' turn. Let's see you in your gowns!" Delores said, stepping down and watching all three girls stand and head to the dressing room. It was so good to see Charlotte on her cane. In no time she would be off of it too.

In a few minutes and with lots of giggling, the three emerged from the dressing room.

Marissa stood before them in her bright yellow sleeveless satin dress. It's belted at the waist and had rhinestone embellishments completely around the waist. It flared out and was knee-length. It complimented her dark hair and eyes, and she looked beautiful.

"Aunt Marissa! You look like Belle, the Disney Princess!" Emma gasped. They all giggled.

"Thank you, Emma," Marissa said, blushing.

"Your mother picked the perfect color for each of you!" the seamstress said, nodding in agreement. Marissa stepped up on the stool first, and the seamstress went to work checking everything.

"Looks good. How do you feel about it?" the seamstress asked.

"I think it is perfect," Marissa said, amazed at her reflection. She couldn't wait to see Dan's reaction to her. Emma must have read her mind.

"Aunt Marissa, Dan is going to see you and say *'Hubba! Hubba!'*" They all laughed.

Charlotte stepped up next and look at that stool nervously.

"You are fine, dear. I can check your measurements without stepping onto the stool," the seamstress said kindly.

"Thank you. I don't want to be back in that wheelchair," Charlotte said, blushing. She looked at her reflection in the mirror. Her strawberry blonde hair popped against that royal blue dress, identical to Marissa's other than the color and instead of sleeveless it went over one shoulder. It made her feel more confident with still on a cane and a little wobbly at times.

"It suits you, Charlotte," Marissa said, beaming at her sister.

"I think it even makes your little freckles over your nose dance!" Emma giggled. "You look like Cinderella! And Aunt Marissa looks like Belle!" Emma gushed. They all laughed again.

"Okay, now your turn, young lady," the seamstress said after she gave Charlotte the nod of her approval on her fitting.

Emma bounced up onto the step stool. She loved this dress. It was similar to the others, but it had cap sleeves, and the color was an ombre yellow to the royal blue. It started out bright yellow like Marissa's dress fading into a lighter yellow almost to the belt, then it had a white belt with the embellishments and then went into a light blue under the belt and slowly faded into a royal blue to match Charlotte's at the bottom.

"You look so lovely in that dress," Delores said proudly.

"I like that it is like Mom and Aunt Marissa's dresses but different," Emma said, approving of her reflection.

"One of a kind, just like you," Charlotte said, wiping a tear from her eye. Soon they would be trying on dresses for dances and one day, her wedding. She was so grateful to still be here for it all.

"Thanks." Emma must have been reading her mind. When she was given the seamstress's approval, she jumped down and ran to wrap her arms around her mother.

"I am so glad to be doing this with you," Emma gushed, sobbing into her mother's shoulder. Charlotte nodded, unable to speak, her own tears flowing. She held onto Emma tightly.

"Me too," Charlotte finally managed.

"So the guys will be wearing black suits. Dan will have a yellow tie, Elliott a royal blue, and we ordered an ombre tie for Bob to match Emma," Delores said, trying to hold onto her composure.

"Oh that is so cool!" Emma exclaimed. They all laughed. "What color tie will Grandpa have?"

"A black one," Delores said, smiling.

"Okay, let's get changed and head out for some ice cream before we go home," Marissa suggested. "Before we know it, we will be back in these dresses for the wedding."

"I can't believe May is almost over. This is so exciting," Emma squealed.

"Yes it is!" Delores said and squealed with her. They all laughed.

* * * * *

The first day of June was upon them in no time. The church had simple decorations on the end of the pews only: white tulle bows with bright yellow sunflowers, white roses, and blue delphiniums. The reception venue had royal blue and bright yellow linen table cloths on all the tables. White candles decorated with the same flowers in a simple arrangement wrapped around them. The caterer would be there with the food and cake and other treats after the wedding as well as the DJ. All was in place.

Delores was in the church bridal room with her daughters and Emma. Charles was in the groom's room with Dan, Elliott, and Bob. Their pastor was out talking with the photographer. It was almost time for the ceremony.

"Mom, you are shaking," Marissa said gently. "Did you have enough to eat? Do you need anything?"

"No, no, I am fine. I just can't believe my life has come full circle. I was just as nervous the first time I married Charles. I wasn't sure what to expect our life to be, and all I had known was the orphanage and some fuzzy memories of my parents, nothing too clear. I remember my mom had a sweet, soft voice and she was so loving. She wore a sweet smelling perfume that had a lavender and lemon scent to it. My dad had a rich laugh, and he was always teasing but loving. I always felt safe until they never came to pick me up at school again... I was so afraid of what life held. I was so afraid of change, but Charles was all I had to cling to, and he made me feel loved and safe again. I was afraid of losing him, and that is exactly what happened, but it was all my fault. I pushed him away... I am afraid of making the same mistakes again..." Delores began to cry.

"Oh, Mom, it is going to be so different this time. You aren't a young scared girl. You are a grown woman who has proven to herself and the world she can take care of herself. You were the best mom you could be and we were always taken care of. You did an amazing job with having no example. Now you know the Lord, and you have grown in him and you have healed so much from the past. You know what life is and what it can be. Let yourself have the best part ahead of you. Don't be afraid. Walk into your future, knowing it is going to be okay," Charlotte said, standing behind Delores, wrapping her arms around her, and looking into the mirror staring at her mom's reflection. Delores put her hands onto Charlotte's wrists and nodded, still unable to speak.

"Mom, you have Dad and all of us too. You will never be on your own again. The Lord never forsook you, but you didn't understand that then. We do now. You are never going to feel alone again. We won't allow it," Marissa said, sitting down next to her mom and putting her arms around Delores too.

"Grandma, he waited for you. He never moved on. He waited for you and you waited for him, even if you didn't understand it. You never stopped loving each other or could bear to love anyone else. You are meant to be. What God put together, no man could pull apart," Emma added, coming to her grandma's other side and sitting next to her too.

"What am I to do with all of you? I love you all so much, and I am so sorry for all the wasted years," Delores said, ashamed.

"Enough of that. We are in the here and now, and that is what matters most," Charlotte said proudly. Delores nodded and wiped away her tears.

"You are all right. Let's do this," Delores said, smiling again. There was a light knock on the door.

"Ladies, is the bride ready?" Elliott asked on the other side of the door. Charlotte smiled at her mom, and she nodded.

"Yes, Elliott, you can come in," Charlotte announced.

The door opened, and Elliott, Dan, and Bob came in. They looked at all four ladies and were speechless. The women all laughed.

"Delores, you are a beautiful bride," Elliott finally managed.

"Wait until Charles sees you!" Dan whispered.

"Thank you," Delores said, beaming. "Now the two of you can go to your ladies."

They didn't need to be told twice. Elliott and Dan had swooped up their ladies into their arms quickly, both finding it hard to express their words to them.

"Miss Emma, it is an honor to escort you today. You look so lovely," Bob said and bowed to Emma.

She giggled. "Thank you, Bob," Emma said and kissed his cheek.

"He is right," Elliott said, beaming at his daughter. "I will need you to get that taser ready, Dan."

"Definitely, Elliott. No boys are going to get through us," Dan said, smiling at this little girl who didn't look like a little girl anymore. Emma giggled.

"Are we ready?" Their pastor was at the open door, smiling in.

"Yes, I think we are," Delores said, smiling. She took her bouquet that matched the girls' bouquets; only hers was a little bigger, cascading, and she took a deep breath.

"I know I am a little late, but may I have the honor of escorting the bride down the aisle?" Lewis asked at the door. He honestly hadn't thought about it until Charles thought of it and called him that morning.

"Oh...well... I would like that very much," Delores said with tears forming in her eyes. Lewis wore a black suit and tie just like Charles. He fit right into the wedding party.

Lewis took Delores by the arm, and they waited behind the others who got in line. Marissa and Dan first, Elliott and Charlotte next, holding her bouquet and her cane with the same flowers and blue and yellow ribbons twisted and tied around the length of the cane for decoration, and Bob and Emma right behind them.

The pastor went to get Charles, and they took their place in front, staring down the aisle, awaiting the wedding party. The music began to play, and one by one, the couples emerged.

Charles drank in the beauty of Marissa and Dan. They looked so good together, and he was so happy to be a part of their lives together from the moment they met and onto the future. The tears were starting to blur his vision, so he wiped them away and winked at Marissa as she blew him a kiss passing him.

Next was Elliott and Charlotte. He was so grateful to the day they came bursting into his life and brought untold happiness back into it. They were such an amazing couple, and he was so happy to see them walking down this aisle. That cane looked like an accessory only, and soon enough it would be gone. They were all so grateful to have Charlotte back.

Then it was Bob and Emma. Oh what at young lady she was becoming. She was such an angel and a dream he had been afraid to dream of ever having in his life and how appropriate for her to be walking with Bob, the best friend he had ever had. She was giggling as she passed him. The couples had parted in front of him, the men stepping behind him and the ladies across from him.

Then he and his pastor exchanged smiles, and he looked down the aisle as the music ended and then the wedding march began. He felt his palms get sweaty just as they had the first time. He felt more confident and assured this time, but the love and excitement to be joined together was the same.

Lewis and Delores appeared, and his breath was taken from him. She was exquisite. An older, more beautiful bride stood before him than she had been the first time. He couldn't believe that the Lord had restored all to him and then some. He broke down this time, the tears could not be held back as they moved closer. He wasn't embarrassed at all. He knew he was blessed, and he knew he had every right to be emotional over all God had done in his and this families lives.

Lewis was beaming, and Delores was wiping tears away with that same handkerchief she had in the first time they were married. She was feeling the same things he was and understood. There wasn't a dry eye in the church, not even the pastor. They all chucked a little.

"All weddings are special, and I am proud to be a part of many a union in the sight of God. This is very special for I have come to know and love this family and see how God has moved mightily in their lives. It is a true joy to be here today with all of them, especially Charles and Delores, in reuniting what once was broken and shall never be again. Years have passed, but the Lord always knew you would be together again, and I am so happy to witness this event and have my small part in it," the pastor said, wiping tears from his eyes.

"I often give advice to couples on the ups and downs of life and how to keep God in the mix of it and hold on tight, but I don't need to explain any of that to Charles and Delores. They are fully aware of all of it. I am excited for what the future holds for them, as a couple and as believers. So let's get right to the point. They have waited long enough. Charles and Delores have written vows to share with each other today, so I will let them begin now. Charles?"

Charles took Delores's hands in his and looked into her eyes and took a deep breath. "Delores, I fell in love with you the first time I saw you. There was no doubt you were the most beautiful girl I had ever seen and still are. You were a few years younger than me, but I didn't care. It took a little work to get your attention, and then your trust. I knew I would love you for the rest of my life, and I have. We made our mistakes, and we were apart way too long, but there has never been a day that has gone by that I didn't think of you or love you. I never thought I would have the chance to look into your eyes again and to tell you how sorry I am and how much I love you. I am so blessed to not only be with you again, but to have been with you when you asked Jesus to be your Savior. As we begin again, this time there are three of us in this, I know the best years of my life are ahead of me. I can face tomorrow because my Savior lives and he has brought you back into my life. I love you, Delores, and vow to never leave again. I love you today, tomorrow, and forever," Charles declared.

"Delores," the pastor whispered. He could barely speak.

"Charles, from the moment you came up to me whistling and winking at me, to you persisting to get my attention and trust, to the love I found in your eyes, my life has never been the same. We made our mistakes, but I always knew you loved me. I thought I had finally snuffed out that love in pushing you away, but the moment I saw you again, once my anger and shock passed, and I really saw you, I saw it in your eyes still. You were patient with me, just as you had always been. When you gave me that Bible with my name on it, I didn't know what to think, but I was so happy and surprised by it. I can't imagine being able to make that prayer with anyone else. You drove in to me the final call on my heart that the Lord had been trying for so long. I finally knew he was real, and I needed him so desperately. When we almost lost Charlotte, I knew a fear I had never known, but you were right there by my side. We have found our love is still there and very real and watched our Charlotte come back to life. We have watched our Marissa fall in love. We have watched our Emma go from a little girl to an enchanting young lady. We have so much more to watch and share together, and I am grateful for all of those things and for what is to come. Charles, I was a foolish girl, but I loved you deeply. I always have, and I always will. I am older and I hope not nearly as foolish as I once was. I love you, Charles, and I will never let you leave again. I love you today, tomorrow, and forever," Delores said from her heart.

"Charles, do you take this woman to be your wife again?"

"Without a doubt, forevermore, yes, I do!"

"Delores, do you take this man to be your husband again?"

"With all of my heart, I will, I promise, I do!"

"It is my pleasure, to pronounce you once again, and never to be broken apart again, husband and wife. Charles, you may kiss your bride."

Charles embraced Delores, and they shared a kiss. Everyone cheered and the music began. Charles walked his bride down the aisle, and they were followed by the rest of the wedding party: their children, granddaughter, and Bob. The guests all cheered and applauded as they exited the church and then followed them.

"Let's head to the reception and celebrate!" Charles yelled out. Everyone cheered and followed them. The caterer was there and the food was laid out buffet style. The DJ had the music going. They all arrived and got their plates of food and ate. It was a wonderful time. The dance floor was filled with couples as the meal came to an end. Charles and Delores served each other the first pieces of cake, and everyone got their piece next.

The DJ announced it was time for the happy couple to have their first dance, so the other couples stepped off the dance floor. Charles and Delores shared a very sweet dance, and as the music came to an end, Delores turned and looked around the crowd. Everyone was still watching, wondering if something was wrong from her behavior.

"Marissa? Marissa, where are you?" Delores called.

Marissa looked at Dan and he shrugged and she went over to her mom. "Mom what is it?" she asked as she rushed to her. Halfway there on the dance floor, Delores threw her bouquet to Marissa. She caught it and was confused until the spotlight hit her, and all of a sudden, Dan stood before her, smiling as wide as he could. He went down on one knee, and Marissa gasped and put a shaking hand to her mouth.

"Marissa Lynn Medlock, I am madly in love with you. The first time I saw you, I wasn't looking for love, but there you were. My life has never been the same since you stepped into it. Colors are brighter, everything smells sweeter, and I swear I hear music every time I set eyes on you. You take my breath away. I am bolder, more confident, happier, and more caring since you have been by my side. Will you marry me, and make me the happiest man alive?" Dan opened the small ring box he had been holding up as he finished. Marissa gasped again.

"Dan, without a doubt, I will marry you and follow you to the ends of the earth. Your family is my family. My family is your family. This was God's plan, and I want to follow his lead for the rest of my life," Marissa said as the tears flowed. Dan stood and put the ring on her finger and embraced her. Everyone cheered.

Lewis and Beth embraced and sobbed. This was so unexpected but so perfect. Lewis had never guessed this is what his son had been talking about last fall. It was the perfect plan to catch her by surprise and to let everyone be a part of their engagement, and he needed the help of Charles and Delores to pull it off. Perfect. His son, once again, had deeply impressed him.

"*Yay*! I have an Uncle Dan!" Emma cheered. Everyone laughed.

As the reception came to a close that night, they all said their goodbyes to Charles and Delores who were on their way to a seven-day cruise—the honeymoon they had never had. Charles had packed up his apartment, and they had moved all his boxes into Delores's house the day before the wedding and turned in his apartment key. He had spent the night at Bob's house. They would unpack him when they returned.

"So when is the next wedding?" Charlotte asked Marissa, checking out her ring again. Marissa laughed and looked at Dan.

"This Christmas," Marissa announced. They were all shocked.

"You don't need more time?" Dan asked, very happy to hear the date was sooner than he expected.

"No, I know what I want, and I don't want to wait another year and a half," Marissa said assuredly.

"We had planned a Christmas wedding so Grace and David would be here, but when we found out they were staying, we still loved the idea of a Christmas wedding," Dan explained.

"You planned around our visits? Oh Marissa, how sweet!" Grace said, wiping away a tear. She dearly loved her new sister and was so happy for her brother.

Marissa hugged her and they giggled.

"Well, Charlotte, I think we can pull this off without any problems, don't you?" Grace said, rubbing her hands together.

"Without a doubt!" Charlotte said, nodding.

"I am so in!" Emma shrieked and they all laughed.

What a Magical Day

Dan took Marissa to grab a quick bite and then to her house after the cleanup from the reception, and they sat on her couch, snuggled up, and looking at the ring on her finger.

"It is so beautiful," Marissa whispered.

"I designed it for you. I couldn't find one that felt right, so Grace asked me if I had an idea in my head of what I wanted. I didn't know I did, but once we took it one step at a time, it all came together. The saleslady showed it to us on a computer and I knew it was right."

"You did? Grace was with you?" Marissa was even more impressed and trying to figure out when he did this.

"Yes. You know that day I took off work and you met Grace and David that night? I didn't ask you to take the day off because I wanted to go ring shopping with my mom and Grace to pick out the ring. I was overwhelmed by it, and I needed their help and support. They were so excited when I asked them that morning. I hated to keep a secret from you, but I knew I would explain it all to you once you had the ring. I thought long and hard on how to ask you. I wanted to take you by surprise since we had already planned so much. I thought your parent's wedding reception would be the perfect time to surprise you. On Thanksgiving, I asked your parents for their blessing to ask you to marry me and if they would help me with the proposal."

"Thanksgiving?" Marissa was swirling from all he had been up to and she had no idea.

"Yes, before we went home that night, I took them aside and asked if I could stop by after taking you home to talk to them. I think they expected I was going to ask for their blessing, but they were surprised by the second request. They were so excited to help though. I met them at your mom's house for coffee. It was your mom's idea to throw the bouquet to you and then I ask. I just had asked them if I could propose to you at their reception. They were happy to help brainstorm on how to do it."

"Oh my, you are a sneaky one, Officer Dan! And my parents too!" Marissa giggled.

"It isn't being sneaky when you are an officer of the law. It is detective work," Dan said in a mock air of sophistication. They laughed.

"You completely surprised me! I never expected that I would be in my parent's wedding and then get engaged at the reception! I love it! I love you," Marissa gushed.

"I love you too. You surprised me too," Dan added, beaming.

"I did?" Marissa was confused.

"Yes. I didn't expect you to want to get married this Christmas, but I am very happy about it."

"Oh, that. When she asked me, I didn't even think about it. It just came out, but I knew it was what my heart wanted. It is all the time I need, and I hope it comes quickly," Marissa said proudly.

"Me too!" Dan laughed. Marissa yawned.

"It has been a very busy day, and I think my princess needs her rest," Dan said, smiling.

"Your princess?" Marissa asked, giggling again.

"Yes, I picked out a princess cut diamond because you are my princess. I will be taking care of you for the rest of your life, Marissa Lynn Medlock," Dan said with authority.

"Really? I guess I never knew the names of the cuts," Marissa said, admiring her ring.

"Yes, and the band is rose gold because I have never seen a band so beautiful, so I knew it was perfect for the most beautiful woman I have ever seen. The band has an infinity symbol on each side of the diamond with tiny diamonds in it because I will love you for infinity," Dan added, feeling proud of himself.

"Oh wow, Dan, I had no idea you put so much thought into every detail. I know you said you had designed it and that was impressive, but to hear why you chose each detail… I am so blessed," Marissa said as the tears welled up in her eyes.

"I love you, Marissa. You aren't alone anymore. You aren't waiting for anyone to love you anymore," Dan said seriously. He kissed her forehead and embraced her. "Good night, my princess."

"Good night, my sweet prince," Marissa whispered as he pulled away to walk to his car, turning to blow her a kiss before he left. "What a magical day."

Marissa watched through the window as he drove away. She was so tired but so excited. She wasn't sure she would be able to go to sleep, but as soon as her head hit her pillow and she finished her prayer, she was out.

* * * * *

"Wow! What a day!" Emma giggled as they drove home from the reception.

"You can say that again. I can't believe Dan proposed to Marissa today! I can't believe none of us knew about it but Charles and Delores! I am in complete shock, but I am so happy. I can't imagine a better time or place to completely surprise Marissa…or all of us! To let us all share in their moment. Wow," Elliott gushed. Charlotte and Emma giggled.

"You sound like us!" Emma giggled as he looked at them both in confusion. He laughed.

"I don't know about you, lovely ladies, but I am starving. It has been a busy day, and I am tired but hungry," Elliott announced.

"Me too!" Charlotte and Emma said together.

"Let's go out. What do you ladies want?" Elliott asked.

"Pizza! Ooey, goey extra cheese, drowning in sauce, and over-loaded with pepperoni!" Emma said, practically drooling.

"Well, after that description, I am in!" Charlotte said, laughing.

"No argument here!" Elliott said, grinning as he turned into the parking lot of their favorite pizza place.

"I am so hungry, and this has been the best day. The most magical day ever!" Emma said dreamily. They all laughed.

"I think you are right, Emma," Charlotte said, beaming. "To see my parents reunited officially and to see Dan and Marissa get engaged. It was definitely a perfectly magical day."

"A Christmas wedding. This year! Two weddings in one year! This is so fun!" Emma gushed.

"Yes, it is a whirlwind for sure. I am surprised to have another one so quickly, but I am not either. Those two are head over heels in love, and Marissa is a woman of action, so she can create the wedding of her dreams without much delay," Charlotte said, nodding.

"I am sure any help she needs will be provided from you, Grace, Delores, and Beth," Elliott said, laughing.

"Yes, this is going to be a lot of fun," Charlotte said, smiling. "A Christmas wedding. I have never been to one, but I have seen them in the movies. They always look so beautiful."

"I can't wait." Emma giggled. "Then I guess we are done with family weddings until I get married."

Elliott spit out his soda and started choking. Charlotte beat him on the back as she and Emma laughed.

"Stop that! No more talk like that, or you will kill me," Elliott managed.

"Sorry, Dad," Emma said, laughing so hard she was crying.

CHAPTER 21

Down to Business

After church, Dan and Marissa went to Marissa's house. He grilled out some chicken that she had marinated in Italian dressing and had some sliced up potatoes wrapped, covered in shredded cheese in foil on the grill as well. Marissa whipped up a tomato and cucumber salad and had a fruit salad she made that morning chilling in the fridge for dessert.

"Thank you, Father, for this meal before us and the woman you gave me to spend the rest of my life with. I pray Charles and Delores have a wonderful honeymoon and a blessed life together. In Jesus's name we pray. Amen," Dan prayed over their meal and looked up to see Marissa beaming.

"What?" Dan felt like something was on her mind.

"I love how you love my family," Marissa said.

"I love how you love my family too," Dan countered. "So I guess it is time to really start planning this wedding since it is officially happening this year," Dan said, smiling.

"I guess so. What do you want to start with?" Marissa asked as she jumped up and ran to the end table by her couch. She returned with a pad of paper and a pen.

"Well what day?" Dan asked.

"I was looking at the calendar this morning. What about December 29? That way we can have Christmas with our families and a few days to tie up loose ends, and it is still close enough for our Christmas wedding theme," Marissa offered.

Dan liked that idea and agreed.

"Good, one thing down. I would like to get married at the church, and we can have the reception at the church fellowship hall," Marissa offered. "It is right there, and if the weather is bad, we don't have to go but one place."

"Good thinking," Dan agreed again.

"I was thinking that you and the groomsmen could dress in light gray suits and red rose boutonnieres. I could have an all-white dress of course and red bridesmaid dresses. I was thinking my bouquet could be all red poinsettias and red holly berries cascading, and the bridesmaid bouquets could be red roses and holly berries. We can decorate with poinsettia and holly berry bouquets on the ends of the pews in the church, and on some tables at the reception and other bouquets red roses and holly berry bouquets. The bouquets on the tables can be in simple vases that are Ball jars and decorated with candy canes all the way around them, white linen table clothes to balance out all the red," Marissa said dreamily as she described it and scribbled out her designs and descriptions on the notebook. She went on thinking of every detail. She was so caught up in it that she didn't realize that Dan was just staring at her, smiling.

Whatever she wanted was what he wanted. She realized how caught up she had gotten in her own daydreams and plans, then she started to blush.

"It's great. It all sounds so perfect. I love hearing your ideas and plans. This will just take some shopping and ordering, and all will come together easily. I love that you are a woman who knows exactly what she wants," Dan said honestly.

"Well good. I am not the little girl who dreamed of her wedding. I just never thought about such things until I met you. Somehow it all just started to bubble out of me," Marissa said, giggling. She hardly recognized herself anymore.

"I love it," Dan said, beaming. "Now what do you want to do for a honeymoon? Fly off somewhere warm, or go somewhere to enjoy the winter weather?"

"You decide. I would enjoy going somewhere warm and tropical, but I would be just as happy going to some little cottage in the middle of nowhere or to a ski lodge. I haven't done much skiing since college, but I enjoyed it. Whatever you would like. You can even surprise me. I don't have to know until we arrive or are on our way," Marissa gushed.

"Surprise you, huh? I like that idea. You really trust me to surprise you and not give you a single clue?" Dan asked, surprised.

"Yes, I do. You can tell Charlotte and she can pack for me so I will have no idea where we are going until we get there or board a plane or whatever." Marissa giggled, liking the idea the more she thought about it. This was something she would have never agreed to with anyone else.

"Deal," Dan said, beaming even brighter. He could have some fun with this.

"Where are we going to live? We both have a house we own," Marissa asked, pondering it for the first time.

"Well, we can pick one of our homes or sell them both and buy one together," Dan offered.

"*Oooh, I like that idea*. I like it a lot. We both have small homes, and for just the two of us, either would be fine, but I like the idea of starting fresh in a new home together."

"That brings up another question. Is it going to be just the two of us, or do you want to think about having a family? We have never talked about that," Dan realized.

"Well… I love the idea of raising a family with you, but Dan… I am forty-three years old. I don't know how easily I could still have a child," Marissa said softly.

"Well there is more than one way to become a family. We could adopt or try to have a child biologically—or both. We could explore any and all options. I never thought I would have children, but being around Emma, watching Grace and David getting ready for their baby, and thinking about a life with you, I could see raising a family. I could also see enjoying a life of just the two of us. I just don't know what you want," Dan offered.

FOR THE LOVE OF FAMILY

Marissa took in all he said and smiled. She hadn't thought about all the options. She wasn't sure what she wanted. "I have never thought about it either, and I also could see our lives going either way. Let's pray about it and promise to be honest about it with each other," Marissa said and Dan agreed.

"Wow, this is really happening, isn't it?" Marissa said, beaming.

"Yes, it is," Dan said, smiling. "No matter what our future holds and who is in it with us or not, we are going to have a good life with God in the center of it all."

"Without a doubt," Marissa said, smiling, but thinking about the idea of having children or not. She just wasn't sure what she wanted. It was such a new idea.

Dan seemed to pick up on her thoughts. "Marissa, I didn't mean to upset you. We just had never talked about children, and I thought we should talk about it. I didn't mean to pressure you at all," Dan said gently.

"No, you are right. I just had never thought about it. Now I don't know what I want or how I feel about it at all."

"No decision has to be made right away, okay?" Dan said.

"You are right…you are," Marissa said, nodding and trying to wrap her mind around it all.

"Let's pray. This is upsetting you," Dan said. He took her hands. "Heavenly Father, we are trying to plan our lives together and see what it might be. We know, Lord, that you already know the end from the beginning. We don't know if children are in our future or not. We pray for your direction and peace in all of it. We know you will guide us on whatever we have in our future. You are the Father of peace and love. Confusion and worry is not from you. We thank you for your leading and thank you for our lives together in your loving care. In Jesus's name we pray. Amen."

"Amen," Marissa said, feeling much better. They didn't have to decide today, and God would lead them. It all would happen like it was supposed to. If any children were to come into their lives, it would be God's will and they didn't have to worry about any of it.

They went on making more plans for the wedding and discussing what they might want in a home. Dan had a buddy at work named Zach, whose wife, Heather, was a real estate agent and decided to talk to her about their plans.

"You should start dress shopping when your parents get back home," Dan said, beaming.

"This is really going to go fast, isn't it?" Marissa said, sighing dreamily again.

"I hope so," Dan said, laughing. "I know what it is time for right now. I am ready for some of that fruit salad."

"That does sound good," Marissa agreed.

* * * * *

Monday morning Marissa called Charlotte and asked her if she could pick her up and take her out to lunch. Marissa couldn't wait to share with her the ideas she had for her wedding and see what Charlotte had to say and suggest.

"Wow, you have some great ideas! This is going to be so beautiful. You have thought of everything already. I am not surprised. I knew you could pull this off easily," Charlotte said as she followed along and looked at the notepad Marissa had brought along. "I am so happy for you!"

"Thank you. I am excited too. We also have decided to sell our houses and pick out a new one together," Marissa said, beaming.

"Oh wow! That will be so fun. What are you wanting?" Charlotte asked, surprised but liking the idea.

"Well, we don't know. We went out and picked up some home magazines for this area at the grocery store after lunch yesterday and started watching home networks on TV for some ideas," Marissa explained. "But… Dan asked me if I wanted to have a family or not…"

"*Really?*" Charlotte was really taken aback on that one. She had never envisioned her sister a mother but knew now more than ever she would be a great one.

"Yeah… I was just as surprised as you are. I reminded him I am forty-three, but he said we could still have a baby or adopt or both… I was just surprised to realize I really do have options. I just never thought about it. He said he hadn't until now. Maybe it is because

Grace is pregnant and we adore Emma… I don't know. I was feeling kind of nervous and uneasy about it at first, but we prayed about it together and are going to let the Lord guide us on what he wants for our lives. We are open to it but wouldn't feel upset if we didn't… unless he really wants kids more than he is letting on…"

"Dan is very straightforward and honest, especially with you. I wouldn't worry about that. Just see where your heart wants and how the Lord leads. Marissa, you and Dan are going to have an amazing life together. If children become a part of it, you will make incredible parents! If you don't, your life will be full and happy still. If it is meant to be, God will guide and you will be at peace," Charlotte soothed. Marissa nodded; she knew Charlotte was right.

"I know what you mean about not sure and never have thought about things before until now…," Charlotte said, looking down at the tablecloth and bit her lip.

Marissa looked at her in surprise. Something was on Charlotte's mind. "What is going on with you?" Marissa asked cautiously.

"Well, when Mom first asked us to be in the wedding, I started to think about rolling down the aisle in my wheelchair and hated the idea. It had never bothered me before. Then I was trying to push myself too hard, and Joel called me on it. We talked about the wedding and what my future held. He told me he was sure he could get me to a walker or cane by the wedding, and in the future, he was sure I would be off of the cane altogether. So then I got excited about my future and realized I could have a complete fresh start. I am so thankful for the years I had at the restaurant. Larry was good to me, and I made wonderful friends there. Larry had to replace me, and I understood that, but it also got me to thinking. I didn't have to go back to the restaurant. I could do something else. I could start a whole new life. I could go back to school… I wondered if I was crazy, so I called Lewis and he came right over to talk with me. He told me how he had a new beginning after losing Paul. He stopped teaching school and went back to school to be a minister and became a chaplain. He told me I wasn't crazy and I could do anything. So I talked to Elliott, and he encouraged me to go after whatever I wanted. I wasn't sure, but I know what I want to do now…"

"*Oh, Charlotte! That is amazing*! It makes so much sense. Your whole life was turned upside down. It's like a butterfly coming out of a cocoon or a phoenix rising from the ashes. *You can start a whole new life.* You have to have been changed by all of this. *This is so exciting*!" Marissa gushed.

"Thank you. I have only talked about it with Lewis that one time and Elliott a few times. I have done a lot of praying and soul-searching, and I think I know what I want to do." Charlotte took a deep breath. "I want to become a physical therapy assistant. I have talked to Joel about it. He thought I would be a great one. It is a two-year associate's degree and then certification for my license. I would work under the supervision of a physical therapist like Joel and help people. Not everyone will have had a major trauma like I have, but I could help people in a new way. The more I pray about it, I feel like it is what I am meant to do now. Joel and Elliott know, but no one else. They both think it is a great idea. I am going to start classes this fall," Charlotte said, beaming.

"Oh, Charlotte, that is amazing… I am so happy for you," Marissa said and jumped up to hug her sister. "When are you telling the rest of the family?" Marissa asked.

"I was going to wait until Mom and Dad get back, but it seemed to come up today. There is a program at the community college, and Joel said it is a good one. He has helped me get my paperwork in," Charlotte said, grinning.

"Charlotte, that is wonderful! I am so proud of you," Marissa gushed.

"Thank you." Charlotte beamed. "I can't believe it has been a year since my accident. I am almost done with this cane."

"You are about to go on vacation and then start school… Wow. *I am so excited for you*," Marissa said, bursting with happiness.

"Yes, we had promised Emma last year before the accident we would go with Kenneth, Cindy, and their girls this year. They usually go the first week of June, but due to Mom and Dad's wedding, they said they would happily put it off a few weeks to accommodate all we had going on. Cindy's aunt has a vacation home in California, so we can stay for free there. So we are going away for ten days. They said we can grill out and eat at the beach house a lot to save money. The girls were fine with it. They were just so excited we could all be on vacation together this year. I guess it is a nice beach house with four bedrooms. Tara and her friend will share a room, and Tracey and Emma can share a room. We will be there on Emma's birthday, so that is exciting too. I still feel bad last year's plans didn't happen as planned, so this will make me feel better," Charlotte said excitedly.

"You need this. You all deserve this," Marissa said and let out a deep sigh. "I am so glad you are okay and are about to have a wonderful vacation and going to school to start a new life. This is so exciting. And then you can help me with my wedding. You will have a lot of responsibilities if you accept my request for you to be my matron of honor," Marissa said, giggling at the end.

"Oh, Marissa, I would love that," Charlotte said, wiping away a tear. "How far we have come in a year," Charlotte said, reaching for Marissa's hand.

"In so many ways. Our lives are so completely different now, our parents are back together honeymooning on a cruise no less, and *our relationship*...," Marissa said, trying to keep the tears from spilling out of her eyes.

"We better hold it together and pay for this lunch. You have to go back to work," Charlotte said, looking at her watch.

"Actually, are you busy the rest of the afternoon?" Marissa asked.

"I was just going to do some house cleaning and start dinner before Elliott got home. Emma is at Tracey's house swimming," Charlotte said.

"How about we go shopping? Do you have a new swimsuit for your vacation?" Marissa asked, smiling from ear to ear.

"Wow, I hadn't thought about that. I guess I do need to go shopping," Charlotte said, giggling.

Marissa picked up her phone and called her boss requesting the rest of the day off. Then she hung up the phone and smiled at Charlotte.

"Let's go!" Marissa smiled. "I promise to have you home before Emma and Elliott get home."

Days Turn into Weeks and Months

Charles and Delores came back from their cruise and settled into life as a married couple. Charlotte didn't need them to take care of her anymore, but they set up weekly dinner parties with both of their daughters and rotated each week who hosted dinner; Charles and Delores, then Elliott, Charlotte and Emma, and Dan and Marissa made a full rotation. They wanted to stay close.

Shortly after their return, Elliott, Charlotte, and Emma joined their friends on vacation. It was so much better than the year before for Emma because she got to share this one with her parents. They did like Kenneth's style of active days followed by lazy days. They ate a lot of meals at the beach house, enjoying it right on the beach, but they ate out too. It was more new experiences and fun for all of them.

Once back, they got busy getting Charlotte and Emma ready to go back to school. Emma was proud that her mom was following her heart and trying something new. Charlotte said as scary as it was to go back to school, it didn't hold a candle to what she faced coming out of that coma. It was time to learn how to use all the tragedy to help others, find some purpose for the pain.

Charlotte found school exciting and fun. Emma was excited it was her last year of middle school and that she would be in high school next year. Elliott joked that he was glad he would have one out of college before the other started. He was happy to see Charlotte loving her classes and was sure this is what she should be doing. Joel was a great help to Charlotte and was looking forward for her to graduate and become licensed so he could hire her to work with him.

As fall came in full swing, so were the wedding plans for Dan and Marissa. Charlotte was her matron of honor and Elliott Dan's best man. Grace and David were also in the wedding party with Emma and Zach, a buddy of Dan's rounding out the wedding party. Marissa knew what dress she wanted; she had eyed it when dress shopping for her mother and had picked out in her mind the perfect red dresses for her wedding party, so they only had to make one trip to pick out the dresses and order them. All fell into place quickly.

Zach's wife, Heather, had both their houses sold before the wedding, and they had found the perfect home. They moved their things into the new home, but they wanted to move in it together, so Dan moved in with his parents for the last few weeks before the wedding, and Marissa moved into her old room at her parents' house. Dan also had his surprise honeymoon all booked and planned out. He was excited to surprise Marissa, and she hadn't wanted a single clue. It seemed harder for him to keep it so secret from her than for her not to have any idea. She was too busy making finishing touches to the wedding.

The holidays came and were so much fun with the addition of David and Grace's daughter, Polly Danielle. They named her in honor of Grace's brothers: Paul, who had passed away as a child, and Dan. Lewis and Beth had been blown away by their gesture and were madly in love with their granddaughter.

CHAPTER 23

The Lord's Leading

One evening shortly before the wedding, Dan and Marissa had dinner with Lewis and Beth. Something felt different; Lewis and Beth both picked up on it. Dan and Marissa seemed to both have something on their mind but weren't talking about it at dinner. It was driving them crazy, wondering what the elephant in the room was, so to speak.

"Dan and I will clean up," Marissa offered since Beth had made dinner.

"Oh no, you won't. Not yet anyway. I can't take it anymore. Something is going on, and you need to tell us what it is," Beth exclaimed. She had tried so hard to be patient and wait to find out what was the meaning for all their nervous energy, but she couldn't hold it in anymore.

"I agree. What is on your minds? It is obvious you both are quiet and keep looking at each other. Is something wrong? Can we help with something?" Lewis was feeling uneasy and was so glad Beth finally addressed it.

"We are sorry to upset you. It isn't anything wrong, but we do need to talk to someone, and we think you two are the two to help us," Marissa gushed.

Beth and Lewis didn't feel any better and just exchanged looks.

"We have done a lot of planning and preparation for our wedding and lives together. We have our home ready to move into when we get back from our honeymoon, and all the wedding plans are in place. We are at peace in a lot of areas of our lives together." Dan stopped and took a breath and smiled at Marissa, taking her hand in his. "There is one area we have done a lot of talking and praying about, and we have come to a decision," Dan continued.

"We decided we want children, but at my age, I really don't feel comfortable trying to have a baby. I know many women do in their forties, but we really feel led to go another way. I don't need to have a child biologically to be its mother. We have talked about becoming foster parents and maybe adopting. We thought fostering might help us get a handle on if we think this is right for us. There are so many children who need good homes and families and are overlooked because they aren't babies. I keep thinking about my mom and how her life could have been so different had someone taken her as their own. We feel so much peace and excitement the more we talk about it. We also like that there is training and classes before you become foster parents," Marissa explained.

"Oh, that is wonderful!" Beth exclaimed. "You both would make wonderful parents. You would be a blessing to a child or children, and they would change your life in more ways than you can imagine."

"We thought as a chaplain and in volunteering at the hospital with the babies and children, if you have any extra advise or know the best way about getting these steps started or if you become aware of a family in need, you can keep us in mind. We don't know when God will move a child or children into our lives, but we will be ready. We really keep thinking about the possibility of keeping siblings together. We picked a house with four bedrooms for a reason. We can find other uses for them, but we wanted to have bedrooms available," Dan added.

"We were wondering about the number of bedrooms you have in that new house of yours, but you hadn't said anything about why you chose that house," Beth said, laughing.

"I am so moved by your hearts, and I am not surprised one bit. Dan, I know you see family tragedies every day. Marissa, I know you have your mother's childhood that must weigh heavy on your heart as well as struggles you felt in your own childhood that might point you both in this direction. What better parents could there be?" Lewis said, tears in his eyes.

"Not to mention our families. There is a lot of love on both sides, and with Delores's experiences and the two of you knowing loss and ability to counsel, we just feel like we are equipped to take this on. We have no doubt, that like you said, Mom, we will be the ones blessed the most from any child or children that become ours. We just really feel the leading of more than one. We keep feeling in our spirits that siblings will be in our future," Dan said honestly, wiping tears from his eyes.

Marissa squeezed his hand and smiled big, tears streaming down her face. This just felt so right; they knew it was God's leading. When the time was right and the right children needed them, they would be ready.

"I can definitely give you a number of a friend of mine who is over foster families to help you begin training and getting started. He will be so excited to hear you are looking for older children, siblings that need a family. Many people start as foster families and move into adopting those children," Lewis said and picked up his phone to look for the contact information for them.

"We would like to call and talk to him and get things rolling after we get back. Dad, could you give him a call and let him know our intentions and let him know we will be in contact when we get back? I just feel an urgency to get this initiated," Dan said, smiling at Marissa. She nodded in agreement.

"I can do that. You two really want to start on this right away? Not wait for a while?" Lewis asked cautiously. He appreciated their hearts and intentions, but they were just getting married.

"We don't know how long it would take to have a child or children placed with us, but we just want to get trained and ready. I can't explain it. I wouldn't have expected to work so fast on this either, but we both keep feeling an urgency," Dan explained. Lewis nodded in understanding.

"Marissa, do you still not know where you are going on your honeymoon?" Beth asked, shaking her head. These kids these days.

"Nope. Dan is trusting me with the wedding, and I am trusting him with the honeymoon. It is kind of fun not being in control and just being taken care of," Marissa said, giggling.

"That is new for you, isn't it?" Lewis said, smiling. He was so happy for Dan and Marissa and so happy to see how the Lord had brought Marissa so far already.

"Yes, it is," Marissa said, smiling at Lewis.

"All right, but I couldn't do it. I trust Lewis and all, but I have to know. How will you pack?"

"My sister will take care of that," Marissa said, smiling.

"Well as long as you are at peace with it, and I know my son will make sure all is taken care of... I just can't imagine," Beth said, sighing deeply.

"More grandchildren... I am so excited for all the future holds for all of us." Lewis beamed.

"I will have to get one of those sweatshirts with all the grandchildren's names on it. My friends at church all have those, and I have been dying for one!" Beth said excitedly. They all laughed.

"That would be wonderful. My family will be so excited too. We are going to tell them all about it when we get back." Marissa added, "So keep this to yourselves for now. We just were dying to talk to someone about it and figure out how to get started."

"Of course, we understand," Beth assured them.

"The Lord is certainly leading the way in your lives. He always does when we let go and let God," Lewis said, sitting back in his chair.

What a difference a year makes. So much joy and happiness born out of so much pain and tragedy. So many lives have been touched and changed, and it was only the beginning of what was to come.

The Christmas Wedding

The church pews were decked out in poinsettia and holly berry bouquets. There were two Christmas trees at the front of the church decorated with white twinkling lights, bright red poinsettias and holly berries, and flocked in fake snow. It was simple but beautiful.

The pastor took his place with Dan in the front of the altar, between the Christmas trees. The music began, and Elliott, David, and Zach came out of the groom's side room to their places as well, behind Dan.

Then Charlotte stepped out, wearing a floor-length red velvet gown that had cap sleeves with a rhinestone broach on the waistband. Her strawberry blonde hair was curled in long ringlets and laid on her shoulders, one side pulled back from her face with a white lace and holly berry embellishments on the barrette. Her bouquet was red roses and red holly berries and sprigs of evergreen branches throughout.

Next came Grace in a matching red velvet dress and her dark brown hair in the same style as Charlotte's. She winked at Dan and smiled at her parents who were beaming and her mother holding sweet Polly in a red velvet dress of her own. She clapped when she saw her mother.

Emma came out in a red velvet dress identical to the other two, but her hair was pulled up with the ringlets falling down around her face. It made her look older, much to Elliott's displeasure, but she was beautiful.

They took their place on the bride's side, and the music ended. After a moment of pause, the wedding march started and out stepped Marissa in a floor-length white silk gown. She had long sleeves and a long train. There wasn't much detail to the dress; it was more subtle, and the bride definitely made the dress. It was simple and beautiful and definitely made Marissa the star and not the dress. Her cascading bouquet of red poinsettias and holly berries was breathtaking. Her hair was upswept with ringlets falling down around her face, like Emma's. She had baby's breath and holly berries stuck throughout. She had a long veil covering her face. Her father stood on one side of her in the same light gray suit as the rest of the men, a white shirt, and bright red tie. They all had a red rose boutonniere with a sprig of evergreen with it. On the other side of Marissa was her mother in a floor-length red gown covered in lace and long sleeves. She had white pearls and a corsage of white roses and red holly berries and sprigs of evergreen. Delores's dress and corsage matched Beth's as well. And Lewis also matched the other men.

Charles and Delores both walked Marissa down the aisle and gave her away to Dan with a hug for the bride and groom then took their place in the front row on the bride's side.

"Well, here we are again with this amazing family growing in size, joy, and love. I remember meeting both Marissa and Dan, shortly before Charlotte, was able to come back to church and on her first Sunday back I was able to baptize Delores, Marissa, and Emma. I caught on right away that Dan and Marissa were quite a match and definitely put together by the Lord as they told me how they met. The Lord brought Dan into the lives of this family at their most vulnerable time, and he and his father were a comfort and support for this family. It has been my pleasure to become Dan and Marissa's pastor as well. I wasn't surprised that we are here today to join them in holy matrimony. Dan and Marissa have written their own vows and would like to share them now. Dan..."

"Marissa Lynn Medlock, I never expected my life to change that June day when I got the call to respond to a serious accident. I was just doing my job. I saw Charlotte and knew she was in trouble. I stayed by her side and contacted Elliott from her phone contacts at the hospital. There was something about them that grabbed my heart. I have no doubt that I was there that day and felt the pull to get more involved in this family by the lead of the Holy Spirit. I just wanted to help them. When I laid eyes on you, my heart skipped a beat, but I tried to ignore it and concentrate on the seriousness of the situation but found so drawn to you and more bold than I have ever been in my life. You have made my life so much better and brought more joy, love, and happiness into my life than ever before. I have only felt such a strong tug on my heart three times in my life: when I felt convicted to ask Jesus into my heart as a child, when I felt my calling was to become a police officer, and when I laid eyes on you and knew I had to know you better. There is no going back in my life on any of those three things. I have never known anyone like you, Marissa, and I know without any hesitation that my life is meant to be experienced and enjoyed with you by my side. I vow to you and your family that I will always take care of you and put you above myself. I will love you like Christ loves the church, and I will be the best husband I can be," Dan said, tears streaming down his face.

"Marissa…," the pastor said softly.

"Daniel Harrold Williams, I wasn't looking for a husband or a change to my life that day either. I was at work when I got the most terrifying call of my life. I rushed to get my mother and get to the hospital. My mind was blown to come face-to-face with my father for the first time in years, and everything was so surreal and overwhelming. Then you walked into the room, and I can't explain how it touched my heart to say hearing how you were there for my sister and had gotten them support before you left and was back to check on them again. You were definitely someone I had to get to know more. I am so glad that my sister is still here with us. I am so glad that I was led to the Lord Jesus Christ by Mary Ann," Marissa said, turning to smile and wave to the sweet lady sitting in the front row next to her mother.

"I am so glad that you were there to teach me about the Lord and the Bible, and your joy in finding out I was newly saved made you even more interested in me. You have taught me about love and the Lord, and I look forward to our lives together and whatever the Lord brings into our life and whatever your surprise honeymoon for us is as well. Because I trust you, Officer Dan, with all my heart and have never felt more loved or safe than in your arms. I vow to be the best wife I can be."

"Dan, do you take this woman to be your wife for the rest of your life?"

"I do."

"Marissa, do you take this man to be your husband for the rest of your life?"

"I do."

"I now pronounce you husband and wife. Dan, you may kiss your bride."

Dan embraced Marissa and gave her a kiss. Everyone cheered. Dan and Marissa turned to face all of their guests.

"I now introduce you to Mr. and Mrs. Daniel Williams."

Marissa and Dan grinned at each other. They shared a kiss and then hugged all of their wedding party and then their parents. They walked down the aisle and headed to the fellowship hall at the other end of the church.

"Everyone, please follow all of us to the fellowship hall for the reception," Elliott announced. He then escorted Charlotte down the hall. David and Grace picked up Polly and followed. Zach and Emma were next, and the pastor followed both sets of parents. The rest of the guests followed.

The food was laid out by the caterer, and a DJ was playing music. It was a wonderful reception and time together.

As the evening came to an end, Dan took Marissa by the hand and smiled. "Mrs. Williams, are you ready to begin our adventure?"

"I think I am. Where are we going?"

"That is the first time you have asked," Dan said teasingly.

"I told you I trust you, but now I am dying to know. I still trust you, but where are we going?"

"Well we are going to stay at a hotel near the airport tonight. Tomorrow morning we leave on a plane." Dan stopped and laughed.

"Okay, so we are flying. Where?" Marissa was excited and dying to know for the first time.

"Well this is an adventure, right? Our whole lives will be an adventure, so I thought we would start it out with the wildest adventure I could think of," Dan said honestly.

"Wildest adventure?" Marissa was intrigued.

"Mrs. Williams, your sister and mine have packed your bags and they are in the trunk of my car. We are headed to Africa for a safari honeymoon!"

"*What? That is so exciting*! I have never known anyone who has actually done that!"

"Me either. It was Grace's idea. I was asking everyone for ideas. David and Grace gave me all kinds of information and helped me plan it."

"*Of course*! They spent three years in Africa! I never would have dreamed of that. I am so excited." Marissa giggled.

"Then let's go!" Dan said, kissing her and waving goodbye to all, and they ran out and jumped in the car and took off.

CHAPTER 25

African Paradise and a New Life

The flight was long, but they were so excited they didn't care. Dan couldn't imagine making such a long round trip twice a year. No wonder David and Grace liked to sleep most of the day when they first arrived.

They were met by their driver holding a large poster with their names on it at the airport. He was a kind older man who welcomed them and took them by jeep to their resort cottage. This was more luxury than rustic. It had a magnificent view and private pool and deck with a grill and hot tub also. They were both overwhelmed with the beauty and luxury of it all.

Dan had planned different sightseeing and animal watching tours, a hot air balloon ride, and even a private sail boat excursion at sunset with a guide who manned the boat and an assistant to serve them dinner and tend to anything they needed. They even braved bungee jumping as well. Dan was so impressed and thankful to David and Grace urging him to plan this trip. They told him they had to experience the beauty of Africa for themselves. Marissa had never dreamed of taking such a trip; it seemed too exotic and possibly dangerous to her, but when she was told their plans, she was excited and trusted that Grace and David wouldn't steer them wrong. She was so right.

It was the best two weeks of her life, and she was soaking up every minute of this experience and looking forward to the life ahead of her as Mrs. Dan Williams. She was keeping a journal of all their experiences, and they were taking lots of pictures to remember this time and be able to share with their family at home. That is what it felt like to them, one big family. No in-laws or outlaws, like people joked about. Her family had known enough discord and pain over the years, and that was over. She knew their lives wouldn't be perfect, but she was ready for all that came their way. Together, and with the Lord, she knew they would be just fine.

Before they knew it, their last night in Africa was upon them. The next day would be busy with packing up and getting ready to go to the airport and the journey home. Dan grilled out some steaks and vegetables on the grill. Marissa threw together a cold salad and got their glasses of lemonade ready.

She set the table on the deck as Dan brought the steaks and vegetables to the table. They sat down and looked around them, holding hands. This had been such an unbelievable experience, they wanted to soak up every bit of it to hold in their hearts forever.

"I am so excited to move into our new home and fall into our new normal as a married couple, the weekly dinners with my family, and we should really start doing that with your parents and David, Grace, and Polly too. It is really fun, and families just don't do things like that anymore," Marissa said dreamily.

"I am looking forward to that too, but it is also hard to leave this paradise, to not have to work and just spend all our time together," Dan said, smiling at her.

She nodded and leaned forward to kiss him. "This is going to be hard to leave for sure. Oh, I have loved it. Thank you, Dan. This was absolutely perfect," Marissa said, looking all around them.

They ate dinner and decided to get in the pool.

"We might have to put a pool in at home. This has been so nice," Dan said, smiling at Marissa.

"No argument here," Marissa said, laughing and lightly splashing him. Dan laughed and started to splash her back more aggressively. They both were laughing and enjoying their last night in Africa.

* * * * *

Lewis and Beth were relaxing in the living room. Beth was knitting Polly a new pink dress with matching hat to keep her warm for the rest of the winter. Lewis was doing a crossword puzzle when his phone rang. He looked to see who it was and shot Beth a look that made her pause to pay attention.

"Hello, Brian, how are you?" Lewis greeted cheerfully. Beth sat up. That was Lewis's friend who worked for the Department of Foster Families.

"Yes, they are heading home tomorrow. Yes, I think they would be interested in starting classes soon. That is why they wanted me to let you know their intentions and were planning on contacting you when they got back. They will need a few days to get rested and settled into their new home and back to work, but they were very excited on getting started, so they could be ready when needed.

"I see... I understand... I will talk to them as soon as I get a chance... Thank you, Brian. Yes, you as well," Lewis said and hung up. He sighed deeply and looked at Beth with tears in his eyes.

"They are needed to become foster parents as soon as possible, aren't they?" Beth asked softly. As excited as they all were to have more children in their family, they knew that meant a child or children's biological family to be in turmoil or tragedy. That was the hard part, especially with older children in need. A lot of times babies are adopted to give them a better life and know nothing else but their adopted family. It wasn't the same for older children.

"Yes. A mother has contacted Brian, and she has just been diagnosed with stage 4 cancer. They don't think she has long, and she has no family. Her husband...was a firefighter, and he died in the line of duty a few years ago. They have no other family. There are three children. The mother wants to make arrangements and choose the family for her children so she can help them make the transition and know they will be okay," Lewis said and began to sob into his hands.

Beth set her knitting down and went to sit next to him on the love seat. She wrapped her arms around him, and they cried together.

* * * * *

Dan and Marissa arrived at their new home and looked at each other giggling. They had been in the home moving everything in and unpacking so it would be ready for their return, but this was new. This was the first time it really was their home and not their future home. Dan opened the door, and they just peered in. It smelled so wonderful, and they looked at each other, surprised.

"Do you smell…apple pie?" Dan asked, confused.

"Yes, I do," Marissa said.

They went in and found a note addressed to them on the table. They picked it up and read it together.

Dear Mr. and Mrs. Williams,

We knew you would be tired when you arrived to your new home, but we thought a fresh warm-baked apple pie and ice cream would hit the spot for a welcome home celebration. The pie is on your kitchen counter, and the ice cream is in the freezer. We have milk, sweet tea, and other groceries in the refrigerator, freezer, and cabinets for you. We thought that would be a great welcome home present for you. There is also a big cozy blanket in the dryer still warming. You just left warm Africa for a cold, snowy home, so we wanted to make it a warm reception.

Welcome home! Get some rest, and then fill us in on all the fun things you did!

Love,

Your sisters, Grace and Charlotte

P.S. This is what you get for giving us keys for emergencies.

They began to laugh and found the pie still very warm on the counter. The kitchen was stocked with all kinds of food and a few frozen complete meals for them to save on cooking for a full week! The dryer was still going, and the blanket was very cozy.

"We have the best sisters in all the world!" Dan gushed.

"We sure do! I will get the pie served, you get the ice cream, and we can sit on the couch under that blanket and eat this pie!" Marissa said, beaming. "Wow…they had to have just left here!"

"We'll eat and go to bed. I am exhausted," Dan said, going for the ice cream in the freezer.

"Sounds good to me. That was a long flight." Marissa was exhausted, but that pie smelled delicious.

Dan's phone rang. It was Lewis.

"Hi, Dad, are you in on this too?" Dan asked, laughing.

"In on what?" Lewis said, confused.

"Guess not. Grace and Charlotte must have just left before we got here. They stocked our kitchen with food and the freezer with casseroles and left a hot apple pie on the counter and ice cream in the freezer and a big blanket in our dryer, still running!" Dan said, still amazed.

"Wow…no, I had no idea. That sounds like them though," Lewis said, smiling. "Dan, can you put this call on speaker so Marissa can hear?"

"Sure. Marissa, my dad needs to talk to both of us. Okay, Dad, Marissa is right here, and I have you on speaker." Dan exchanged confused looks with Marissa. This sounded serious.

"Welcome home to you both, and I know you are both tired and need to settle in, but I needed to talk to you right away. I got a call from Brian at the Department of Foster Families. He wanted to know if you and Marissa can start classes either later this week or next. There is a family of three siblings in need of placement soon. He thinks this might be a good fit for you two, and I agree. I can give you more specifics tomorrow, but there are three children. Are you interested?"

Dan and Marissa locked eyes. They knew they both felt the same way. They weren't expecting to be getting children this quickly, but if they were in need and the Lord felt they were the ones to take them, they were ready. Marissa nodded.

"We are ready, Dad. You got our attention. What do you know?" Dan put his arm around Marissa, and she rested her head on his shoulder.

"Their father was a firefighter and passed away in the line of duty a few years ago. Their mother hasn't been well. She went to the doctor and was diagnosed with stage 4 cancer. She doesn't have a lot of time left, and she wants to find the family to take her children and help them begin the transition so it might be a little easier on them," Lewis managed to get out. "That is all I know."

"Thank you. We have Brian's number. We will call him," Marissa said, tears flowing freely. They said their goodbyes and they hung up.

"Call him now," Marissa said. Her heart was racing.

Dan made the call.

"Hello, this is Brian." Brian didn't recognize the number on his phone's caller ID.

"Hello, Brian. This is Dan and Marissa Williams. I have you on speaker phone so my wife can hear you," Dan said.

"Dan and Marissa... I thought your dad said you were just getting home tonight? I must have misunderstood him," Brian said, thankful for their call.

"We did. We have been home for about ten minutes. My dad called to ask us about the classes and said there were children in need. We pressed for him to tell us all he knew now. We are very interested in taking classes as soon as possible and meeting with this mother. If she thinks we are the ones to raise her children, we would be honored to do so. Does she know I am a police officer? Would that be a problem for her or the children? Dad said they lost their father in the line of duty as a firefighter. They may be scared off by my being a police officer," Dan said.

"Wow, thank you for calling me so quickly. We can start you in classes any day this week, and I thought about that too, Dan. I brought up the potential families I thought would meet her criteria, and I had told her about the two of you interested in going to start classes. From what she had told me she was looking for, and what I knew about you from Lewis, I felt you would be a good possible match. It is unusual for me to do so, when a couple hasn't officially been certified as a foster family, but I know your dad, and I felt a strong leading from the Lord to mention you. She handpicked three potential families, and one of those was the two of you. She respected the fact that you served your community. That was a big priority of her husband, obviously, and he would like that. I can set up the meeting for you and her this week as well. You won't be taking custody of them until she passed or had to go into a nursing facility or hospital. She knows all the possibilities and wants to find the right home for her children and start the bonding process and for you to know her as well to help all of you in this process. She is quite a woman. She knows her time is short, and she is all business. She wants to know her children will be okay," Brian said, trying to hold it together. "This isn't a usual circumstance we have here, but it has happened before."

"I understand. Marissa, when do you want to start classes?" Dan asked.

"Tomorrow," Marissa said, clinging to Dan, her heart breaking.

"I agree," Dan said, holding onto Marissa tightly.

"Wow, thank you so much. The classes are held at the community center on Sheridan Lane. It starts at seven in room 418B. I will be teaching this set," Brian said, so grateful for couples like Dan and Marissa.

"We will be there," Dan said and hung up. Marissa had written the information down quickly. They held each other in silence. Their hearts went out to this family. This amazingly strong mother...her children who had lost so much already...

"This is happening so quickly. We haven't even told the rest of the family," Marissa said, shaking.

"I know. Dad can tell them for us and catch them up. We just need to pray, and if this is God's plan for us and these children, then we will be ready. He will guide us," Dan said pointedly. Marissa agreed.

"Dear heavenly Father, we come before you humbled by your love and plans for our lives, whatever they may be. We pray for this mother, in all she faces physically and in the decisions for her children. If your will is for her to be healed, we ask for that. If you are to receive her into your arms, then we pray for the right family to be given these three children. Be with them every step of the way and all of their lives. We pray, Lord, that she is saved and that her children know you as well to help them through more heartache than they have already suffered. Lord, if we are the ones to take on this great responsibility and are given these children to love and raise, we pray your Holy Spirit to guide us. If another family is meant for these children, we pray for them to know you and to be led by your Spirit in the years to come. We leave all of this in your capable, loving hands, Father God. In Jesus's name we pray. Amen," Dan prayed as he shook and tears rolled down his face.

"Amen," Marissa said and sobbed into chest.

After gathering themselves, they ate their pie and ice cream quietly and then put the dishes in the sink to soak. Dan took Marissa by the hand, and they went to rest. They had made a long journey home and now they needed rest for tomorrow.

His Hands and Feet

Dan and Marissa slept most of the day. They got up and had one of the wonderful casseroles left for them by their sisters and got showered and ready for their first foster parent class. They felt so many emotions but felt like they were very much in line with what God wanted them to be doing.

Dan had called Lewis and asked if he could let the rest of the family know what they were embarking on, and they would update everyone as soon as they could. It was Monday and they were supposed to go back to work on Wednesday, but they called their bosses and explained the situation and both were told to take the full week off and come back the next week. They wished them well in their endeavors.

They headed to the community center to begin their first class and get information on how all of this worked and talk to Brian after class to set up a time to meet with this mother. This wasn't usually how any of this worked out, but when dealing with people and families in need, a lot of times there were circumstances that were not text book.

* * * * *

Lewis had called everyone and asked them to come to have dinner with him and Beth. They would order in pizza, so nothing fancy; but it was also an important family meeting concerning Dan and Marissa, and they needed to get right down to business. All were concerned and promised to be there.

Charles and Delores arrived first, as requested to show up early. Charles and Delores were very concerned.

"Please come in," Beth said when she answered the door.

Delores clasped Beth's hands in hers. "Beth, we are very worried. Did something happen to Dan or Marissa in Africa or on the way home?" Delores asked in the doorway.

"No, nothing like that. They are fine. We haven't had a chance to get any information out of them about their trip yet. This is about something that they talked to us about before they left. They wanted to talk to everyone else personally about it, but things happened way faster than expected, and so they are going forward and asked for us to explain for them. They are fine. Please come in and let us explain," Beth said sincerely.

Charles and Delores exchanged confused looks but nodded and followed Beth into the living room.

Lewis heard them arrive and met them there. "Please have a seat, and let us explain," Lewis began.

They all took a seat.

"The day after Christmas, Dan and Marissa sat us down to ask for our help. They had been doing a lot of praying and talking about if they were to have children and if they were, in what manner. Marissa was concerned about trying to have a baby at her age, and the more they talked and prayed about it, they felt they knew what they were meant to do. They wanted to become foster parents and maybe lead to adopting children. It just felt right for them. They wanted to talk to us because they thought since I was a chaplain and Beth volunteered at the hospital, we could help them get started in this journey," Lewis explained.

"Oh...well that makes perfect sense. One or both of you would surely know how to help them. I understand," Charles said, nodding.

"Foster parents…adopting…so they are looking for older children without families…not a baby?" Delores felt a flood of emotions. She was touched they would think of children that were older and hurting and had no one, children like she had once been. She was so proud.

"Yes. They felt led to want older children. They also had a burning in their hearts for siblings, a family needing a home and to stay together," Beth added.

"Oh my… I am so surprised, but I am not… Those two are…," Charles said, shaking his head and covering his mouth with his hand. He was trying to hold himself together.

"You said they were planning on talking to all of us personally, but things have changed?" Delores said, remembering. She was taking in the information stoically. This was hitting her heart deeply, but she needed all the information.

"Yes, the night before they came home, I got a call from my friend Brian who works at the Department of Foster Children. I had touched base with him after the wedding to let him know Dan and Marissa wanted information about starting classes and applying to be foster parents," Lewis explained. "He called me to ask if Dan and Marissa were serious and would be interested in starting classes this week or next. The need is great, but there was a special circumstance that he was alerted of, and even though they hadn't started the process, he felt that they might be the right couple for this family."

Lewis stopped to let them soak in the information and so he could take in a deep breath. Charles and Delores were surprised by this development too and picked up on how Lewis and Beth were emotional about what was coming next. Charles and Delores looked at each other, and Delores swallowed hard.

"What is it? You said family, so is it more than one child? Siblings?" Delores pushed on for information. She looked from Lewis to Beth.

"Yes. It seems that there are three children. We don't know, boys or girls or ages of the children. Their father had been a firefighter. He passed away a few years ago in the line of duty," Beth began and pursed her lips together. That part was very hard for them, given their Paul had wanted to be a firefighter. She licked her lips and went on. "Their mother has been very sick, and she has been diagnosed with stage 4 cancer. She wants to make sure her children are taken care of, and she wants to pick the family. She wants to get to know them and help them bond with the children and to make this as easy and smooth as possible for the new family and her children especially," Beth managed.

Lewis was standing with his back to them. His hands were on the mantel of the fireplace and he was shaking.

"Oh my...," Delores said. "What a horrible situation...what a difficult task for her and these children, but at the same time...what a blessing to know that she can be sure she knows who will have them and to try and help them..."

"Yes," Beth said, taking Delores's other hand. She wasn't sure how Delores would process all of this with having been an orphan growing up in an orphanage after her parents' death in a car accident. Charles squeezed her hand in support. Lewis turned to see how Delores was doing, tears in his eyes.

Delores was shaking, but they all were. Their heart went out to this family, but they were sure that Dan and Marissa, if God's will, would be perfect for this family.

"Where are Dan and Marissa now?" Delores asked. She was keenly aware she was holding it together much better than the others.

"They were starting foster care classes tonight. They didn't want to wait. They got the rest of the week off work and are starting to meet guidelines by the state. Brian told the mother about them and let her know that they were just starting the process. Nothing was approved yet, but she liked what she heard about them. Her husband being a firefighter, she connected with Dan being a police officer. She handpicked three couples, and she wants to meet all three and go from there," Lewis explained.

"You would think that might scare her off, afraid for another loss...but if it is God's will for Dan and Marissa to have these children, then it wouldn't," Charles said softly.

"Yes. I was thinking that too," Beth said. "Marissa asked for us to tell you both first. She wanted to make sure you both knew before the rest of the family and to give you more time to digest it as well."

"I understand. She is a good girl and wanted to make sure I was okay," Delores smiled proudly.

"It all happened so fast, and they didn't expect to start classes this month even, but the call came," Lewis said. He didn't want them to feel slighted for not knowing in advance.

"We understand," Charles said, nodding. He could tell Delores felt as he did, and they didn't feel snubbed. They knew Dan and Marissa wouldn't do that, nor would Lewis and Beth. They considered them good friends, not just their daughter's in-laws.

"I feel so many things, but Charles is right. We understand how it all snowballed so unexpectedly. I just keep thinking, as a mother, what this must be like for her...and I keep thinking of the children. I didn't have warning, and I didn't lose one parent at a time. It was one big shock. I just can't imagine how hard this is for all of them. If they become Dan and Marissa's children, we will all love them as our grandchildren no different than Emma and Polly. My heart just goes out to their pain and situation," Delores said quietly, tears spilling out of her eyes.

"Yes," they all said at once in agreement with Delores.

"I think we should pray, pray for this family and for Dan and Marissa," Delores said, standing up. Charles and Beth stood up, and Lewis came over to them. They all held hands. "I would like to say the prayer, if that is okay," Delores said and looked around as they all nodded in agreement. They couldn't think of anyone more appropriate to lead this prayer than Delores.

"Dear Jesus, please, Lord, be in this situation. You know every detail of the entire situation, and you know this mother and each of her children like no one else ever could. Lord, we pray for the health of this mother. We pray for healing for this mother. We pray for a miracle for her, Lord. If she is too tired, and you will be receiving her, we pray she is ready to meet you. We pray for these children and all they are facing and will face, Lord... We pray for the right family to receive them, that they know you and will raise them in love and full knowledge of who you are. Lord, if it be this family, we know that Dan and Marissa will love them and do for them what they can as if they were their blood children. There will be no difference to them Lord, or us. If it be us, guide all of us in the coming weeks, months, and years to help them in this life and make them feel and know they are loved by us unconditionally. Let your will be done, and let us be your hands and feet in this life. In Jesus's name we pray. Amen."

Tears flowed freely, and they all held onto one another's hands, praising God and thanking him for moving in this situation and for being the holy God that he is.

* * * * *

The class gave a great introductory to the world of foster families and how this beginning process usually takes shape. Dan and Marissa took vigorous notes and hung on every word that Brian said. There were three other couples there.

"I am going to pass out the schedule for the rest of the classes. If you have any schedule conflicts, contact me. My number is on the bottom of the page, and we can get you in with another class and instructor to complete the process for you. We understand how busy your lives can be. We will make it work for you. If you think this might be something you want to know more about or definitely know you want to do this, complete the paperwork and we will see you in the next class, either with me or someone else if needed. If you feel like this is definitely not for you, at least at this time, we thank you wholeheartedly for trying us out. At no point are you locked into this with no turning back. There are more children needing homes than there are foster homes available, but we want families who want to do this and for the right reasons. Thank you all for coming out tonight to be here. Have a good rest of your evening, and I hope to see you at the next class. Good night." Brian spoke from his heart. The other couples nodded and thanked him. They gathered their belongings and left quickly. Dan and Marissa stayed put.

Brian smiled at them and came over to shake their hands again. "Thank you so much. I can't imagine just getting married, just getting back from Africa, and being here the next night. That speaks a lot about your hearts. We need more couples like you, but this isn't for everyone, and we know that," Brian said honestly.

"We weren't expecting for this to start up so quickly, but when my dad called us, we knew in our spirits that this was bigger than us and we would do whatever the Lord led us to do," Dan said.

"When Lewis told us...how could we not respond to what we were being asked to do? We had already felt this was in our future, but to hear that you thought of us, even with us not started in the process yet and that she wanted to meet us...that just is undeniably the leading of the Lord," Marissa said.

"Yes, and if we aren't who she feels is right, that is okay. The Lord knows we were obedient, and we will pray for them and her and the family who becomes their family too. We will be ready for whoever God leads us to be a family to," Dan added.

Brian nodded and wiped away a tear. These were the couples he prayed for every day for these kids, all of them, in all situations.

"Thank you. I don't usually bring up or contact couples who have only shown interest, but your names just kept burning in my spirit... I tell you, if I weren't a Christian, I wouldn't have lasted in this job. I don't know how others deal with all we see and deal with in this profession without God. I really don't," Brian said, pursing his lips together to keep control of his emotions.

"What is next?" Dan asked. He knew from his line of work exactly what Brian meant. He felt the same way.

"Well, I talked to Laura this morning. She understands that your first class was tonight, and you hadn't even been given the paperwork until tonight. She doesn't care. She wants to meet you. She said if you were right for her children, she would know it. She is a Christian, and she has been in prayer. She is trusting God to guide her to the right couple, and she said she felt a tug in her spirit when I told her about the two of you. She knew this class wasn't until seven tonight. She met the other two couples today, and she was reserving all judgment until she met with all three couples and pray about it. She wanted to know if you could meet her tomorrow," Brian explained.

"What time?" Marissa asked.

"How about 9:00 a.m. at my office? Here is my card. She won't have the children with her. They will be at school. She is trying to keep their life as normal as possible," Brian said and sighed. "She is a good mom. We usually see home lives that are very different from this situation."

Dan nodded and patted him on the back. He understood.

"We will be there," Marissa said through her tears. They had thought about becoming parents, having a family, finding children who needed a family, but she really hadn't really stopped to think about these situations and what they were really like. She felt so naive and foolish and maybe selfish. These children, Laura's children, and all foster kids have been through so much. They didn't deserve any of it.

"Thank you," Brian said, shaking their hands again before he led them out to the parking lot. "Just be yourselves. This isn't just a one-way street, you know. She has to make a decision, but so does whoever she picks. If it doesn't feel right to you, if you don't think this is God's plan for you, then you can say no."

"I understand what you are saying, but we are serious about this, and if God brings us to that decision, we know what it is. Laura and her children didn't have a choice in this, or we wouldn't be standing here right now. This is so unordinary, from you thinking of us to her picking us also. It feels like God is all over this," Marissa said from her heart. Brian nodded and got in his car to go.

"Where to?" Dan asked as they got in the car. "Home or Mom and Dad's house? They might all still be there."

"I can't talk to them tonight. I love them all, and I know they would be so supportive. I know they are praying for us, and that is enough. I just want to go home and be with you, pray and go to sleep."

"Home it is," Dan said quietly. He understood and was relieved it was what she wanted.

* * * * *

Elliott, Charlotte, and Emma were very curious and concerned about this family meeting Lewis had called. They had been told to be there at seven. They knew it had to do with Dan and Marissa but had been told they were fine, but they needed a meeting. That didn't make them feel more peaceful about the whole situation. When they got there, they found David and Grace pulling up too. Charles and Delores's car was already there.

"What is going on?" Grace asked. She looked just as concerned as they were.

"We don't know," Charlotte said softly. Grace nodded.

David got Polly out of the back seat and they all went in.

They found the others in the living room, drinking coffee. There was a pot and more mugs out. And a thermos too. Lewis, Beth, Charles, and Delores seemed quiet but calm. They offered a kind smile to the worried looks of the new comers.

"Hello, everyone. We have fresh coffee, and the thermos has hot chocolate," Beth said as she swept a giggling Polly out of David's arms.

"Is everything okay?" Grace asked. "Where are Dan and Marissa? This is about them, right?"

"Yes, they have asked us to talk to everyone. We asked Charles and Delores to come at six to talk to them first. It was requested by Marissa, and we agreed it was appropriate," Lewis explained.

Grace and Charlotte grabbed each other's hand. Elliott and David exchanged worried looks. Emma ran to sit between Charles and Delores. They smiled at her and held onto her. Delores kissed her hand.

"Come in and sit down. They are okay. Things are happening in their lives, and it is happening way faster than anticipated, and they want you all to know about it but are taking care of the situation as it is unfolding and can't be here tonight," Lewis said calmly.

"As it unfolds? Faster than anticipated? They just got married and home from Africa last night? What is going on?" Grace asked, more confused than ever.

"Please sit down," Beth urged. "We will explain all of it."

They all found a seat and took off their coats and waited quietly.

"Let me explain it all before you react in anyway, okay?" Lewis asked, looking from Grace to Charlotte to Emma. They all nodded.

"Dan and Marissa were talking and praying about whether to have children. They felt led in their spirits to explore fostering. They were wanting not only an older child in need, but it was really on their hearts to request siblings, to keep them together." Lewis paused to let them all take in what he had shared.

They all seemed to relax a little and smile in understanding. They knew Dan and Marissa, and although they were not expecting this, it was not surprising that they would make a decision like this.

"They came to us the day after Christmas, just days before the wedding, because they felt so strongly about it. They thought we might have connections through Lewis's job and my volunteering at the hospital. Lewis does have a friend in the Department of Foster Families. They wanted him to contact him and let him know they were very interested, and when they settled into life after marriage, they wanted to start classes and see what doors the Lord opened. Looking back, it is interesting that they felt so strongly for us to reach out to get this initiated right away. It had to be God," Beth said wistfully.

"Yes, I think you are right," Delores said, a tear in her eye.

"So anyway, the night before they returned, I got a call from Brian. He wanted to know if I thought they would be interested in starting classes this week or next. He seemed like it was urgent that he knew...and then he explained why..." Lewis stopped suddenly. He seemed emotional, and he turned away from them. They all looked at one another. They had never seen Lewis like that before.

Beth handed David his daughter and went to embrace him. Charles and Delores looked at each other.

"There is a family in need, and as unusual as it is and not customary to consider a couple who have not really even started the process to become foster parents, only showed interest, he felt led to consider Dan and Marissa. He has been in contact with them, and they are at their first class tonight to get the formalities underway, but they are possibly going to be considered for the foster family for these three siblings," Delores explained.

They all looked at her, surprised. Three siblings? Considered already? This had to be God.

"The father was a firefighter and died in the line of duty a few years ago. The mother now has stage 4 cancer. She wants to handpick the family for her children and help them transition in the time she has left," Charles explained.

"That mother...her bravery...her poor broken heart...," Grace whispered as she looked over at her baby girl in her husband's arms.

"Those children have lost so much already, and now they are losing their mother. I know Dan and Marissa would be able to give them the stable home, love, and support they need. A trust bond will have to be made and a lot of healing. I am so in awe of their mother. In all she is facing to find the strength in her weakness to do this...it is understandable but so difficult," Elliott thought aloud.

"So what happens next?" David asked, cuddling Polly closer.

"Well, I imagine they will meet the mother, continue on with classes, and see what the mother wants to do next. She understood that they hadn't been certified as a foster family yet but was very interested in meeting with them," Lewis managed.

"That is a lot to take on right after getting married, but if any-one can handle it, those two can. They felt led to do this, and for all of this to unfold so quickly, it sounds like God is working it all out, so they will be fine," Charles said.

"We understand now. Thank you for telling us, and we are thankful they wanted to keep us in the loop. When they add to this family, in whatever manner, we will be here to support all of them and let any child or children know they have a big family now," Charlotte said, smiling at her mother.

She couldn't imagine how this was affecting her heart. Delores smiled warmly back at her and nodded in agreement.

Laura

Laura watched from the window as her children played in the front yard, running around and throwing snowballs at each other. They were the joy of her life, and she had never expected to leave them to grow up without her. She never expected for Aaron to die either. They always knew the danger of his job, but you still never think it will happen to you. She knew something was wrong with her when she was sick but wasn't getting any better. It had been going on for too long. By the time the tests were done, she was expecting the doctor's report. She wasn't trying not to have faith; she just knew somehow. She felt like the Lord was preparing her. She didn't feel alone or forsaken; she felt cared for and loved. She knew God would make a way for her children. The peace that passes all understanding surrounded her.

She had prayed about her children and for God to help her make sure they were going to be okay. She had to make sure it was settled and in place before she left them. She didn't want them to just go into a situation with strangers, and most likely be split apart. They were brave children and strong in the Lord, but they deserved something better than that. She had tried to talk to adoption lawyers, but most people wanted babies. She was advised to talk to the Department of Foster Families. She knew she wanted a home with Christian parents. She wanted a home where there weren't a lot of other foster children, and she wanted a home that would be a forever home, not just passed on through the system. She was nervous about contacting the Foster System for that reason.

She was told there were a few families who currently had no other children, who had just had theirs leave to go back to their biological families, and one that was just getting started and whose goal was to find children, hopefully siblings to keep together and to adopt them. Something stood out to her about this last couple, but she wanted to talk to all three couples. She had to look at all her options and prayed the Lord to guide her in this process. She knew she was tired, and it was time to go rest in heaven before too long, but she knew the Lord would not forsake her or her children in their future.

She had told the children she had cancer and that she was going to go to heaven to be with Daddy. They took it as hard as any child would, but she told them that she was going to find them a family that would love them like their own and keep them together. Jesus would help her find the right family. They were quiet when she had told them that. They knew she would take care of them, and as hard as it was to lose her, living with strangers was scary. To know their mom would pick the family helped a little, but it was still scary. She had prayed with them on giving them all peace and bringing them a family that would love them and that they would fall in love with too. They hadn't talked more about it. She was waiting until she had found a couple to introduce them to because she wanted to keep everything as normal for them for as long as possible.

After watching them board the school bus, she got ready and headed to Brian's office. He was a nice man who cared about children and she trusted him. She was set at ease about the Department of Foster Families upon meeting with him the first time. She had met the first two couples, and today she would meet the last couple.

She had met with Mitchell and Linda first. She could tell they cared about children, and they proudly told her of past foster children they had had in their home with the same love and pride as they did their biological children who were grown. That did impress her, but she didn't like that they said they only went to church every once in a while. Her children were used to going on a regular basis, and they would need that even more with losing her. She didn't want them to struggle more with less of a faith-based home and church family support system.

Next she had met Ted and Rachel. They had two of their own children still at home, they were in fifth grade and eighth grade. Ted had been a foster child himself, so it was important to him to become a foster parent. He had had some good homes and not so good homes growing up in the system. He wanted to offer a good home to children in need. She could see how sincere they were, especially with Ted's background. They would be a better option for her children, and she applauded that they took in foster children while raising their own. However, she wanted her children to have a lot of attention in the beginning with dealing with their grief. She knew that might be selfish, but she was on the hunt for the best possible home for her children. She wasn't ruling Ted and Rachel out; she just wanted to see all her options, and she knew God had a plan for her children.

Laura arrived at Brian's office and saw a couple heading into the building as she parked her car. She watched them, wondering if they were Dan and Marissa. She saw how they smiled at each other and how he took her hand as they went in. There was a warmth to them that she liked already although she reminded herself she had no idea if that was them or not.

She was trying to reason with herself to stay neutral. There was just something about this last couple, that when Brain had told her about them, she felt a strong stirring inside her. She was impressed that they had just gotten married and had wanted to become foster parents to become parents. They had no other children, and Brian said he knew his father because he was a hospital chaplain. That made her happy too. She took a deep breath and prayed before she went in to meet with them, as she had done the previous two couples.

"Dear Jesus, guide me in finding the right family for my children. You know my heart and what these children are going to need. Please provide a family that will love them as their own and be able to support all they will go through and lean on you to raise them and be a strong support and spiritual guide as well as a home full of love.

In Jesus's name I pray. Amen." Laura felt peace flood her soul, and she headed inside.

When Laura got to Brian's office, she saw the same couple inside his office. They were seated, smiling and talking with Brian, holding hands.

"Laura, it is good to see you. Come in," Brian said when he noticed her smiling at the door, watching Dan and Marissa.

Laura came in, and immediately Dan and Marissa stood. They smiled kindly at her, and she could tell they were nervous. Brain made the introductions, and she shook their hands and sat down in a chair across from them. They sat down as well.

"Well, let me begin. My name is Laura Sinclair. I married my husband, Aaron Sinclair, fifteen years ago. We had met through a friend of mine. Aaron was her neighbor growing up and was in the academy becoming a firefighter, and I was in college to be a preschool teacher. We only dated a few months before we got married. When you know it is right, you just know, I guess. He was a kind man who loved the Lord with all his heart. He taught a Bible study in our home once a week. He had a deep voice and a laugh that warmed your heart. He was a big guy but as gentle as a teddy bear. He loved his children and me with everything in him. He was so proud of them, and they adored him. We had trouble getting pregnant at first, but Aaron said when the time was right, it would happen. We traveled a lot those years before the children came, and I was at peace about it. Then it must have been time because they came," Laura said, chuckling, lost in her memories.

"My oldest is Nathan, and he is ten years old. He is a smart boy, and he loves the Lord, and he really feels a strong need to be the man of the house now. He is protective of his sisters and me, but I try to remind him he is still a boy and that it is okay to have fun and be a boy. He loves video games, basketball, and he likes a good book too. Aaron always read to the children, and he pushed them to have a love for reading. He always told them that no matter how much money you have, you can go anywhere in a book. All my children have taken that to heart," Laura said proudly.

"Then there is Naomi who is eight years old. She loves all things pink and girlie. She loves to paint her nails and all the princess things. She is a smart cookie too. She is as sweet as sugar. She loves to make crafts and draw and write. She is a little on the shy side, but if there is something she wants to do, she has more courage than I can imagine. She surprises me all the time. She wants to be a preschool teacher like me and act in plays at the community center for fun one day." Laura beamed. "I always tell them to follow their hearts and dreams.

"My little one, Nicki, is six years old. She is a ball of energy and fun! She has the biggest heart and jumps into everything with both feet. She is my talker! I have to slow her down and remind her to take a breath. She just laughs and tells me she doesn't have time for that. She doesn't know a stranger, and she wants to be everyone's friend," Laura said, laughing. "She also has an interesting fashion sense that might just be due to her age, but she wears her bold choices proudly, and I let her.

"I taught until Nathan was born. I wanted to be a stay-at-home mother until my children were all in school. I ended up back at the same preschool teaching once Nicki was in full day school. I was able to make it until Christmas break but unable to go back. I didn't know how long I would have strength to keep working. I had to keep my strength up for my children and finding them a new family." Laura paused to take a breath. "I am so blessed to have had that time with each one of them.

"Two years ago my husband died in a fire in the line of duty. You always know that is a possibility, but you never expect it to happen to you. My children and I have found a new normal and are very close. This news was very hard for us to swallow, but I am grateful that I have the time to make sure they are taken care of in my absence. You think I would be angry, but I don't have energy to waste on that. I have to take care of my children now. They have taken the news of my health and my mission to take care of them with great strength and courage. I know they are being strong for me and one another." Laura paused to gain composure and wipe away her tears. She had had tissues ready.

Dan and Marissa hung onto every word she said, holding onto each other's hands and trying to be strong for her. Their hearts broke for her. She was a very proud mother and by the way she described her children, she had every right to be.

"We find our strength in the Lord, and that carries us through. They are good children, full of love, energy, and joy. They know their manners and how to behave, but they are children," Laura said proudly. She beamed as she thought about them.

"I know the two of you just got married, and I am impressed that you are willing to become parents right away, especially someone else's children. What can you tell me about yourselves?"

Marissa smiled at Dan and nodded for him to start. He looked back at Laura.

"My name is Dan Williams, and I grew up in a Christian home. My dad had been a schoolteacher, and my mom a stay-at-home mom. I have two younger siblings. Grace has a husband and a baby girl now. They spent three years in Africa as missionaries. They came home when they found out my niece Polly was on the way. Grace is a nurse. My little brother, Paul, was diagnosed with leukemia when he was three years old. We lost him. He had wanted to be a firefighter and was obsessed with fire trucks, and that is all he wanted to play. When we lost him, my father seemed especially lost. My mom went into mode of hanging onto Grace and me extra tight. She began volunteering at the hospital, rocking babies and spending time playing with sick kids while their parents were working. She felt like she was doing something that mattered. She really felt like she had to find a purpose for the pain, and she still does it today," Dan said, smiling. He was so proud of his mother.

"My dad took her lead and became a minister and is a hospital chaplain. That is actually how I met Marissa. I was the first responder to her sister's car accident. I stayed with her and followed the ambulance to the hospital. I called her husband and waited for him to get there. Talking with him, he just touched my heart, and Charlotte too, who was still unconscious. Elliott mentioned they had a twelve-year-old daughter, and I knew they needed support. I called my dad to come be with Elliott. I felt a drawing, and I kept checking back in with the family at the hospital. I was charmed by Charlotte and Elliott's daughter, Emma. I also met Marissa, and we just connected. And here we are. I didn't know if being a parent would be in my future. I never thought it would. Once Marissa and I were becoming serious, I started to wonder. I see a lot of families and situations in my line of work. I started to wonder if adoption or fostering might be in our future. I knew my future was with Marissa and whatever else God had planned for us would happen in his timing," Dan explained.

"Oh my. You have experienced family loss and grew up healing from that. Hearing that your brother had wanted to be a firefighter... that touches me," Laura said honestly.

"I grew up with my mom and little sister, Charlotte. It wasn't a picture-perfect home. My parents fought a lot when I was little. When they weren't fighting, it was wonderful. My parents split up. My mom just really pushed my dad away and kept telling him to leave, and he finally did. I was five and my sister was two. We never heard from him again while I was growing up. I was very broken for years, worse than I realized. My sister recently told me of the nightmares I would have all the time growing up, crying for my dad to come back. I never realized that I did that. I was good at basketball, and that was where I hid in my pain. I was good and got a full scholarship for college. I have coached a girls' basketball team at the community center since I got out of college. Those girls meant the world to me, and in some cases, I was the only family they had. I work at a bank and have worked my way up to branch manager. I can't say I was close to my sister at all. I was mean to her, and my mom and I took out our pain on her. I am ashamed to say." Marissa looked down at her lap out of shame but then looked back to Laura again.

"Charlotte has always been the sweetest, most loving and forgiving person I have ever met. Right before her accident, she found our dad and reconnected with him, but I didn't want any part of him or her anymore. When I got the call from Elliott about the accident... I was broken. I was in shock and I couldn't face it." Marissa licked her lips and continued, feeling very emotional, "Charlotte got saved as a child at vacation Bible school, but I never had an interest.

I was too angry and hurting. I found myself compelled to reexamine my belief in God as I saw how different Elliott and Emma handled this difficult time. I was listening to what they said and all that Lewis, that is Dan's father, was saying. I found myself wanting to believe, and I met a lady in a restaurant…a complete stranger, who led me to Christ. I have reconnected with my earthly father as well as my heavenly Father. I have an amazing relationship with all my family. My mom also found the Lord, and my dad was the one who led her to Christ. He found Jesus after he left us but didn't know how to come back. My mom had returned all his letters and cards. I found that out during this time too. My mom was orphaned at the age of six. Her parents were in a car accident while she was at school. She was told by a police officer, and they took her to the orphanage to live. She married my dad the day after high school graduation because she had to move out of the orphanage. They were in love, but my mom had so much pain from her childhood she was scared and lost. They never divorced or wanted to be with anyone else and had a wedding last June on their original wedding anniversary to make their coming back together official. My family and Dan's family have really become one family. We spent Thanksgiving and Christmas together and plan on continuing that new tradition. Dan's parents helped us meet Brian, and we hadn't told anyone else about our plans. We had Dan's parents tell my parents, and later last night, Dan's sister and her husband, as well as my sister and her family together so they know what is going on," Marissa explained.

"Wow. I love that your families are that close… Welcome to the family by the way. I appreciate your honesty and heart you have shared with me. No one is perfect, and when we are hurting, we do the best we can, especially if we didn't know the Lord. I am truly touched by your stories. What you both have experienced and your family as well." Laura was moved beyond words. She felt strongly in her heart that this was the family for her children. She still needed to pray about it and ask a few more questions, but her heart felt so light knowing this part was just about over.

"May I ask you a few questions?" Laura asked. They smiled and nodded. "I know Dan is a police officer. You said you are a branch manager at a bank. That is impressive for a woman of your age. You must work full time. How will you manage the children's afterschool childcare until you get home from work?"

"Yes, I am a branch manager at a bank. I started as a teller while in college and worked my way up. Dan and I work until five, but his mother has offered when we had children to pick them up from school and take them to her house. She would make afterschool snacks, help them with homework, and play with them until we picked them up," Marissa explained.

"I like that. You really have put a lot of thought into all of this. You both are serious about this, and that touches my heart," Laura said, exhaling. This decision was becoming more and more apparent to her. Her spirit was at peace, and she really felt like she was connecting with Dan and Marissa. "How often do you go to church?"

"We go every Sunday to both services and on Wednesday," Dan answered. Laura exhaled.

"That makes me happy. How did you find your church?" Laura asked.

"Well, I was going to the one I was raised in with my family all my life. When I met Marissa and we actually began dating and she was newly saved, she had started to go to church with her sister's family. Her parents did as well. Her dad moved back here to help with her sister's recovery and to be close to them. I started to attend that church as well. I liked it, and it felt right to attend with her," Dan explained.

"I see. I like that you did that, Dan," Laura said, nodding.

"Laura, I assume that from what you have said and by asking that question, you are regular attendees as well?" Marissa asked.

Laura nodded again. "Last night after we had spoken with Brian, he shared a little about you. He told us you were Christians. Dan and I talked about it last night. If you choose us, if we are the right fit for your family to be our family too, we want to attend your church. Your children have been through so much and will be going through so much that we feel they will need their support system and as much familiar surroundings as possible. We also want to keep them in the same school. They will need as much of their lives as possible to be routine and familiar. We think it will be very important for them," Marissa added.

Laura burst into tears and bent over, burying her face into her hands. Dan and Marissa looked at each other, and then Marissa hit her knees and wrapped her arms around Laura.

"You have no idea how much I have prayed for that. I wasn't sure how to ask that of someone but was going to leave that in God's hands. That would mean so much to them, to me too," Laura said, trying to regain composure. "You really are the best family I could hope to find for my children, and I know they will love you. It might be hard at first, but as they heal, they will come to love you," Laura said, smiling through her tears.

"If we could change this and you be well, we would do that for you in a heartbeat. We are praying for it. If this is going to happen and we can be the family to love and raise your children, it would be an honor," Marissa said through her tears.

Laura nodded and embraced Marissa. They cried for a few minutes, holding onto each other. Dan and Brian watched these two women who were connecting on a very deep level. There wasn't a dry eye in the room.

"Well, we need to pray together," Laura said, standing. She took Marissa and Dan's hands. Brian joined hands with them as well.

"Dear heavenly Father, we come to you with this plea. Guide us in the coming days and help us to make this transition as easy on these children as possible. Help them to open their hearts to Dan and Marissa easily. Guide Dan and Marissa in how to love and raise these children and be their family for the rest of their lives. There is no question in my heart or soul that this is your leading. Let me help them in all I can for as long as I have left. In Jesus's name, I pray. Amen."

"Amen," the other three said.

"Now, I need to talk to my children and then have you meet them. Then we can go from there. Brian, any guidance you can give us on how to help this process go as smoothly as possible, I would appreciate it," Laura said assuredly.

"I definitely will. I suggest since you have found each other, with this unique situation, that you can go ahead and go through a lawyer and make this adoption complete. I know you started there, but the best place to find a family wanting older children and siblings was with us. Now that you have made this connection and decision, I would go to the final step now. I would suggest to Dan and Marissa to finish the foster family classes to help prepare you on how to help the children in this process. These are still children joining a new family who have suffered loss. I think it would be helpful to you, but I won't need that paperwork, and you won't need the certification. God has guided you onto your rightful path and family. I feel so strongly that this is God and this is the right decision for all of you, especially Nathan, Naomi, and Nicki," Brian said. "I know a lawyer who can help you in this next step."

They all nodded in agreement. There was no question in any of their hearts that this was the answer to all their prayers.

As they talked a little longer, they discovered that Dan and Marissa's new house was in the same school district as they attended now. When Laura heard their home had four bedrooms, she began to cry again. She was so overwhelmed by God's provision and guidance in all of this. She was tired, but so much peace flooded her soul. She went home to nap until the children came home. Dan suggested he drive her car for her and she ride with Marissa home so they would know where she lived and because they could see how drained she was. She accepted. They were such loving people who cared for her and not just her children. That touched her heart, and she knew her children would be able to see that, and that would mean the world to them.

* * * * *

Dan and Marissa went home. They were even more impressed with Laura than they had been when Brian first told them about her.

"You can tell she is not feeling well, but her light shines bright," Dan said.

"Yes, it does. My heart just breaks for her, but if she and her children have to go through this, I am honored that we would be chosen to become part of their family," Marissa said, a fresh tear rolling down her cheek.

"I agree," Dan said, nodding. They were truly humbled.

"What if they don't like us?" Marissa said, concerned.

"I think it will be fine. I don't think the Lord would guide us to them if it wasn't going to be in their best interest. It may be hard for a while. They are going to go through all the stages of grief, including anger. My dad and your mom might be the best thing for them, all the family, but with dad's counseling skills and your mom's experiences, I think we are in a good position to help them in every way anyone can," Dan reassured her.

Marissa nodded. "You are right," Marissa said, sighing deeply. "When do you think we will hear from Laura?"

"I don't know. Maybe tomorrow? She is a woman of action, and she doesn't want to lose any time on this," Dan said gently. Marissa nodded.

"I think continuing with the classes is going to help us become the best parents we can be. I like that we are going to go forward with the adoption. I don't want them to question their future," Dan said.

Marissa agreed.

"I can't wait to meet them: Nathan, Naomi, and Nicki. I love them already," Marissa sighed dreamily.

* * * * *

Laura rested and spent the rest of the day in prayer. She knew she needed the Lord to help her talk to her children and to help start this transition for them. It wasn't going to be easy, but she felt strongly that Dan and Marissa Williams could handle it with God's help.

Laura sat at the window, anxiously awaiting for the school bus. She was excited to see her children and to love on them.

They came in and told her about their day as they unpacked their school bags and began their homework. Laura sat with them and helped them and just drank them in: their little faces, their smell, and their laughter and chattering. If only she could live on the joy they brought her, she would live forever.

After homework, they helped her make dinner. She had suggested homemade pizza. Nathan and Naomi exchanged looks and Nicki cheered. They loved homemade pizza, and that was usually a weekend treat. Laura knew the older two were on to her.

They rolled out the dough and made four small pizzas. Laura put some green peppers, mushrooms, and sausage on hers. Nathan loaded his with pepperoni. Naomi put some leftover chicken on hers and some barbecue sauce instead of the tomato sauce. Nicki wanted only cheese on hers and lots of it.

Once the pizzas were in the oven, they settled into the living room. Nicki was reading to Laura, and the older two were playing on the floor with their own toys quietly. They just wanted to be close to Laura. Nicki was getting better at reading, and she was so proud to read to her mommy.

After they had dinner and did the dishes, Laura told them she wanted to talk to them in the living room.

"I feel really tired. Can it wait until tomorrow?" Nathan asked, heading to his room.

"No, it can't, Nathan. I know you don't want to talk about this, but waiting until tomorrow won't change anything," Laura said gently.

Nathan froze in his tracks and exhaled. He came back and sat down next to Laura. Naomi was on her other side and Nicki sat on her lap. Laura had been praying through dinner and dishes to give her strength for this conversation.

"You know I am not going to be with you very long. I am tired, and I am not going to get better. I am going to heaven to be with Jesus and Daddy. It doesn't help to avoid it. I promised you I would make sure I handpicked who would raise you. I would find a wonderful couple to become your family. I have done a lot of praying, *and I mean a lot of praying,* about this. I met a couple today that I know in my heart is the best possible match for our family. They are a Jesus-loving couple with a big family who will all love you very much," Laura said with as much excitement and strength that she could muster.

"A big family? How many kids?" Nathan asked slowly.

"No other children. I mean aunts and uncles, cousins, and two sets of grandparents for you," Laura explained.

They all seemed to relax a little.

"Where do they live? What school will we go to?" Naomi asked.

"They don't live far from here, and you will go to the same school. They wanted to make sure of that themselves, even before we realized they lived in the right district. They also want to switch to our church. They want to keep you in as much familiar surroundings and support that you already have. I was praying for that to be a possibility, but I never expected it would be their suggestion. It really drove home to me that I was right in feeling they were the right family," Laura explained.

"Wow. I would like aunts, uncles, cousins, and grandparents!" Nicki said, excited. Laura appreciated them being open, and she knew that Nicki really didn't fully grasp what the older two did. Even in losing her daddy, it was still hard for her to understand losing her mommy.

"When do we meet them?" Nathan asked guardedly.

"Tomorrow," Laura said softly.

"Tomorrow? What?" Nathan wasn't happy at all. This was too soon.

"Nathan, hear me out. We are going to have dinner with them and then go to our church together. That is all. Start out slow," Laura explained.

"Oh. Well, okay," Naomi said softly. "Do you think they will want to go to our church?"

"It was Marissa's suggestion. They wanted to take us out to dinner and then come to church with us."

"Marissa? That is a pretty name," Nicki said, smiling. "What is his name?"

"Dan. They are Dan and Marissa Williams," Laura said, relaxing a little. The girls were taking it well. Nathan still looked angry. She understood. He took losing his daddy very hard, and now he was being told he was losing his mom and going to move in with strangers.

"Nathan, will you keep an open mind? For me?" Laura asked gently.

Nathan softened. "I would do anything for you," Nathan said, tears in his eyes.

She put her arms around all her children and held them tight. Nathan cried hard. The girls soon joined in too. Laura cried too. She had found out, when they were grieving the loss of Aaron, that it helped to be open and honest with each other, better to share their heartbreak and their joys.

When they had gathered themselves and got them ready for bed, she called Marissa.

"Hello," Marissa answered.

"Hello, Marissa. I spoke with the children, and it is a go to meet for dinner tomorrow before church. When they heard you would keep them at the same church and school, they were very relieved," Laura said, smiling.

"Oh good. We will pick you up tomorrow at five before church," Marissa said, smiling at Dan.

"Do you have room for all of us?" Laura asked, surprised.

"Yes. Um, well we traded my car in for a minivan this afternoon," Marissa said, blushing.

"Good choice. Thank you, Marissa. We will see you then," Laura said, smiling. She loved them already.

Introductions Are in Order

Nathan sat glaring at the TV and was determined to not watch for Dan and Marissa's arrival. Laura sat next to him with her arm around him. She knew this was so hard for him. As the oldest and the older brother, he felt extra pressure and responsibility. She wanted him just to be a ten-year-old boy again. In ways, that would probably never happen, but in all the ways it could, she wanted it for him.

Naomi and Nicki sat at the window, watching for Dan and Marissa excitedly. They were curious, but the reality of who they would become for them wasn't really upon them yet.

They got excited when a van turned into the driveway. A very nervous Dan and Marissa knocked on the door. The door opened wide and fast. Two adorable little girls were beaming up at them.

"Hello! My name is Naomi Rose Sinclair. This is my little sister, Nicki Lynn Sinclair," Naomi said before Dan and Marissa could say anything.

"Well, hello to you both. This is Daniel Harrold Williams, but you can call him Dan. My name is Marissa Lynn Williams. We have the same middle name, Nicki!" Marissa said, her heart bursting at the sight of them. They giggled. Nicki lunged forward and hugged Marissa. Tears filled Marissa's eyes. Dan put his hand on her back for support. He had tears in his eyes as well. They were so precious and so welcoming. They weren't sure what to expect.

"Come in, please," Naomi said, stepping back from the doorway to let them in. Nicki took Marissa by the hand and led her in. Dan followed.

"Well, I see the girls have introduced themselves. Nathan, please turn off the TV now and welcome our guests," Laura said gently.

Nathan stiffened but did what she asked. "Hello. I'm Nathan, Nathan Aaron Sinclair," Nathan said, looking at the ground.

"It is very nice to meet you, Nathan. Your middle name is after your dad. Mine is too. My dad's name is Lewis Harrold Williams," Dan said kindly.

Nathan looked up at him. He knew he was trying and they seemed nice. He would try too. "So your dad had that horrible middle name, and he decided to share the pain?" Nathan asked, smiling.

Laura was about to scold him, but she saw his smile and Dan laughed.

"I kind of always felt that way too." Dan chuckled.

He and Marissa gave Laura a warm smile. "Hello, Laura, it is nice to see you again."

"It is good to see the both of you too," Laura said, exhaling in relief that this was starting out okay.

"Are you really taking us out to eat and going to church with us?" Nicki asked.

"Yes, we are. We thought it might be a nice way to meet you, and we are looking forward to going to your church and meeting your church family," Dan said, smiling at her.

"Thank you," Nathan said softly. They all looked at him in surprise. "Thank you for coming to our church. It is the only church we have ever gone to."

"There is a lot of change going on, and we can't fix so much of what we wish we could for you, but if we can do anything to help you feel more secure, safe, and familiar, we want to make sure that happens," Marissa said sincerely.

Nathan nodded and swiped at a tear in the corner of his eye.

"I'm hungry. You get to pick. Are we going for burgers and fries, pizza, tacos, or what?" Dan asked cheerfully.

"I really like burgers and fries," Naomi said shyly.

Nicki jumped up and down cheering.

Nathan nodded when they looked to him.

"Let's go then," Dan said, gesturing toward the door. Marissa led the way, and the children followed.

Nathan looked back to see Dan help Laura lock up and make sure she was okay. She was weaker now than she was a month ago. He saw it, and it scared him. He did like how Dan was looking after her. They were good people. They just weren't what he wanted. He wanted *his mom* and *his dad*, but that didn't seem to be an option.

They got to the fast-food restaurant, and Dan got everyone's order. Marissa led Laura and the girls to a table. Nathan offered to help Dan carry the food to the table. Dan was impressed with him, and Laura was proud.

Dan smiled at Nathan, but he looked at the ground. He did take the first tray of food, and Dan took the second.

"What's your job?" Naomi asked Dan.

"I am a police officer," Dan said. The children looked at him.

"That is a dangerous job, but an important one. My dad always said someone has to be the strong one and take care of everyone else, no matter the danger. It isn't a choice. It is a calling. It says a lot about someone. My dad was always right," Nathan said proudly.

"Thank you, Nathan. I agree with your dad. Your mom has told us a little about your dad and all of you. From what she has said, I believe that," Dan said, smiling kindly at him. Nathan sat up straighter; he liked that.

"I don't mean to be rude, but can I ask you something?" Nathan asked quietly. Laura looked nervous.

"Nathan, you can always ask us anything. There are going to be some hard days ahead, and we want to be your friends, friends you can depend on," Dan said honestly, looking him in the eye. "Honesty and openness is very important. We hope to prove to all of you that we want that in our relationship. Friends that can become a family, without taking away anything from the family you were born into, we just want to be added to your family."

"I think you might have answered my question... You don't expect us to call you Mom and Dad, do you?" Nathan asked.

"No, we don't. We know you have had an amazing father and mother. We aren't trying to replace anyone. We could never do that. We do hope you accept us as your family in time. At some point if you wanted to call us something like that, you would be welcome to do that, but know that you will never be expected or asked to do so. We are what you want and need us to be, that is our hope. You can love us as a bonus mother and father in your life without calling us by anything but our names," Dan answered.

"I appreciate that," Nathan said, looking back down at his plate. Laura wrapped an arm around him. He was being so brave and mature, but she knew he was hurting. She could tell in all the emotion he was fighting with, he did like and respect them. God was definitely moving in their hearts.

The rest of dinner was lighter conversation. Nathan got out what he needed to know right then and the rest could wait another day. The girls liked that Marissa was a bank manager and giggled about girl power. That made them all laugh. They thought she must be very important. Nathan was impressed that she was a basketball coach.

"Really? I love basketball." Nathan smiled and took a drink of his soda.

"Yes, *really*." Marissa smiled. She was glad they seemed to be connecting with all three of them. Laura looked so pleased.

They went to church, and it was very similar to their own church, and the pastor knew their pastor. Laura had done a lot of talking and praying with him, and she had kept him up to date on what was going on with their family.

"Thank you for coming here and for all you are doing. I know it means so much to Laura, and it will mean the world to those kids. I appreciate you keeping them here so we can love on them."

"We feel it is best for them," Dan said, shaking his hand.

Nathan stood next to Dan and was smiling at him. Dan realized and smiled back and put his arm around his shoulders.

Nathan found he liked that. He missed his dad a lot, but this was nice. He realized maybe this was God giving him a father back. He was sure his dad would like Dan and Marissa a lot. This wasn't what he wanted, but he felt like it would be okay, and he was trusting God for the rest. His parents had made sure their children knew Jesus and had a strong faith and foundation in Christ.

They took the Sinclairs home and said goodbye. Laura suggested that they come over on Saturday and let them spend more time with the children. Dan and Marissa agreed. The girls cheered, and Nathan smiled.

Over the next few weeks, Dan and Marissa spent a lot of time with the Sinclairs. Laura taught Marissa how to braid the girls' hair. Dan and Nathan played video games. Laura watched as they all played basketball out back. It was a warm winter day, too cold for Laura, but they were all bundled up and waved at her from her spot at the window watching them. It seemed to be going well. Nathan even was bonding with them, but he hung close to his mom, making sure Laura was comfortable and taken care of. He was a very devoted son. Aaron would be so proud of him.

Dan and Marissa invited Laura and the children to a Saturday family dinner at Lewis and Beth's house. The whole family would be there. Laura was looking forward to meeting more people who wanted to become family to her children. They were excited too and begging to meet them. Dan and Marissa had just wanted time to bond with Laura and the children before they introduced the rest of the family to them. They didn't want to overwhelm the children by moving too fast.

* * * * *

The next Saturday, Dan and Marissa picked up Laura and the children and headed to Lewis and Beth's home.

"Please, if any of you feel at any time you are wanting to go home or if you are tired, Laura, you can just let us know and we will take you home," Marissa said as she watched them put on their seat belts. They smiled and nodded.

"So you live close to us?" Naomi asked shyly.

"Yes, just a few streets away actually… Would you like to see our home?" Dan asked.

"Yes," all three children said at once.

"Well, let's go!" Dan said, laughing.

"Now wait a minute, they were not expecting company today. Are you sure you are okay with this?" Laura asked, a little embarrassed.

"Oh, it is fine. It is a good idea. We just hadn't thought about it," Marissa said reassuringly. Laura nodded and smiled.

They pulled up to the house, and Laura smiled. It was beautiful. Her children were going to be well taken care of, loved, and be raised by good people who loved Jesus. That is all she wanted.

"Let's go in," Dan said and got out of the van. They headed up to the door and went in. The children looked around smiling. This was a nice home. Bigger than theirs, but it felt homey to them.

"Let me give you a tour," Marissa said, smiling. She showed them around the first floor living room, kitchen, half bath, a game/play room, and dining room. Upstairs was the four bedrooms, and each had an attached bathroom, a washer and dryer hidden away in what looked like a hallway closet.

"We get our own rooms and our own bathrooms?" Naomi asked in shock.

"Yes," Marissa said, smiling.

"Which room is whose?" Nathan asked.

"Well, you are the oldest. Which one do you want?" Dan asked.

Nathan smiled and chose one. The girls claimed theirs as well.

"It's empty in there," Nicki said, looking around at the empty rooms.

"Yes, when you move in, we will put all your things in there. We thought it might help you to have everything like you are used to having. If you prefer to decorate in a different way, we can do that, whatever you think would make you feel more comfortable," Marissa explained. Laura pursed her lips together. She was so touched by how much thought and care Dan and Marissa put into every detail and decision. They would be great parents.

"I want mine exactly the same," Nathan said.

"All right, you have dark blue walls. I will get that painted for you," Dan said.

"Can I help you?" Nathan asked. Dan smiled and nodded.

"We share a room right now, and it doesn't really have a theme. I would like a pink room and a princess theme," Naomi said shyly.

"That sounds perfect. Your mom and I can help you pick out all the details and get it ready for you," Marissa said. Laura smiled and nodded. She would like that.

"What about you, Nicki?" Dan asked.

"Hmm... I don't know," Nicki said, puzzled.

"Well, we will check out different themes, and you can decide," Marissa said, smiling. Nicki loved that idea and hugged Marissa.

"Well, now that is starting to come together, let's go meet the rest of the family," Dan said, smiling.

Laura loved that the children were making great strides in bonding with Dan and Marissa and getting comfortable with some of the changes to come. God is good all the time.

* * * * *

They were the last to arrive at Lewis and Beth's house. Nathan was counting the cars already there: four cars. They weren't kidding when they said they had a big family.

"Are you nervous?" Dan asked, seeing Nathan's expression.

"A little. We just have us. I'm not used to a lot of people," Nathan admitted.

"We meant what we said. If you feel overwhelmed, even if we haven't eaten or are eating, just say the word. We can go," Dan said honestly.

Nathan nodded. He knew it was going to be okay; it was just new. He trusted that Dan and Marissa would be true to their word, and that was enough to settle his nerves.

"I will be okay," Nathan said, smiling at Dan.

Beth and Delores opened the door as they approached.

"Welcome! I am Beth, Dan's mom, and this is Delores, Marissa's mom," Beth said excitedly.

"Hello!" Delores said, beaming at them all.

"Hello, I am Laura, and these are my children: Nathan, Naomi, and Nicki," Laura said happily.

"Where is everyone else?" Dan asked.

"Well, we didn't want to be too much for everyone. We are all so excited. We actually drew straws to see who could open the door, and I won!" Beth giggled. "We had decided whoever won could pick one more person to join them at the door. I thought it was only fair to choose Delores. The rest are in the living room."

"You drew straws to see who got to meet us first?" Nathan said in shock.

"Yes. We are really trying to be on our best behavior and not scare you away," Delores said, smiling.

"I don't think anyone has ever been that excited to meet us before," Naomi said, smiling.

"Well, that is a shame. They are all missing out," Beth added. Naomi smiled and hugged her. Nicki jumped into Delores's arms. Nathan waited his turn for his sisters to hug them both, and then he went in. He had never had a grandma, and here were two!

Laura fought back her tears. This was definitely more than even she had dreamed of for her children. Dan and Marissa led the children in. Laura hung back and tried to find the words to say something to these amazing women who had just helped her children relax and not be nervous.

"Laura, it is an honor to meet you and your children. We all wish it were under different circumstances, but we want you to know we will love you and your children with all of our hearts. You are all our family now. We aren't taking your children. Our family is growing by adding *all four of you*," Beth said wholeheartedly.

"Absolutely," Delores said and embraced Laura who began shaking. "Laura, we love you and are praying for you. As mothers, we can't imagine what you are facing and the strength you are finding in all of this."

Beth put her hand on Laura's back as Delores held Laura in her arms. Laura began to sob. She felt so loved and safe. She never expected anyone to welcome her into their family. She was just so focused on her children's welfare. She was so grateful and overwhelmed.

"We are all here for you in any and all ways you need. If you need a driver or someone to do errands for you, if you need someone to talk to or some company—anything at all—we are in this with you 100 percent," Beth said sincerely.

"I don't know what to say… I never dreamed…" Laura was so overwhelmed by their love and acceptance. She gathered herself and pulled back but took both women by the hand.

"Laura, I have lost a child, and Delores has lost her parents as a child. We have known great loss, and we have known great love. We are family, and we will get through all of this together," Beth said gently.

Laura nodded. "Thank you. I had been wondering how I was going to handle things as I got weaker… I just couldn't worry about that yet," Laura admitted.

"We understand as much as we can. If at any time today you feel tired and need to lie down, we have a guest room on the first floor. You can rest in there," Beth added.

Laura was so grateful. She had worried about a long day away from home, but these wonderful women had thought of everything. She was sure the rest of the family would be just as loving to her family.

The three women headed into the house. They found the rest of the family in the living room. Naomi was seated next to a couple and holding their baby. She was talking to them about the baby and how she wanted to be a preschool teacher like her mom. Nicki was talking with another couple and their daughter. She was telling them all about seeing Dan and Marissa's house and getting her own room. The three of them were trying to help Nicki come up with a theme ideas for her room. Two older gentlemen were talking to Nathan. Dan and Marissa were standing on either side of Nathan. They knew he needed the most support in all of this. Later the girls would need them more, but Nathan was keenly aware of what was to come, and as strong as he was, he was very fragile. They wanted him to feel their support and love. The love they all were showing her children warmed her heart. Everything was really going to be all right. Beth and Delores stood on either side of Laura as they watched her take in the family and her children with them. Both women took Laura by the hand and stood by her side, not saying anything. They felt the presence of God so strongly in that room.

They all went into the formal dining room that was seeing a lot more use this past year than ever before and would continue in this new trend. Beth made her lasagna and chocolate cake. Beth had made chicken parmesan and lemon bars. Charlotte made vegetable soup and some cherry Jell-O; she thought Laura might need something lighter. Grace made a huge salad and garlic bread.

There was a lot of conversation at lunch, but the children seemed to blossom with all the attention and activity. After they ate, David and Elliott offered to clean up, sending the rest of the family back to the living room to play games. Laura watched for a few minutes and then asked Beth if she could lie down. Beth showed her to the guest room. She smiled and listened to the family and her children playing charades in the living room as she drifted to sleep with a smile on her face. She was getting weaker, but it didn't scare her anymore. Her hard work was done. They had the adoption underway, and she knew all was going to be okay.

Transitioning

Days turned into weeks, and the adoption had gone through with no problem, the children keeping the Sinclair name as they wanted. It had been Dan and Marissa's idea to ask them. They thought they might want to keep it the same. They told them it was okay because they were not replacing Aaron and Laura in their lives; they were just joining the Sinclair family. The judge was touched that this mother had found her children's new family and how Dan and Marissa were bonding with both the mother and children. He gave his best to all of them. The children would stay with Laura until she passed. They had decided that Dan and Marissa would move in with them in the end to help take care of Laura and the children. Laura was so touched that she was a part of their lives as well. She knew that would help her children in the months and years to come.

Dan had gone to Dad and Donut day with the children, and they had asked Marissa and Laura both go to Mom and Muffin day at school. Laura was so pleased. Dan and Marissa felt so blessed. They got the girls' rooms all decorated and Nathan's painted. He wanted everything the same as his current room so it would be moved later. As the school year was drawing to a close, Laura was getting much weaker. She was in a wheelchair and true to their word. Her last public outing was to Nicki's kindergarten graduation. She had made it to all of their kindergarten graduations but never expected it to be the only graduations she got to attend. Dan had made sure to get as many pictures of Laura, especially with each child and all together as he could and ones of Marissa and Laura together, as well as some with him and Laura. For the years to come, they could hold onto their memories and these pictures.

Dan and Marissa's family, Laura's new extended family, were there for her and the children. Charles and Delores took care of her home, cooking and cleaning. Lewis and Beth were there often too, and they all took her to appointments and did her grocery shopping.

David, Grace, Elliott, Charlotte, and Emma were there often as well, helping in all the ways they could, helping the kids with homework and school projects. They made sure the children knew they were a real family. Grace, being a nurse, was a great help to Laura, and she would not need to call in hospice care. She had family equipped to care for her.

"Laura, is there anything that you really want to do with the children before...?" Marissa asked.

"I was just thinking about that," Laura said then paused to take a breath; she was on oxygen at this point. "I want to throw the children a big birthday party, one for all three of them, each with their own cake. I won't be here for their next birthday, but I want to have one more party with them."

"You got it. Tell me what you want, and I will make it happen," Marissa said, excited. She thought that was a great idea.

"Let's talk to the children and see what they want," Laura said, smiling. She wasn't going to ask, but it had been on her heart.

They children loved the idea. They only wanted their new big family to be there and to have it in their home. Even though it would be tight, everyone agreed. They decorated the house with streamers and balloons and three cakes with their own theme for each and with their next age number candle. They had homemade pizza and cake and ice cream. Laura didn't eat, but the children made her favorite pizza anyway. It was a wonderful day. The only gifts were from Laura to her children. Marissa had gone out and bought what she had asked for and wrapped it up for her.

Nathan got a 5 × 7 wooden framed picture of the last family picture they took as a family with his dad shortly before he passed away and a gold pocket watch with the inscription:

To Our Nathan,

You make us so proud. You can be anything you want to be through Christ who strengthens you.

Love,
Dad and Mom,
Aaron and Laura Sinclair

The girls both got a gold locket necklace with the same picture in it and the same inscription to them on the back. They loved it and held onto their mother and cried. She held onto them with all her might. The rest of the family sat quietly, praying and crying.

Soon after, Laura needed to lie down. Grace and Charlotte helped to get her into bed. The girls climbed up into Marissa's lap and held onto her. She just held them tightly. They didn't say a word.

Nathan looked like he didn't know what to do. He just paced around, looking like a caged animal.

They all knew time was growing very short. Dan and Marissa had brought two small bags to move in that night. The couch turned out to be a bed so they would sleep in the living room. Grace had set up a cot in Laura's room to stay close by her side.

"Nathan, do you want to go outside? What do you need?" Dan asked.

"I don't know. I mean, I just don't know," Nathan said and kicked the wall. Dan went over and hugged him. Nathan tried to push away, but Dan held on, and Nathan wrapped his arms around him and began sobbing.

Emma buried her face into her mom's shoulder. Charlotte wrapped her arms around her. It wasn't fair that Laura was dying. It could have so easily been Charlotte that had died. It was just so horrible. Elliott put his arm around Charlotte. Tears flooded their eyes.

Lewis and Beth held onto each other tight, as did David and Grace, and little Polly cried from their grip on her. They let up and soothed her. Delores turned to Charles and buried her face into his chest. He held onto her tightly.

"I'm just so angry," Nathan cried. "I feel so guilty. Here we are so happy to have you all in our lives. We are getting so much, and my mom...she is losing everything!"

"She needed to know you were going to be okay. She wanted you to have all this. You know that, right? She has held on until she knew you would be okay because that is what an amazing mom like your mom does. She is going to go to heaven, and she will be waiting for you there. All the feelings you have are very understandable, and I want you to know you are safe to feel and express whatever you need to with all of us. If you need to go for a run, we will be with you. If you need me to take you to the gym and let you work out or beat on a punching bag, say the word and I will have you there. If you need to go somewhere and scream, I will take you there. If you want to go to church or talk to your pastor, I'll make it happen. God led us to your mom, and we are your family, not a replacement—an addition to the family, the amazing parents God gave you. What we don't want is for you to feel guilty for being happy or feeling loved. That is what your parents wanted for you, and if you didn't find that, their hearts would be broken," Dan said as he held onto Nathan.

Nathan sobbed and held onto Dan with all his might. He was listening and nodded. He knew what he said was right, and it was good to hear. He needed to hear that. He needed to know whatever he needed would be available for him and his sisters.

Nathan pulled away, gaining his composure back. He smiled at Dan and looked at Marissa, holding onto his sisters. Tears ran down all their faces. He looked around at the room overflowing with people who loved him.

"I love you all. We love you all," he said, looking at his sisters who nodded. "God gave us the best parents in the world, and when he needed them back, he gave us the best family in the world. My mom made that happen with the help of the Lord," Nathan said. He looked over at Delores and went over to her and took her hands in his. "Grandma Delores, I am gonna need you a whole lot," Nathan managed.

"I will always be here for you, Nathan. All of us will be, but I understand what you mean," Delores said hoarsely and embraced him tightly. She closed her eyes tightly and prayed silently in her heart. "I understand now. What I went through prepared me to be here for my grandchildren. You never forsook me. I just didn't accept all the times you tried to tug at my heart. I will do everything in my power to help these children in the hard times ahead. Thank you, Jesus, for always being there for me, even when I couldn't see."

* * * * *

It was only a few days longer, and Laura passed away with her children, Grace, Marissa, and Dan by her bedside. The rest of the family were out in the living room quietly praying.

They stayed in Laura's house a few more days. The day after her services and burial, they moved Nathan's things to his new room and the rest of the girls' things and went on a vacation. Dan and Marissa thought the kids needed a change of scenery, and when they got back, the children would spend their first night in their new home as a family.

It was just what they all needed. Nathan and Naomi remembered going to the beach and seeing the ocean with their parents, and they were excited for Nicki got to go again to see it. She had just been so young the last time; she had pictures of it but no memories of her own. They went to Florida and enjoyed the beach for a couple days and then surprised the children with a few days at Disney World. The girls cheered, but Nathan looked unsure.

"Does it feel right to go to the happiest place on earth right after you lose your mother?" Nathan asked guiltily.

"It was your mom's idea. This vacation was her idea. Your mom thought the beach was a good idea because she knew you and Naomi remembered going with her and your dad. She thought it would bring you comfort, and she had said they had always wanted to take you kids to Disney World," Marissa shared. "Nathan, your mom had changed her life insurance to go to us and asked us to take you to Disney for her and your dad, to fulfill their last wish to do with you that they never got to do."

"Really?" Nathan asked, the tears streaming down her face. "Wow. It makes sense... Did you know that is where they went on their honeymoon? They went to Disney World," Nathan said, beaming.

"They did?" Naomi asked, surprised.

"Yeah, she told me once. She showed me the pictures," Nathan said, remembering.

Marissa brought out the photo album Laura had given her.

"She thought you might worry about going to Disney, and she said you would remember what she told you but just in case, show this to all of you."

They all poured over the pictures of a very young Aaron and Laura Sinclair at Disney and laughed over the pictures.

"My mom is the best. She always thought of everything," Nathan said proudly. She always blew him away.

"Yes, you are right," Marissa said wholeheartedly. Nathan hugged her.

"Let's go have some fun and make Mom and Dad proud," Nathan announced. They all cheered.

Adjusting

Dan and Marissa and the children had a wonderful time on vacation. They found it easier to smile, laugh, and just feel like children again with the change of scenery. A very well-needed get away. While they were gone, the rest of the family moved all of Laura's furniture and belongings to a storage unit for the children to have later. They took all the photo albums and anything the children might want or had requested to Dan and Marissa's house and cleaned the house for potential buyers. Dan had been in contact with the real estate agent who helped them buy their house and put Laura's house up for sale. It sold quickly, and the money was divided up and put into three saving accounts for the children. That could go for their first car and college or whatever they needed in the future after graduation. After taking care of all Laura's financial affairs, the remainder of the insurance money also went into the three saving accounts for the children. Marissa set it all up at her bank; she had discussed with Laura what she had wanted to do, and Laura was very pleased with the idea.

The evening they returned from vacation, they were all exhausted, and Dan and Marissa tucked them all into their own beds and told them good night after praying with them. Marissa got up in the night to check on them and found all three children curled up together in Nathan's bed. They each cuddled a stuffed animal sprayed with their mother's perfume.

The next day, they had been invited to Charles and Delores's house for a big welcome back breakfast. The children ran up to the house and were excited to see Grandpa Charles and Grandma Delores. They gathered around the kitchen table to eat and talk all about their adventures in Florida.

"Did you know this vacation was our mom's idea?" Nicki asked proudly.

"We did know that. God sure gave you the best mom ever," Charles said, beaming. They all had been so impressed and changed forever by having known Laura Sinclair. She had been a gift in all their lives, for the brief time they knew and loved her.

"Yeah, she knew our only vacations we would remember was going to the ocean with her and our dad. Nicki was too little to remember, but she has seen the pictures. I had forgotten until Marissa reminded me that my mom told me that she and our dad had gone to Disney World for their honeymoon. That is funny," Nathan said, laughing.

"I think it sounds like a great idea. That is what I want to do. Maybe I can get married at Disney World, like a real princess!" Naomi said dreamily. They all laughed.

"You just might, Naomi, but let's not rush that, okay?" Dan said, chuckling.

"Okay," Naomi said, smiling big.

"What is a honeymoon?" Nicki asked.

"When you get married, you go on a little vacation to celebrate," Nathan explained.

"Oh, okay," Nicki said, satisfied with the answer. "I don't know where I will go on a honeymoon. I think I will ask my husband, and we can decide together."

"That is a very good idea, Nicki. Unless you do what Dan and I did," Marissa said, laughing.

"What did you do?" Naomi asked, leaning forward, very interested.

"Well, I was busy with the wedding plans, and in talking about it, I thought it might be fun for Dan to just take care of that and decide and set it all up and surprise me. Aunt Grace and Aunt

Charlotte packed my bags for me. So I found out as we were leaving the wedding reception that we were headed to Africa for a safari honeymoon. It was fun and a real adventure!' Marissa gushed.

"Wow. That is a lot of trust," Naomi said. "I don't know if I could do that."

They all laughed.

"You just went on a honeymoon last year too, right? You just got back together and had a wedding?" Nathan asked Charles and Delores.

"Yes, we did. We went on a cruise to a bunch of islands. It was like a floating hotel resort, and every few days we stopped on a new island," Delores said, beaming.

"Wow. That sounds so cool. I want to do that!" Nathan said, smiling.

"We know Dan and Marissa met when Aunt Charlotte had her accident. My parents met through a friend and she set them up on a blind date. How did you two meet?" Naomi asked Charles and Delores.

Charles and Delores looked at each other and smiled. The old memories weren't so painful anymore. They remembered them well.

"Naomi, it all began at school. I was in the seventh grade, and Grandma Delores was in the fifth grade. My family had just moved to town, and back then, the elementary and middle school was in the same building. They just had all the middle school kids on one side of the building and the elementary kids on the other. I saw your grandma, and she was the prettiest little girl I had ever seen. I didn't care if she was a fifth grader. She was beautiful...," Charles said wistfully.

"I don't know how beautiful I was, but I didn't let anyone get close to me. I was on my own and looking out for myself only. Your grandpa Charles would come around and try to talk to me or offer me some of his lunch. I misunderstood what he meant and didn't take that kind gesture as it was intended..." Charles and Delores both burst out laughing.

The children looked from each other to Marissa; they didn't understand what was so funny. Marissa shrugged and looked at Dan smiling. She had never heard any stories from when they met and were growing up. She was as intrigued as the children were. She wished Charlotte was here to hear this too. She would be sure to tell her every detail.

"Well, our story isn't like your parents or Dan and Marissa, who met and hit it off and the rest was history. Instead of riding off into the sunset, we took a wild roller-coaster ride. The good, the bad, and the ugly through God, we made it back to each other and are now riding off into the sunset together in spite of ourselves," Delores said, chuckling and shaking her head.

"Please tell us! We have to hear this," Naomi coaxed. Nathan and Nicki nodded and leaned in, smiling too.

"Well, all right, we will tell you," Charles said teasingly. It was a wild story with lots of twists and turns, but it was theirs, and maybe it was time it was told.

Dan and Marissa adapted to becoming parents quickly and were so thankful for their blessings. It wasn't easy. There were a lot of dark days and long sorrowful nights. Each child handled their grief differently, but Dan and Marissa found the training from Brian's classes was very helpful. The family was there to support them all. The grandparents were the best at connecting with the children and helping them through. Nathan really clung to Delores. He felt a special connection with her.

The children loved how their big family not only loved them but loved their mother. She was often brought up in conversation, and they would ask them to share their memories of both their parents. They wanted them to keep their memories alive in their hearts and know that nothing was taboo. Dan and Marissa hung Aaron and Laura's wedding picture and family photos up on the walls and took one together as well. In time, the girls began calling Dan and Marissa by the names of Dad and Mom. Nathan never did, and that was just fine. He grew close to them and trusted and loved them, and they knew it.

Charlotte became a physical therapist assistant and began working with Joel two years after she finished being his patient. She found her new job very rewarding, and she was able to use her story to help motivate her patients and letting them know there was hope and she understood because she had been there too. Elliott, Charlotte, and Emma continued their yearly vacations with Tracey and her family.

Before they all knew it, the girls were choosing colleges. Tracey headed for California, but Emma stayed close to home like they had planned that first summer vacation so many years before. Tracey became an interior designer and stayed out west. Emma became a social worker and worked at the hospital her mother had been taken to after her accident. Emma was able to create and manage volunteer programs at the hospital and did her best to make sure no one in the hospital waiting with or on a loved one felt like they were alone or hungry.

Charles and Delores had a full life together and with their big family. They were best friends with Lewis and Beth which was so wonderful since they shared grandchildren. Lewis and Beth became additional grandparents for Emma. Polly and her younger twin sisters called Charles and Delores Grandpa and Grandma too.

David and Grace talked to Nathan, Naomi, and Nicki and got their blessing and approval to name their twin daughters Erin and Lauren after their parents. They were touched and loved that truly were a part of this family, and that included their parents as well. Dan and Marissa reminded them that Aaron and Laura Sinclair lived on forever in their hearts, memories, and most importantly, through their legacy, their children.

Nathan Sinclair became a firefighter like his father. Naomi lived out her dream of marrying the love of her life after college at Disney World and became a preschool teacher like her mother. Nicki became an art teacher at the elementary school she and her siblings had attended. She started a drama club at the school as well, and they put on plays twice a year, some were ones she wrote herself. She also took part in performing in plays at the community center.

ABOUT THE AUTHOR

Amanda J. Gowin lives in Indiana with her husband, Randy, and their two young sons. Amanda loves her family, friends, and being a part of her church. Through life's ups and downs, it has been her faith and relationship with Jesus that has brought her through. She has often found that the lessons taught to her by her Children's Church teachers and family are what have helped her the most in life.

It has always been her dream to tell stories that make the characters come to life to show your first impression of someone might not be accurate. Amanda is a firm believer that with Jesus, you can do anything and that those who are hardest to love usually need it the most.

CPSIA information can be obtained
at www.ICGtesting.com
Printed in the USA
BVHW072344020321
601492BV00005B/375